Lord Kingsford's Quest

by

Donna Davidson

A SIGNET BOOK

SIGNET
Published by the Penguin Group
Penguin Books USA Inc., 375 Hudson Street,
New York, New York 10014, U.S.A.
Penguin Books Ltd, 27 Wrights Lane,
London W8 5TZ, England
Penguin Books Australia Ltd, Ringwood, Victoria, Australia
Penguin Books Canada Ltd, 10 Alcorn Avenue,
Toronto, Ontario, Canada M4V 3B2
Penguin Books (N.Z.) Ltd, 182–190 Wairau Road,
Auckland 10, New Zealand

Penguin Books Ltd, Registered Offices:
Harmondsworth, Middlesex, England

First published by Signet, an imprint of Dutton Signet,
a division of Penguin Books USA Inc.

First Printing, March, 1995
10 9 8 7 6 5 4 3 2 1

Printed in the United States of America

Uncaged Desire

Woolfe was dark. Hair coal-black, hanging loosely over his collar. Dark blue eyes hidden by thick Celtic lashes no man ever deserved. Dark skin, tanned like oak, drawn closely over that wonderful bone structure that had so entranced Taryn years ago. He was not handsome but rather something worse—dangerously attractive.

He reminded Taryn of a caged animal she had once seen, a black wolf, powerful and frightening, prowling to and fro. She had longed to let the black wolf loose, even knowing that he would likely kill her should she open the door. Like the animal, Woolfe's deeply tanned face spoke of faraway places and a life she could not imagine. As for what he might do to her should she open the door of her heart, she had every assurance it would be deadly. Even knowing that, she felt drawn to him. And like the wild thing that had so mesmerized her, damn him, he knew it, and smiled. What kind of animal had he become that would be amused by this power?

Taryn knew she was about to find out. Woolfe was going to kiss her. . . .

Dedicated to
Carolyn Kistler Worthen,
my neighbor in Japan and California,
a dear friend who made the writing
of this book possible

Thanks to those wonderful people
whose skillful assistance gave this story
texture, direction, and merriment

Ann Alt
Greg Alt
Allan Davidson
Kimi Sasakura

and to two exceptional editors,
Jennifer Enderlin, whose enthusiasm
for this story gave it birth, and
Jeanmarie LeMense, whose insightful editing
gave it a full and happy life

Prologue

1801, Kingsford, England

Woolfe Burnham moved quickly back into the shadows of the lilac hedge separating Kingsford Hall from the stables. With eyes far too old for a boy barely twelve, he watched Claudia Chastain hurry across the courtyard toward the open stable door.

Raising her elaborate evening gown above the dusty stones, she picked her way on white-slippered toes, the essence of her anger swirling around her like an acrid perfume. She stopped abruptly as her husband, Oliver, strode from the stable, her brows lifted inquiringly toward him. Oliver smiled briefly, then turned back to watch the door. Claudia's attention followed, eyes lit with anticipation.

Woolfe, alerted to deathly silence, joined the vigil.

Oliver's henchman, Quinn, lumbered out of the stable, dragging a small child behind him, his full lips moving soundlessly as his fragile captive struggled against his powerful hold. A dirty lantern suspended from a tall, weathered pole cast elongated shadows onto the cobbled courtyard, dark reflections pirouetting in a sinister dance.

At a wave of Oliver's ruffled sleeve, the hulking Quinn released the child onto the stones and moved back into the darkened perimeter of the stable yard. *Taryn*, Woolfe thought, Claudia's newly orphaned niece, a noisy, cheerful child whose presence in the Hall had endeared her to the servants since her arrival last week. Indeed, the village was buzzing with the news. What was she doing out here?

Taryn scrabbled to her feet, the hem of her nightgown falling to her ankles as she looked around defiantly, a diminutive warrior bedecked in white lace and dirty feet. At the sight of Oliver's wife, the child's face crumpled, and tears followed already wet paths over her rounded cheeks. "Aunt Claudia, it's my puppy. He h . . . hanged him."

She flew to her aunt, arms outstretched.

Claudia stopped the small hurtling child with a quick snap of her wrist, tangling long, slim fingers of one hand into the child's snarled hair to keep her at arm's length. She jerked the girl's surprised face upward into the light. "Did I not tell you to cease arguing with me?"

Unbelieving, Taryn's horror-tinged whisper echoed into the damp night air, "*You told* Quinn to do that?"

"My precious sister spoiled you, Taryn, and your wealthy father indulged your every whim. You must learn that those days are now over. I am the one who makes the rules, and you are the one who obeys without arguing."

Taryn's chin wobbled, then rose stubbornly. "My father gave me that puppy, Aunt Claudia; you had no right to have him killed."

Her aunt leaned down, and briefly in the lantern's glow their mirrored faces radiated a striking similarity of exotic beauty—then Claudia's features contorted, dispelling the image. "Had you obeyed me, it would not have been necessary. You have brought it upon yourself."

Taryn twisted to free herself, frantically reaching upward to pry herself free from Claudia's painful grasp. Her tiny fingers entangled in Claudia's elaborate coiffure, eliciting a screech from her aunt—and a back-handed slap that cut a gash across Taryn's upper lip.

One drop of blood fell from Claudia's ruby ring onto her satin slippers, and she stepped back, her eyes narrowing at the offensive sight. Without taking her gaze from her spoiled slipper, her words fell like sizzling acid from soft, perfect sculpted lips. "Quinn, teach this imp from hell a few manners."

Taryn's wild eyes flicked across the cobbles as Quinn moved into the lamplight. His hand moved effortlessly, and the tip of a long, tightly braided whip snaked out of its curled position on his shoulder and slipped onto the rough stones before him.

Woolfe shuddered at the familiar sight, and he quickly looked at Claudia to gauge the depth of her fury. His heart pounded at what he saw in her face. He quickly shifted his attention to Oliver, for Quinn was Oliver's man and did not act without his permission.

Oliver's cold eyes gleamed as he nodded his acquiescence

at Quinn. As the creature moved forward, nausea rose in Woolfe's throat. Even after years of being at Oliver's mercy, Woolfe could not believe Oliver would hurt his wife's niece, a delicate child of less than nine years.

Guilt seared through Woolfe. He shouldn't have held himself aloof from the child. He should have talked to her, warned her that any defiance would innocently cry challenge to the couple's perverted brutality, summoning forth pain in an inescapable, engulfing torrent. Even in the week Taryn had been in Kingsford, Woolfe thought, he could have taught her to remain quiet no matter what occurred—even now she might save herself by wilting into a defeated heap on the ground to satisfy her tormentors. If only . . .

Taryn's chin lifted in rebellion, and Woolfe's breath caught as her wavering voice defied them. "I shall tell Lord Fortesque, Aunt Claudia, and he will take me home to live with him. I shall tell him you hanged my dog, and you will be thrown into Newgate Prison."

Claudia sneered at the child. "Your parents are dead now, Taryn. So, tell me how Lord Fortesque will hear your useless whining when you will never see him?"

"He is my guardian and will come to see how I fare—or I shall send him a message."

"You are a child, Taryn. No one will believe you, and as for sending him a message, your Uncle Oliver will never frank such a letter to that fussy old man in London."

Taryn's tongue ran across her lip, stopping to worry at the cut directly above her slightly tilted front tooth. "He said he would come, Aunt Claudia, and he will see what you have done to me. And when he takes me away, you will not be able to spend my father's money any longer." The child's face shone with satisfaction.

Woolfe's cynical expression softened at the child's triumph, and his shoulders shook in unaccustomed laughter. Amazed at Taryn's adult grasp of her status in life, he took a deep breath and relaxed, curious to see how Claudia would react to the girl's inescapable logic.

In answer, a flash of light shone briefly on the woman's bejeweled hand as she signaled to Quinn, and the whip sang through the air. The child's gown split at the shoulder, and she fell to her knees, whimpering in pain and disbelief.

Quinn drew back the whip in a sinuous gathering of power—and a scarlet flash of rage exploded in Woolfe's head.

He charged forward to stop the unspeakable weapon from touching this tiny, innocent child. He threw his arms around her, shuddering as he anticipated what was coming.

At the sound of the second whip crack, Taryn cringed and cried out—then she stilled, comprehension dawning in her tear-filled eyes. Her head snapped up to stare at her rescuer.

"Get that boy away from her!" Claudia's angry scream joined Oliver's furious growl.

As the whip hissed up into the air once more, Woolfe willed his mind to soar beyond the pain by riveting his attention upon something else, abandoning his body to suffer alone. He looked at the child, concentrating his fierce attention on every detail. Purple eyes staring in wonder at him—like violets, he cataloged, as the third whiplash bit into his flesh. Hair almost white, and most enchanting, just beneath her cut lip, a small tooth slightly tilted as if cuddling its mate for comfort.

Taryn erupted into a ball of fury, screaming as she tried to push Woolfe aside. "*Leave him alone! I shall do as you say.*" Woolfe stared at her, amazed that her quick little mind had charged straight to the speediest solution possible.

Oliver stopped the whip in midair. "Enough, Quinn." The aborted stroke echoed like a gunshot, sending shivers down Woolfe's back. Taryn whimpered deep in her throat.

Oliver cocked his head to the side, a handsome, fair-haired gentleman, eyelids fluttering almost closed as he listened to his own thoughts. "I believe the child has given us a solution."

Claudia's angry protest snapped back. "I want her whipped, Oliver, not the boy."

Impatience flickered briefly across Oliver's normally impassive features, but he spoke in even tones. "Think, Claudia. The girl is right. As joint guardian, Fortesque will most certainly be poking his nose into her business, and he may believe her."

"She has always been a haughty little baggage. I mean to break her."

"Look before you, Claudia." Oliver motioned to the huddled figures on the stones. Taryn had pulled away from Woolfe's protecting embrace, and was at that instant lifting his shredded shirt away from the lacerated back, tears streaming down her cheeks as she tried to lessen his pain.

"Taryn," Oliver said calmly, his eyes opaque as the child raised her agonized face to him. "You are right, of course. We must not mar you, lest it give Fortesque any concern. However, young Woolfe means nothing to your guardian, nor will anyone be surprised that this worthless boy has once more been disciplined. You, however, will know that the punishment for your disobedience will be immediately visited upon Woolfe."

Taryn's eyes widened as she perceived his meaning, and her words flowed without thought. "No, you cannot—"

Woolfe stiffened and opened his mouth to warn her, but even as Taryn gasped at her mistake, Oliver answered her defiance with a nod to Quinn. The whip danced once more, barely missing her fingers while slicing a new red stripe into Woolfe's white shirt. Without waiting for Taryn's response, Oliver offered his arm to his wife and said, "You must change your slippers and tidy your coiffure, my dear. Our guests will be arriving any moment."

"What will Woolfe's Uncle Richard say when he discovers how you are using him?" Claudia asked, hurrying beside her husband.

"His dear uncle will say what he has always said, my dear. He will ask for my steward's report—which he never reads—and ask for the money I shall inform him is available—which he will promptly gamble away. As for Woolfe, Richard will tell me to carry on and make a man of the little savage."

Claudia glanced back at the two children huddled together. "Get her away from that boy this instant," Claudia hissed. "He's a disgrace, and I do not want her associating with him when she is to be our son's wife."

"Nonsense, my dear. Let them cling together. She will guard him as he did her. It is better than hiring a nanny or locking her in her room. And," he said, brushing a bit of hay from his sleeve, "it costs us nothing."

Chapter One

Spring, 1803, Kingsford

"Want to go fishing, Geoffrey?" Woolfe asked casually, casting an expert gaze out over the end of the pier. A brisk breeze roused the gentle waves into a green froth and whipped the ends of Woolfe's loose shirt. He turned to study his cousin, wishing that his Uncle Richard would leave Geoffrey at Kingsford instead of taking him back to London to learn the ways of a wastrel gentleman. Geoffrey, although considered an adult at eighteen, was too gentle and unsophisticated to withstand the easy temptations of that life.

"C-c-can't," Geoffrey replied. "M'father's wanting to leave by noon." Looking longingly up at Woolfe's open-necked shirt, Geoffrey tugged at his own elaborate neckcloth. "I c-c-came down to see you before his valet gets him stuffed into his c-c-clothes and pours a bottle of ale into him."

Woolfe looked sharply at his cousin. "You only just got here last night. Why did you come at all?"

"M'father's in dun territory, out at the heels. C-c-come to squeeze the ready out of Oliver. Oliver's been pleading poverty, but m'father's sure he's a rascal and k-k-keeping it to himself."

"I've been telling Uncle Richard about Oliver for years, Geoffrey, and I don't care if he was your mother's brother, the man acts like a deranged potentate here in Kingsford. He's got people tugging their forelocks and bowing to him—sometimes I think he believes Kingsford belongs to him."

"You aren't serious?"

"Listen, Geoffrey," Woolfe said urgently, encouraged by his cousin's incredulous stare, "do you think your father might be willing to listen to me now that he's angry with Oliver?"

Geoffrey glanced quickly at his cousin, then looked down at his feet. "Sorry, Woolfe. As soon as Oliver brings out the c-c-coins, m'father will forget it all and think Oliver's a fine fellow. In any c-c-case, no one can tell m'father a thing, not about you and not about Taryn. Even when he's sober, he doesn't want to hear about anyone's problems." His voice grew pensive. "He's k-k-killing himself with the bottle and throwing his blunt away on the tables. So far he's not been pushed to hazard the estate, but it's only a matter of time."

Woolfe nodded, disgusted with himself for even mentioning it. He motioned to the slanted triangle of shade next to the fishing shack. "Sit down, Geoffrey, you'll bake in those clothes." At Geoffrey's hesitation, Woolfe nudged him forward, and his cousin went willingly enough, like a friendly puppy, shy and eager to please.

As they sprawled against the weathered shack, Geoffrey sighed. "We haven't been so lucky with our fathers, have we?"

"At least Uncle Richard wants you with him. My father left without so much as a wave good-bye."

Geoffrey replied slowly. "Uncle Justin, your father, a pirate. I c-c-could hardly believe it when I heard the stories." In an effort to lighten the mood, Geoffrey nudged Woolfe's elbow. "Wish he'd drop by and unload some of his stolen gold. We c-c-could all use it."

Woolfe tried to smile, for Geoffrey hated to see anyone even mildly disturbed, and didn't deserve to be subjected to Woolfe's black mood.

Encouraged, Geoffrey explained. "After all those good years with Uncle Justin as steward, m'father's never forgiven his brother for disappearing like that. Then Oliver offered to run things, and his idea of good management is to keep a steady stream of brandy and a trickle of money coming to pacify m'father. Most of the time it's enough, but underneath, m'father isn't so far gone not to know Kingsford's going downhill."

Geoffrey lifted his face to catch a cool gust of air blowing up off the water. "I think that's why m'father's deserted you, Woolfe. He's still furious with Uncle Justin for leaving."

A bitter laugh escaped Woolfe's tight throat. "Uncle Richard's story is that he has given me over to Oliver for training. He claims Quinn's whip will keep me from becoming a 'savage' like my father."

Geoffrey sighed. "It's hard to love them—our fathers—isn't it?"

"Go ahead and love your father, Geoffrey—I hate mine. If I

ever see him again, I'll show him what a whip feels like myself."

Autumn, 1805, Kingsford

Woolfe closed the book and stretched before the fire, idly watching Taryn's pink tongue rub over her tilted front tooth as she concentrated on the toasting fork in her hand. He reached up to push back an errant strand of her hair that threatened to dangle into the flames, and as his fingers lightly stroked her hair, he was filled with the warmth her presence always brought. She was a cheerful little companion and grateful for the small pleasures Woolfe arranged for her, be it discovering birds' nests or berrying or visiting the tenants to play benefactress with her small offerings.

He mused, "I thought with Uncle Richard so ill, Geoffrey might think ahead and start paying attention to the estate, but he says country life is like being buried alive. If Kingsford were mine, I would—"

Giles snorted. "It will never be yours, Woolfe, and no one wishes to hear your endless theories on farming." He turned from the rain-streaked window and folded his arms across his chest, the lace at his sleeves falling in graceful folds.

"Giles," Taryn said softly, "I want to hear it."

Woolfe paused, knowing that his own presence was responsible for Giles's unusual foul mood, for the boy was usually sweet-tempered and malleable. Between Claudia's fanatic coddling and Taryn's soft heart, Giles would never mature, but instead would forever plow ahead like a horse with blinders, seeing only the treat he wanted—his mother's adoration, and Taryn's exclusive attention. And he was jealous of Woolfe.

Deciding not to give in to Giles, Woolfe replied in a reasonable voice, "Someone ought to care before Kingsford is ruined beyond fixing."

Giles stepped toward Woolfe, the boredom vanishing from his face. "Are you criticizing my father?"

Taryn spoke quickly. "Of course not, Giles." She sent a warning look to Woolfe and added, "Woolfe just reads all those books to see what folk are doing in other parts of the country."

Ignoring Giles's choleric complexion, Woolfe turned his attention back to Taryn. He pulled his long legs up to his chest and wrapped his arms around them, leaning his chin upon his knees. "Suppose you had a pond like ours, Taryn, and Kingsford got their fish from it. Then one year they took all the fish out, and not even one was left. What would happen when someone needed fish for their table?"

"Who cares when we have the river and the ocean right at our doorstep?" Giles retorted, dropping down on the rug beside Taryn.

Taryn patted Giles's hand as she concentrated on Woolfe's riddle. "There would be no fish, ever again."

Woolfe nodded, pleased with her answer. "It is the same with all things, Taryn. A slothful farmer plants the same crop over and over again, and never even hurdles the sheep over the ground because he's too lazy to care that the land needs feeding. We have never tried anything except broadcasting the seed here, which the sea breezes promptly blow up against the brush. Have we even tried dibbling here or crop rotation . . . or," he asked, exasperated, "turnips?"

"Turnips?" Taryn giggled. "What has that to do with anything?" She held the toast up under her nose and inhaled. "Ummm."

Giles absently reached over and took the toast from the fork. "Why do you care what happens to Kingsford, Woolfe?" He spooned up a dollop of jam from the pot on the tray between Taryn and Woolfe and plopped it onto the toast. Using the back of the spoon to spread the red concoction, he then dropped the sticky, crumb-covered spoon onto the carpet and began taking bites until his mouth was full.

Taryn rescued the spoon and wiped away the debris from the carpet with a napkin while Woolfe answered Giles's question. "It means nothing to me personally, of course. I shall make my own fortune."

Taryn stared at Woolfe, her eyes frightened as she tried to speak. "You'll leave Kingsford?"

"Of course he will, Taryn," Giles said, laying his hand over hers. "There is nothing for him in Kingsford. I cannot imagine what has kept him here so long."

Woolfe's eyes narrowed as he studied Giles's profile, then shifted his gaze to Taryn's hand lying so tranquilly under Giles's. "I want to be rich, Taryn. Everywhere there are people making fortunes, and I am as clever as they are."

"Oh Woolfe, then will you come back?"

"Perhaps," he murmured, some nameless emotion driving

his words. "Perhaps I shall buy Kingsford. The price of a worthless estate should be reasonable by then."

Giles scowled, but Taryn's face broke into a smile, and she serenely gave herself a happy ending. "You'll come to rescue us."

Woolfe fell silent, insisting fervently to himself that he would be *happy* to leave Kingsford. It was torment to see Taryn's guardians smothering her fighting spirit on one side—and Giles exploiting her soft, nurturing heart on the other. Taryn's father's will had given his blessings to Giles's and Taryn's betrothal, leaving her wholly under Claudia's control. Taryn's father must be burning in Hell, Woolfe thought with vicious satisfaction.

No matter how he tried to give Taryn a balance to counteract her family's selfish influence, the truth was that he had found no means to safely rescue her—and no one was going to help him.

Taryn's London guardian had long since died and been replaced by a man who considered Oliver 'admirable' for taking in his orphaned niece. Uncle Richard now suffered ill health, and Geoffrey—although sympathetic to Woolfe's concern regarding Taryn—had no resources to offer Woolfe, living as he did from one quarter allowance to another in a lazy life of pleasure.

Giles was right, Woolfe thought, he must concentrate on making his own way. He would read every book here in the Kingsford library to arm himself, to enable him to match wits with the rest of the world. He would accept offers from the fishermen to learn to sail. He would join the smugglers who traversed the channel to France and understood the meaning of profit.

Only when he was wealthy and powerful would he be in a position to help her—if she even wanted it by then.

Summer, 1807, Kingsford

Bright sunlight danced in through the open kitchen door, investigating the room like a new visitor, nodding in approval as it crept across the spotless stone floor, twinkling in shining delight as it floated up the side of the new Rumford stove, and gave its benediction to the fragrance emanating from the oven's depths.

Martha, Cook's youngest daughter, knelt upon a chair,

avidly watching her mother tuck a cloth over the large basket. Cook addressed the tall young lady standing nearby. "This is for Rose Simpson, Miss Taryn. There's gingerbread for the older girl and provisions for a couple of days."

"May I go with her to see the new baby, Mother?" Martha begged. Black curls bounced around her rosy, heart-shaped face as she jumped to her feet, her hands clutching the edge of the basket to show her readiness.

"May she?" Taryn asked, exchanging with Cook an expression that betrayed their mutual inability to deny the eager child her boon.

"If you wish," Cook replied. "Alyce and I got an early start this morning and can spare the little rascal for an hour." She bent over to lift Martha's face and brush gingerbread crumbs off the corner of her mouth. "Be good now." Cook's own face mirrored that of her children: flushed cheeks, laughing blue eyes, and shiny black tresses.

Alyce, Cook's older daughter, hurried to open the door as Taryn lifted the basket. Martha skipped ahead of Taryn, too impatient to walk, too excited to wait to see the newest addition to Kingsford's small village. Taryn shifted the basket so it would balance on her hip and laughed. "Go on ahead, Martha. You may tell them that I am coming if you wish." With a whoop, the girl flew down the shortcut through the trees.

Sedately, Taryn walked through the shaded woods, humming as she contemplated the gorgeous day. The trees were thick now, and undergrowth crowded the path, and the scurrying sounds of woodland creatures ceased briefly as she passed.

Ignoring its fainthearted fellows far below him, a wryneck continued pecking against his chosen tree. Taryn stopped and looked up to search out the colorful bird. Smiling, she cleared her throat, amused when he responded by earning his name and twisting his neck as he was wont to do when disturbed. The bird's colors outshone even Giles all decked in sartorial splendor, ready for a strut on the town—blue superfine coat patterned in yellow and black, yellow neckcloth, white brocade vest, and blue trousers—well, blue tail feathers, she amended.

She shifted the basket to the other side, then resumed her walk, accompanied by the woodpecker's industrious tapping. A few feet farther she became aware of another rhythmic sound—footsteps behind her.

She slowed, her heart pounding, for she knew that step—it

was Woolfe's, his long legs bringing him along one step to her two. Another feeling shivered through her as she turned to watch him approach, one she had felt lately when she encountered Woolfe. Mature for his eighteen years, he had changed so much this last year, becoming more solitary, often staying away for days at a time. Still so dear to her, her childhood champion, yet grown a stranger.

"Hello," she offered, wondering why he looked so serious.

"Taryn," he said, coming alongside her and lifting the basket off her arm. He shifted it to his other hand and flung an arm around her shoulder as they strolled forward. The casual action made her nervous, for she'd grown into a woman's body early last year, tall and rounded and wishing no one would look at her. Having him touch her now felt strange, awkward, as though she were someone else entirely.

They passed out of the trees into a patch of sunshine just as she looked up at him. She gasped, coming to a stop. "What happened to your face, Woolfe?"

He dropped his arm off her shoulder and faced her. "Quinn," he replied, brusquely, with no elaboration. He was tense, poised like a stag, full of courageous energy and apt to lope off arrogantly into the woods at any minute.

She studied his face. A bloody welt streaked down one side, hugging his hairline and defacing the curve of his ear. Bruises already turning blue covered one cheekbone, and his lip was split and puffed.

"I've never known Quinn to beat anyone with his fists," she said, confused at Quinn's departure from using the whip.

"No one has ever stood up to him before," Woolfe replied, a trace of satisfaction lacing his fierce words.

Terror, stronger than she had ever known, began pumping through her body in a thundering cadence. "What happened?" she whispered, knowing that it didn't matter, really, for Woolfe was doomed.

Woolfe began walking again, and she followed him into the next stand of trees, hurrying to stay close enough to hear his words. "He snapped his whip at my face, showing off to his friends. I lost my temper, and without thinking, I grabbed it and pulled him to the ground. His friends began laughing at him, so he came after me."

"And he beat you."

"He tried. I left him unconscious on the ground." He said it as if it didn't matter, as if it were a commonplace occurrence.

"He will kill you, you know," she blurted. "He won't fight fairly. He will come from behind, and you won't have a chance." She knew it was going to happen, and her throat ached so hard she couldn't say another word. She stopped walking as a storm of pain froze her where she stood. Tears, unbidden and unwelcome, streamed down her face.

Woolfe turned and retraced his steps to stand before her, dropping the basket carefully onto the path and enfolding her in his strong arms. She slipped her own arms around his back and held on as if he would be torn away from her if she let go.

How long they stood thus, she would never know, even years later when she thought about it. After a while, though, he leaned back and cupped her face in his large hands. Slowly, he lowered his head and touched her lips with his own. It was a magic moment—a communion of souls saying good-bye—for they both knew he would have to flee.

Woolfe's lips were swollen and sore, yet she knew he felt no pain as he lifted his lips, looked at her, and lowered them again. It was a gentle kiss, but it stirred something in her she had never felt before, a warmth that was the sweetest feeling she had ever known.

Then, like a window opening, the truth materialized in her heart and brain—she did not want to let him go. None of her life meant anything if Woolfe left. He was her anchor, the reason for molding her days to please everyone, indeed, the force that gave her life meaning. Woolfe lit her days with moments of true happiness, and she treasured the encounters with him that made the rest of her life bearable.

She loved him.

Did he, wonder of wonders, love her?

She searched his face and caught her breath. Usually so closed and wary, his face now blazed with love and resolve. "We can leave Kingsford together now or wait until you are ready," he said, and she gasped at the daring thought. His hand caressed her cheek to calm her. "Do not worry about Quinn, Taryn; I am not afraid of him."

She could say yes, she could beg him to stay with her—or she could go with him. But, what about his plan to become wealthy, to make his fortune?

If he stayed, his life was forfeit, either at Quinn's hand or by hanging for killing Quinn—Oliver would see to that. If she went with him, Oliver would pursue them mercilessly to keep her fortune within his grasp. Even if Oliver did not find them, how could Woolfe make his future with her dragging him down? He hadn't even enough money, she was sure, for passage to another continent, much less enough money to maintain them at the other end of a voyage.

How many years had Woolfe suffered for her? Could she ask for still more, for the rest of his life, for the end of his dreams? The bright light of her newly discovered love intensified, then coalesced into a fierce, narrow beam of resolve to save him.

She couldn't say she loved Giles, or deny her love for Woolfe—she knew she could never speak such words. But then, she would never need to be forceful, for whatever rejection she dealt him, he would accept, no matter how nebulous.

He would expect it.

She had only to find the courage to speak. To speak the truth.

"You know I am to marry Giles, Woolfe. It's all arranged in my father's will."

She would never in all her life forget the look in his eyes at that endless, traitorous moment. He put her from him then, firmly, without hesitation. He was leaving, she thought; she might never see him again. The thought terrified her. "Will you ever return?"

"You have made your choice, Taryn, and there is nothing else for me here . . . I shall never return."

She fought the panic within her. How could she do this—to herself, to him? She clamped her teeth on her lower lip to keep from screaming the truth aloud as he left her, striding quickly away without looking back.

She watched him until he disappeared, then shakily picked up the basket and slowly turned to complete her almost forgotten task. Her heart wept silently all day as she went through the colorless motions of living. And upon her pillow that night she wept great sobbing tears—for a love she had known only for a moment, and for a man she would never see again.

The next morning she found a present at her bedroom door, one Woolfe had left with Cook yesterday morning before he met Taryn in the woods. It was a soft, lavender ribbon—the identical gift he gave her each year, for he said it was the color of her eyes. He'd wrapped the ribbon in a threadbare, monogrammed handkerchief that his father had left behind, the best he could do, for he had none of his own.

As she held the ribbon to her breast, she realized she'd forgotten that today was her birthday—a day that Woolfe had always tried to fill with laughter and little surprises. Somberly, she wondered if birthdays would ever again seem joyous, for the friend she'd always secretly considered God's greatest gift to her had just walked out of her life forever.

February, 1813, Kingsford

A cold, blustery wind blew across the cemetery, whipping the cloaks and scarves of the mourners assembled to bid farewell to Richard Burnham, late Earl of Kingsford. Before the grave stood Geoffrey, the new earl, oblivious to the uneasy glances of the other mourners as they hesitated to leave en masse now that the vicar had committed the late earl's soul to the mercy of his Maker.

"Giles," Taryn murmured, trying to keep her voice level. If Oliver and Claudia suspected what she was about, she hated to think to what lengths they would go to prevent another such opportunity as this. "I would like to have a private moment with Geoffrey. If I ask Claudia if I may stay, she will . . ."

"I know," Giles replied. "She will throw a fit and accuse you of something ridiculous . . . I don't know why she does that."

"Could you . . ."

Giles waved his leather-gloved fingers. "She won't know what happened until she is ensconced in her parlor with a cup of tea." He turned jauntily toward his parents.

Dear Giles—he did his best to act as a buffer between his mother's temper and Taryn, and had been a great comfort since Woolfe's departure. She watched him walk away, miserable at how she planned to deceive him.

As Giles herded Oliver and Claudia into the family coach, Taryn moved slowly forward to position herself beside Geoffrey, watching in relief as the other villagers began leaving, walking back to hearths that would put welcome warmth back in their bones. Taryn sighed and murmured to Geoffrey, "Stay a moment and talk to me."

Geoffrey's head turned slowly as if awakening from a sleep. "Oh, Taryn, it's you. Sorry, I c-c-can't seem to b'lieve he's really gone."

"I'm sorry about your father's passing, Geoffrey . . ."

Geoffrey nodded absently and offered Taryn his arm. Nodding at the vicar to signal his satisfaction with the service,

Geoffrey took a deep breath and drew her beside him, slowly walking down the lane. "You wanted to talk to me? About Woolfe?"

Taryn's heart lurched. "Woolfe? You've seen him?"

Geoffrey frowned. "No, I have not, and I am worried. It's been too long, and every time he does this to me, I have him dead and buried before he shows up again." He took a step forward, then felt a tug on his arm. Stopping, he looked down at Taryn. "What's the matter? You aren't going to faint, are you?"

Taryn attempted to find her voice while the road whirled before her. "No, really, I am fine. It must be . . ."

"What a beast I am, frightening you with tales of Woolfe's absence. Pay no mind to me, Taryn, and tell me what you wanted to say. Although," he added, "I have an idea what you wish to discuss."

Geoffrey smiled at Taryn's confused frown and drew her forward along the ice-encrusted lane. "I promised Woolfe that if ever I could, I would see to your getting free from your aunt and uncle."

"Woolfe asked you . . . ?"

"Every time I saw him, even when you were children together, but m'father wouldn't listen. How do you feel about it now, though? Do you want to stay here and marry Giles?"

"Oh," she said, her throat raspy with emotion, forcing her thoughts away from the subject of Woolfe. "It's not that I don't have a fondness for Giles, I do. But even though it seems they indulge his every whim, I do not think Oliver would allow Giles to manage my money, even if he tries to. Oliver would never let that wealth out of his grasp."

She felt like a melodrama heroine, portraying her relatives in such appalling terms, but anything less might not convince Geoffrey how serious she was. "Oliver terrifies me, and Claudia makes my life miserable. Sometimes, I don't think I can stand any of them one more minute, much less the rest of my life. If only my father's will hadn't decreed we marry . . ."

"I don't believe it did," Geoffrey replied, shaking his head.

"What?" She stopped walking, her hands falling to her sides.

Geoffrey turned back to face her. "I don't believe your father's will said you *had* to marry Giles. Only gave you permission if you wanted to, seeing you were so fond of each other as children."

"But I have seen it myself. Oliver has a copy."

"Yes, he might at that," Geoffrey said slowly, "but it's only a c-c-copy, and evidently been tampered with." He frowned and studied her confused face. "I have seen the original and, as I remember, it says you *may* marry your c-c-cousin, but there is no betrothal agreement. In fact, when you reach your majority, you have access to a sizable fortune, set up in trust, of course. If you wish, you could set up your own household, but you'd need a proper chaperone. Bacon-brained idea for an unmarried girl, but your father was an unusual man—I suppose that's how he got so rich."

"You're sure?" she asked shakily. "Oh, Geoffrey, will you help me? Help me get free of them? I cannot do it alone, for they would just lock me in and force the marriage. I won't reach my majority until next summer, and until then, Oliver and Claudia have guardianship over me."

"Well, let me set my solicitor loose on the problem. If Oliver has gone so far as showing you a forged will, we should see if he has placed his own man as trustee. It shouldn't happen, but it seems c-c-clear he has done some c-c-careful planning behind the scenes already. Perhaps as a relative, I could replace your guardian in London just to keep your aunt and uncle c-c-constrained. Until then, you must avoid marrying Giles. It c-c-cannot be done overnight, you know."

"Will you do it, though? It's my only hope."

"Hmm," Geoffrey mused. "Have to look into it when I return to the city."

"You'll be careful not to mention this to anyone, Geoffrey? Any hint that I am not willing to marry Giles, and Oliver will act immediately."

Geoffrey stared at her, then said gently, "As you wish, my dear. I'll get things moving for you, and then we will talk again. Until then, it's our secret."

Early Summer, 1813, Kingsford

Oliver watched the smugglers bring in the last crate—French lace and bolts of silk—and deposit it on the pile of merchandise stacked in the middle of the storeroom. "I'll let you know when we need to deliver the load," he said, "we'll meet up here at the Hall as usual."

The men scurried out the back way, silent lest they wake the scanty crew of servants in the deserted Hall. Oliver came after, closing doors as he went, kegs of brandy in the adjoining room, and exotic foodstuffs, paintings, furniture, and more in the next. After the last door stood closed and locked, he leaned back against it, alone in the basement with his eyes closed, his face close to ecstasy as he totted sums in his mind. He sighed finally, ready to return home. Quinn waited at the back door with his torch flaming to light Oliver's way.

He wasn't alone.

A short man, his cape flapping in the evening breeze, stood nearby. A flash of embroidered pink revealed his foppish taste in waistcoats, and shiny white satin covered his thighs. "I've bad news, Chastain."

Oliver waved Quinn away and glared at his visitor. "Have you lost your mind, Fletcher? What would people think to see the Kingsford solicitor coming to the country at night like this?"

"I just returned to London from my hunting box in Scotland, only to hear distressing news. I could have let you read it in the newspapers like everybody else, Chastain, but this is too serious. As steward for the Kingsford estate, you could be in a lot of trouble, and if the records are examined too closely, my career is over."

"Hell and damnation, get on with it."

"Geoffrey, Lord Kingsford is dead—murdered by a damned traitor to the Crown." Fletcher shrank back at the expression on Oliver's face. "And that's not all. His cousin, Woolfe Burnham, the new Lord Kingsford, is alive after all. He was at Lady Crowper's ball a few nights ago. The Prince Regent was in attendance and—"

"Why have I not heard of this before? Claudia and Giles are in London—why haven't they notified me?"

"I called on them. Mrs. Chastain refused to leave your boy, Giles, who has been in bed with the ague. She hadn't heard the news, although Geoffrey's burial was today."

Oliver clenched his fists. "I'll go to London and take care of Woolfe. If he disappears once more, no one will think anything of it. In the meantime, you do what you can with the damned documents."

"What if he is on his way here?"

"I'll set men on the highway to watch for him. Now, get the hell out of here."

Fletcher bobbed his head up and down, cleared his throat to speak, then thought better of it. He turned to clamber into the dusty coach waiting in the driveway, and seconds later the coachman snapped the reins and started the horses.

Oliver watched his informant leave. His fists clenched as he turned almost blindly back toward the house and opened the front door. A thin, sour-faced woman hurried forward, irritation evident in every marching step she took. Upon seeing who her visitor was, her pinched expression transformed itself into a welcoming gleam. "M'lord," she said, using the undeserved title.

Approvingly, he nodded. "I am off to London tomorrow, Parsons. I shall check over the Hall as usual before I go." He walked into the parlor and reached for the brandy decanter on the sideboard.

"Very well, sir," she said smugly. "You'll find everything in order. Young Martha's finishing in the bedrooms, and she will be out of your way in a few moments."

He stopped and tipped his head to the side, his handsome face relaxing. Smiling, he downed the brandy and headed for the stairs.

Chapter Two

Taryn stood, signaling an end to the vicar's lengthy visit. In response, that worthy gentleman heaved his bulky frame off the settee, setting into chiming protest the crystal prisms ornamenting the hand-painted lamp on a nearby table. Taryn's perfectly modulated voice rose in a gentle swell to diplomatically disguise the creaking of her visitor's corsets.

"Thank you for coming, Reverend Sefton, and for your condolences on Geoffrey's passing. And thank you for bringing the improving tracts. I do so look forward to discussing them with you each week."

Beaming at his pupil, the vicar removed his spectacles and industriously cleaned the thick glass ovals with a large, lace-trimmed handkerchief. "Charming young lady. Such a pleasure to find such elegance in this backwa . . . umm, country village." He positioned the glasses on the upper bridge of his nose and carefully slid them into place over each ear. That ritual concluded, he shook himself, much like, Taryn thought, a large animal finished with its ablutions. As his clothing, bunched into rolls from sitting, rippled downward and settled into place, he addressed her once more. "I observed the coach leaving this morning, Miss Burnham. Has your uncle gone to attend to estate matters?"

Taryn dipped her head in a delicate, affirmative motion, her thick braids a shining tiara of modest elegance. "My uncle left for London this morning after hearing of Geoffrey's death. I suppose it's all over the village."

The vicar nodded and cleared his throat, his understandable anxiety revealed as he spoke. "And Woolfe Burnham, the new Lord Kingsford, do you suppose he will wish to visit his estate now and make changes—a new broom, so to speak?"

Taryn's hands gripped tightly together, and her smile wavered. Sweet, gentle Geoffrey dead—and Woolfe now Earl of Kingsford. Inside her chest a dozen butterflies danced, and within her brain a waterfall of thoughts roared and splashed and jumbled into a pool of chaos. Grief for Geoffrey's loss held sway, but malevolently awaiting attention was the ominous fact that she no longer had a champion to rescue her.

The vicar cleared his throat, reminding her that her aborted conversation was of utmost importance to him. She pried her thoughts away from her troubles and offered her visitor a hesitant smile. "I do beg pardon, Reverend Sefton, my thoughts wandered. It is so complicated . . ." Granting her instant forgiveness, he waved his pudgy hand in encouragement to finish her story.

Wanting only to hurry him on his way, she continued. "You are, of course, my uncle's own choice, and if he remains as steward, nothing will change." There, that should calm him.

The vicar seemed appeased momentarily, then all the creases of his plump face compressed into a scowl. "But, if Lord Kingsford replaces your uncle with another steward?"

She moaned inwardly and closed her eyes. Rubbing her temple, she looked at his stubbornly persistent face, furious with herself for letting this conversation ever begin. "Should Lord Kingsford wish, we could all be displaced."

"My dear Miss Burnham, I had no idea! Why this is infamous, to think that you . . ." The vicar's words trailed off, and Taryn could see that his thoughts had completely outstripped his ability to speak. He tried again. "But surely, this is your own home?" His brain finally caught up to his tongue, and he protested his own words. "Unless your uncle built this lovely cottage on Kingsford land?"

The "lovely cottage"—an imposing eight-bedroom mansion—indeed stood on Kingsford land, as did the village, the small seaport, and the farmland that rose out of the valley and sprawled across the hills. A few homes were leased to summer people each year, which swelled their population, but even those remained under Kingsford control. Although she was certain Oliver had secured the matter of their home properly, it was impossible to guess what Woolfe might do, should he ever hear of his inheritance.

Taryn clenched the edge of her dress, more irritable by the minute, as the vicar chased the wild possibilities to ground. "But, Miss Burnham, are you not related to Lord Kingsford? Forgive me for intruding, but surely he would not abandon a kinswoman?"

She sighed. "I am sure there is no need for your concern in my behalf. Our fathers were distant cousins, and I am

Woolfe's only remaining blood relative." Undoubtedly that would satisfy him. She stepped toward the door, hoping to draw him after her. Sheeplike, he followed; unfortunately his questions tagged along.

"And your aunt and uncle, how are they placed?"

She turned as she reached the doorway. "As is true of so many families, the lines become somewhat tangled. My Aunt Claudia is no relation to the Burnham family since she is my mother's sister. Neither is my Uncle Oliver a blood relative, but rather is brother to the late Geoffrey's mother, a connection that brought him the opportunity to serve as steward to the Kingsford estate."

The vicar nodded as he pounced upon the most promising kernel of hope. "You are then Lord Kingsford's heir. Oh, not if the estate is entailed, but if it is not?"

She shook her head helplessly. Was there no end to this?

He smiled. "In that case, if Lord Kingsford is dead—"

A scream from the direction of the kitchen broke into his floundering dialogue. Taryn turned immediately toward the sound, then stopped. Turning back to the vicar, she said softly, "Perhaps you might see yourself out, Reverend Sefton, while I see to this domestic matter." She extended her hand, and with an imperceptible pause, he returned the courtesy. Accepting the quick brush of her fingers with obvious regret, he protested, "I feel it is my duty—"

Pretending to have not heard his words, Taryn turned and hurried from the parlor. Down the stairs she ran, her slippers thudding softly on the carpeted stairs leading to the ground floor. She could feel the boards jarring as the vicar followed closely behind. She turned toward the sound of Cook's mournful cries at the back of the house. As she passed through the door to the kitchen, she wished that closing it would somehow stop the inquisitive vicar's progress.

Taryn halted just inside the room, searching for the expected cut finger or painful burn. Freshly sliced bread sat deserted in a heap on the long wooden table, and the mouth-watering fragrance of mutton and vegetables rose cheerfully from the pot on the stove. The comforting serenity of the kitchen registered briefly on Taryn's senses, only to fade immediately as she beheld the frightening sight of Cook leaning against the kitchen door, her fingers pressed against her mouth while tears ran from horror-filled eyes.

A small child deserted her post beside Cook and ran to meet

Taryn. Clutching Taryn's hand, Jolie, the young orphan employed to assist in the kitchen, tugged and pulled Taryn to the door, pointing to the unexpected entourage trudging slowly up the graveled pathway.

Taryn stopped beside Cook, and watched with a strange sense of foreboding as Kingsford's sullen-faced servants carried a large bundle, wrapped unceremoniously in a stable blanket, into the kitchen and deposited it quickly on the stone floor. The two servants then stepped backward, anxiously sidling toward the open door.

The taller man looked at Cook and mumbled, "It's Martha, missus." Taryn watched in silent horror as Cook pulled the blanket aside. No, Taryn's mind screamed in silent protest. No, not Martha.

"She done herself in. Jumped out the window," the servant added. "We found her this morning."

A numbness crept through Taryn's body as Cook dropped to her knees and gathered her precious daughter into her arms, weeping heartbrokenly.

Conscious that she had to do something, for Cook's sake, Taryn broke from her trance. "Get Alyce," Taryn murmured to the wide-eyed Jolie. "She is in the sewing room." Cook would need her other daughter beside her. Taryn knelt and pulled Cook's head upon her shoulder, absorbing some of the burden of the woman's beloved child. Poor Martha. Her black curls were matted with dirt, glass, and blood, and her dress was torn from neck to shoulder.

Rocking to and fro, Cook gently began removing bits of glass from Martha's hair, crying piteously. "It isn't so, is it, miss? Our Martha never did such a thing as jumping out a window. Why, she turned white as my pastry just climbing over the stile!"

Taryn spoke to the largest of the two Kingsford servants. "Tall Johnnie, when did this happen? Did you see her fall?"

Tall Johnnie blinked rapidly and gulped. "No, miss. Samuel here found her out back this morning. Must have happened last night."

Taryn's thoughts whirled, so sure that Martha—cheerful, laughing child that she was—would never have considered such a thing. How could she?

Yet, who knew better than Taryn how deceiving outward appearances could be? Could Martha have been despondent without their knowing it? She thought back, trying to remember if the fourteen-year-old had seemed unhappy last Sunday, her first half day off since entering service as maid at Kingsford Hall.

No, she remembered Martha cheerfully entertaining the staff with a little mocking imitation of Parsons, the Kingsford's cantankerous housekeeper. That ill-tempered, self-righteous madame, Martha had related, spewed her wrath freely toward any creature unfortunate enough to be within striking distance. Martha, as all the servants in the household before her, had become nimble-footed indeed in the week since she had been employed at Kingsford Hall. Martha had laughed while telling the story.

Other than the housekeeper's temper, the work at Kingsford Hall was not difficult. The few servants willing to work in the damp, neglected place fought a halfhearted battle against peeling paint, dry rot, and smoking fireplaces. Perhaps Martha fell, Taryn thought, searching for a reasonable answer; perhaps a rotting window gave way.

She started guiltily when the vicar broke into her thoughts. She had forgotten he was there. "My dear Miss Burnham, this is no place for a lady. If only Kingsford had a magistrate, he could take care of all these unpleasant details. Why, you should not even *be* in this kitchen, much less . . ."

An overpowering wave of rage poured over Taryn, reminiscent of the temper that brought her—and subsequently Woolfe—such grief in her childhood. How dare he intrude so insensitively on her grief and assume she wished to be anywhere other than here with Cook, who had stood in place of a mother for all these years? She w*anted* to mourn Martha, who was like a little sister to her. How dare he be so cold, so obtuse?

And why was he not comforting the poor mother? The old vicar would have been on the floor with his arm around Cook, describing the lost child's wonderful attributes, and promising her distraught mother the wonders and happiness of heaven.

Rapid footsteps sounded in the hall, signaling the arrival of Cook's older daughter, Alyce. Little Jolie entered first, holding the door open for Alyce, who took in the scene at once, her face crumpling in dismay. Taryn stood to embrace her friend briefly, then watched helplessly as Alyce knelt to comfort her mother.

In the background, the vicar droned on with his string of pompous pronouncements. Finally, one statement broke through her grief and silenced the room. "A suicide cannot be buried in hallowed ground."

Taryn turned to him, her dulcet expression held precariously in place—with mayhem in her thoughts. This man was leaving now, she vowed, if she had to chase him out with a broom. With ease of practice, she assumed the empty-headed, socially accepted pose that the vicar expected. "Oh, you poor, dear man. How could I put you through such a wrenching experience. Let me show you out as I had intended before this occurrence interrupted us." She led the way from the kitchen to the front door.

Turning as they reached the front door, she said between gritted teeth, "Dear Reverend Sefton, please do not distress Martha's family until we have investigated the truth of her death. I cannot believe the servants had the story right." She fairly pushed him out the door, gushing once more at his forbearance with the day's events.

The next few hours were distressing to them all. Martha was laid out in an unused bedroom, each servant offering to take turns sitting with her. Taryn administered a sleeping potion to Cook and saw her to the attic bedroom she shared with Alyce.

As day's end approached, Taryn prepared a cup of tea and carried it out of the kitchen, intending to savor a quiet moment alone in her bedchamber. The knocker banged, and Albert, the footman, jumped to answer it. Taryn's heart sank as the vicar waddled importantly inside, his eyes alight at finding his prey so quickly. Nodding at her, he took his time to shed his dove gray cape, pulling his matching gloves from each chubby finger with the precision of an artist, and dispensed them to Albert. "My dear Miss Burnham, I have been to see the housekeeper at Kingsford Hall and have settled everything."

Albert stilled, alert to the vicar's words. After laying a blanket of peace over the household staff, Taryn had no wish to have the vicar rip it away with his unguarded words in Albert's presence.

Taryn forced back the frustration that nibbled at her waning reserve of strength and spoke in a careful monotone. "Albert, see that the fire is refreshed in the parlor. Reverend Sefton, won't you join me?" She slowly followed Albert up the stairs, taking deep, self-composing breaths with each step.

As Albert finished his work and departed, Taryn seated herself in the only chair not given over to crocodiles and lions's feet, a graceful Hope design, whose curving legs and clawed feet had not disgraced itself when the Egyptian style had come into fashion. Her Aunt Claudia had recently declared the Egyptian style "exploded," and planned to search the London warehouses for something new. If luck was running in Taryn's favor, the search might take months.

Waiting for the vicar to lower his bulk at the first opportunity as was his custom, Taryn was amazed to find him instead pacing the room. In a rare surge of authority, he had evidently traveled to Kingsford Hall to gather the particulars, and returned with a light of righteous fervor in his eyes and a dramatic sense of purpose.

The vicar stopped before the fireplace and warmed his ample backside before the blazing fire. His face, still chilled from his hurried outing in the cool sea breeze, glowed with an unaccustomed flush of health; clearly, authority agreed with him. His rosy chipmunk cheeks puffed in and out like a bellows, inflating consequence into the moment. Finally, he leaned one arm on the high mantel and turned, stretching a little to maintain his balance.

He struck a pose, and Elizabeth felt a gurgle of laughter rising through the heavy layers of grief. No matter how she vowed to regard him with respect, this tendency to levity overtook her. She clamped her teeth in a tight vise to confine her offending lower lip and, from somewhere, produced a serious expression. As he began his tirade, her precarious expression turned to horror.

"She's a suicide," he pronounced. "She was too pretty for her own good and much too excitable, the type to fall into a decline over the smallest of things. Parsons assured me that only that day Martha had become hysterical over the slightest of reprimands and spoken most disrespectfully to her. She generously gave her one more chance to save her job, but it was obvious she couldn't face the shame, and rightly so. She therefore took her own life. Jumped out of the window. Parsons, the housekeeper, was most cooperative, indeed, all that was proper. It overset her sensibilities terribly to speak out against the girl, but I insisted that truth must prevail."

Elizabeth gasped, and he glanced at her with a triumphant raise of his chin. "Ah, yes! Well may you join me in indignation that such an insult to a good, Christian woman has come to pass. I assured her that this would not be covered over with a cloak of respectability. We shall make an example of her. We shall—"

Taryn exploded. "You shall do no such thing! You have no right or authority to make any decisions about anything!"

Reverend Sefton's mouth dropped open, and his face erupted in scarlet blotches. His eyes watered and blinked rapidly. "Dear child, whatever do you mean? It certainly is my express duty to forbid any unclean soul burial in the church cemetery—surely you can see that."

"Forbid her burial . . . you . . . you can't make that decision when she certainly would not take her own life! Were you there when Martha died? Where is the evidence that she killed herself? Are you going to take the word of that viper-tongued housekeeper over respected people I have known all my life?"

He surprised her by stepping closer to her with an aggressiveness he had never shown before, and out of hiding crept forth a gleam of something not unlike animosity. "I am taking the word of a righteous church-going woman, and when your uncle returns, he will no doubt reaffirm my decision."

He smiled sweetly, not a pleasant sight. "And how long until she must be buried? The sun grows warmer each day." He paused and then said with a distant, preoccupied musing, "I don't believe there is any reason we shouldn't follow the old tradition in a case like this. Burial at the crossroads in the old manner with a stake in the body to keep her from rising and haunting the neighborhood. Of course, I do not believe in such haunting, but it will satisfy the ignorant, superstitious villagers."

Dear God, what was she to do? How could she prevent him from issuing a directive to a selected famer or two, and the deed was done? She daren't cross him again, for he would only react like the spoiled brat that he was, fighting viciously for his own way.

She paused for a moment to collect her thoughts, then favored him with one of her Aunt Claudia's haughty smiles. Without a trace of apology to her vow to show the man respect, she proceeded to overrun every argument he might muster—with a series of outrageous lies.

"Reverend," she began with a confiding tone, "do you recall your question earlier today regarding the new Lord Kingsford's intentions—whether he intended to return home or not?"

His face was almost comical, so caught off guard was he. She did not intend for him to keep pace with her, and continued before he barely had time to close his mouth. "You must have sensed my hesitation to give you an answer."

The vicar's face cleared, obviously grateful that his response required only a nod. Taryn continued in a low voice. "Few people know the story, but I know I can trust you to keep a confidence."

He pasted on a condescending smile and opened his mouth to compliment himself. She spoke instead. "Years ago, before Woolfe Burnham left, he asked me to marry him." The vicar frowned, then his eyes darted to the side, a habit he favored when faced with a dilemma of choice, especially one of social fence-sitting. Confusing the issue for the vicar was that, although unspoken, everyone in Kingsford knew she was Giles's intended wife.

The vicar's present impasse was whether he should give credit to the unknown Woolfe Burnham, or follow his slavish obedience to Claudia and Oliver, who ruled the town of Kingsford.

Taryn brought the vicar's attention back to her. "I wished to marry Woolfe, but he said that I was too young to decide and, in any case," she lied, "he wished to make his fortune before offering for me. He has traveled the world and has amassed a great deal of wealth. I expected him to return last week, but Geoffrey's death must have delayed him once again."

The vicar could not resist protesting. "But I thought you and Giles—"

"Oh, that is just a hope of my aunt and uncle, of course. Giles and I have no intention of marrying. We are first cousins, you know."

"Not an unheard of connection when a family wishes to consolidate property and fortune, surely, Miss Burnham."

"Dear Reverend Sefton, my cousin Giles has no title; neither will he inherit a great fortune or property from his parents. Since we have only a cousinly fondness for each other, marriage between us would serve no purpose. What better consolidation could there be, then, than to marry Woolfe Burnham? Then both his estate and my fortune would be secured for our children."

The vicar gulped and blinked. He removed his glasses and whipped out his handkerchief to clean them. His hands shook so badly that he dropped the spectacles at his feet, and as he retrieved them his obvious dismay gave her tremendous encouragement to continue. She frowned. "I cannot help but be worried at Woolfe's return, of course."

The vicar's labored breathing stilled as he waited for her explanation.

"He has such a bad temper, you know, unlike the easy-going Geoffrey or Geoffrey's father, Richard. No, Woolfe is more like his own father."

Obviously, the vicar had not heard the entire story of the family disgrace. She bit back a smile. "The younger son."

Now he looked even more confused.

She lowered her voice to a whisper. "Justin, the pirate."

The vicar's eyes darted to the side once more as he did his social calculations. "But," he protested, finding his voice at last, "can the son of such a man inherit?"

"Who would object? Not I." She shuddered dramatically. "Who would withstand a rich man with such a violent temper? The lawyers would love him, and there are no other heirs. Even the Prince Regent is not above accepting donations to his coffers for smoothing the path of a wealthy and generous man." She had no idea if this was the truth, but Woolfe had vowed never to return, so what she said did not matter.

"As I said, I am worried about his return, Reverend Sefton, as you should also."

"Me?" The vicar gulped.

"Indeed. Woolfe used to spend hours in Cook's kitchen, eating her wonderful treats. What he might say to your burying poor Martha in such a terrible manner when she is daughter to Cook and sister to our childhood friend, Alyce, I cannot imagine."

That was the end of the vicar's pose. He dropped into the nearest settee, surrounded by crocodiles and sphinxes. Beads of perspiration broke out on his nose and upper lip and his glasses slid down his nose. Off came the spectacles and out came the handkerchief. He polished the ovals of glass, mopped off his face, and tucked everything carefully back in place.

He looked so helpless. It occurred to Taryn that he was a relatively young man, and this was probably his first position. As a younger son of his well-to-do family, he had no real experience with the life he had been thrown into. She took pity on him and brought the conversation to its finale. "It would be different if we knew for certain that Martha had taken her own life. You have spoken to her on several Sundays, and I know you sensed her purity of spirit. I am sure there has been a mistake, and the kindest thing would be to quietly bury her tomorrow in the churchyard. It would mean nothing to my uncle either way, and to the new Lord Kingsford, it would mean a great deal."

She rose as she always did to indicate that his visit was at an end. Automatically, he rose with her. "Thank you, dear Vicar. I shall come by tomorrow and discuss the burial service." He left without a word.

Thankful for the refuge of her own room, she was just dropping off to a well-earned rest when she heard the sound of a cart traversing the road. She sat up, her heart pounding in fear. For a moment the sound of wheels made her think it was the Kingsford carriage, bringing Oliver and Claudia home. As the cart passed by and the sounds faded in the distance, she realized the enormity of what she had done.

From whence had come today's reckless defiance—the angry scheming she had exhibited today . . . reminding her so much of the wild child she had subdued so many years ago?

If her guardians even heard about the incident, all her hard work would be for nothing. If Claudia heard of Taryn's interference, and thus learned that Taryn actually *cared* about the outcome of the incident, nothing would stop her from seeing the poor girl dug up and banished from the churchyard.

Fear snapped at the edges of her exhausted slumber.

Chapter Three

As the coach followed the narrow coast road, Woolfe Burnham quietly lifted his long legs and arranged them in the opposite corner of the coach, careful lest he awaken his companion, and—albeit unconventional—mentor, Kyoichi Asada. A muffled sigh escaped as he arched his back and stretched, a poor substitute for the brisk walk his muscles craved. His stockinged feet pushed against the squabs of the luxurious carriage his friend and former employer—master spy for England, Lord Hawksley—had insisted he use for this journey.

Without opening his slanted eyes, Asada murmured in his maddeningly probing way, "Considering that you have no use for women, it is ironic that this errand can be laid upon the doorstep of two of their kind."

Woolfe, caught in the uncomfortable vise of truth, denied it firmly, "Nothing of the kind. I am now the heir. I cannot turn my back upon that."

"You go to see the love of your childhood."

"Taryn? I was a friend to the girl, Asada, no more. I go to examine the estate, sell it to the highest bidder, and leave."

"And you go at the bidding of that sorceress."

"Elizabeth?" Woolfe's granite expression softened. Elizabeth, who had turned down his recent proposal because she—whose dreams and visions came true—had *seen* very different futures for them both. Indeed, she had urged him hurry to Taryn, insisting she was in trouble and that, *if he wished, Taryn could be his.* Although he knew from experience that Elizabeth's visions described an accurate scene, by what demented twist of fate would Elizabeth's vision see him wanting the one person whom he could never have?

"And," Asada added in a sleepy voice, "you have come home because you cannot resist solving a mystery."

"Mere curiosity? Nonsense."

Asada opened his eyes, now fully awake and obviously

ready for a stimulating argument. "Your infantile curiosity has landed us in the thorns many times, Woolfesan."

Woolfe's dark expression lightened. "You mean the *briars*?" Seeing the scowl narrowing Asada's eyes to slits, Woolfe couldn't resist baiting his Japanese friend. "Perhaps you are correct. I have often enjoyed contemplating what delicious ravages time might have visited upon my childhood tormentors."

"If you wish to revenge yourself, then do it, else cease dreaming. I have told you many times, Woolfesan, frivolous thoughts drain the fighting spirit."

Ignoring the familiar lecture, Woolfe elaborated dreamily. "I see Quinn with his whip-wielding hand crippled and useless."

Asada slumped into the corner of the coach, disgust wrinkling his teak-hued skin into a mask of disapproval.

Woolfe pursed his lips and said dreamily, "Claudia's teeth are all missing."

The smaller man sighed heavily.

It was all the encouragement Woolfe needed. He mused, "And Oliver's gone senile and impotent."

Asada snapped to attention, his muscular back giving him a height and presence that had given many larger men reason to pay attention. "Woolfesan!"

Biting back a grin, Woolfe said solemnly, "Very well, let Claudia keep a few teeth."

Asada choked and fell backward, shaking with laughter. After a moment, he spoke in a solemn voice. "A child's fading memory does not erase the evil from our enemies, Woolfesan." He shrugged his powerful shoulders. "Oliver's physical potency may wane with age, but fury at such loss will only make him more cunning. Do not allow arrogance blind you to the danger of that one." He mumbled, "*Mekura hebi ni ojizu.*"

Woolfe reached for the strap as the coach went sharply round a bend, translating automatically, "Blind men do not fear snakes?"

Asada grunted, reaching swiftly for his own strap as the coach began veering from side to side in erratic rhythm to the frenzied sounds of a cursing coachman and frightened horses.

A loud cracking noise gave a second's warning. The coach tipped sideways, hesitated, then crashed heavily on its side, twisting and screeching and sliding along the road. Inside, the air exploded. Splinters of wood, silver flasks, boots and bricks flew and slid and smashed.

Asada groaned as he fell upon the door that was now the floor. Woolfe's long legs slid downward as his hand strained to keep its purchase on the leather strap now above him. The smell of oil spilled from the broken lamp Asada lay upon filled the coach. The lamp opposite, now a dangling chandelier above Woolfe's head, burned cheerfully on.

Into the settling quiet, the angry voice of the protesting coachman rose—a gunshot blasted, silencing the coachman and sending the horses into another frightened surge. The coach scraped another few feet forward as the horses attempted to free themselves from their heavy burden.

"Danger, Woolfesan!" Asada whispered, pushing with amazing strength against Woolfe's lower torso in an effort to help him up.

A deadly calm flowed through Woolfe's veins—a relic from childhood episodes under Quinn's whip, and a phenomenon for which he had often been grateful in his travels with Asada, and in his employment under Lord Hawksley. He lifted his other hand to grasp the strap, then pulled his muscled legs upward from the tangle below. Sweat broke out across his forehead as he braced each foot against an opposite seat and heaved a deep breath into his lungs.

"Asada? Are you all right?"

"*Hai.*" The interchange barely made a ripple of sound. Asada began moving quietly.

A low voice outside the coach snarled, "You've killed the coachman, you fool!"

"He shouldn't have reached for his gun." A callow, youthful voice, Woolfe noted, full of heated excitement.

"Aye, you've a taste for blood, Jimmy. One of these days, someone will kill you for your reckless ways." Disgust hoarsened the older man's reply.

"Are ye here to snivel or do a job?"

The older man cleared his throat and bellowed, "H'lo, the coach."

"We are coming out, sirs." Asada whined loudly. "Please calm yourselves." Asada grinned briefly at Woolfe as he twisted the door handle above him and let Woolfe push him upward. He crawled out, making noises like a man in pain. Crouching on the top of the upended coach, he reached down to offer his hand to Woolfe. "One moment, sirs. We are almost out." To Woolfe he murmured, "Pretend to be hurt."

"Holy damn," one voice muttered as Asada faced them to slowly pull Woolfe out of the carriage. He dragged him over the edge of the opened door, then plopped Woolfe's length out upon the coach like a wet fish. Woolfe curled into a ball and rolled over, then unwound slowly and slid down the side of the coach, coming to a weak-kneed stand. He moaned horribly, his thick, straight hair covering his face as his legs wobbled like a drunkard's.

"Stand and deli—"

"Stand?" Asada screeched from atop the coach. "You try standing when you've been tumbled behind a runaway team!"

At the opposite end of the toppled coach, Asada began crawling toward the edge, mumbling loudly, "I suppose you want my money!" He rolled over onto his stomach and slid until his feet hung suspended over the wheel. The younger robber automatically reached for him, but quickly stepped back as Asada fell awkwardly onto the wheel, his seemingly clumsy scrabbling making it swing back and forth. The robber watched for a moment, then disgusted, stepped forward to hold the wheel still.

Asada screamed, obviously out of control. "I suppose you want my master's jewels inside his pocket!"

"Hey, Willie—" The younger robber turned excitedly toward his partner. The older man nodded, moving toward Woolfe.

"Well, shoot him," Jimmy snapped. "I want those jewels."

Asada screamed in his ear, "Not the jewels!" Startled, the young robber jerked back, and Asada's powerful leg shot outward and kicked him in the chest. He dropped like a rock, choking and gasping for air.

"Jimmy—" The older man turned toward his partner and aimed his gun at Asada.

Behind him, Woolfe's hand swung through the air like an axe in full swing and struck the back of the robber's neck. The gun dropped. He joined his fellow on the ground without a sound, and lay unmoving with his eyes wide open.

The younger robber rolled onto his back, his expression wild, and pulled a knife from his boot. Asada flew through the air, his powerful kick catapulting the vicious young robber over the edge of the road and down the sharp embankment.

Asada stepped back and looked triumphantly at Woolfe. "Discipline and practice."

Woolfe shrugged his shoulders. "Dirty fighting."

Asada muttered, "Impudent barbarian," and, dragging the dead robber onto the side of the road, placed the miscreant's hat over his face. Impatiently he lectured Woolfe, "You hesitated, Woolfesan. Another second and he would have pulled the trigger."

"I do not like killing, Asada. If not for the fact that he *was* going to shoot you, I would only have stunned him."

Asada sighed. "You are too tall and too slow. You must work harder. Already I have spent years training you, and still I fail."

Woolfe knelt beside their livery-clad coachman lying motionless on the cold ground. Shaking his head, he removed his long coat and wrapped the coachman in it while Asada released the frightened horses from the tangled traces.

Woolfe tightened his grasp on the reins of the restive mount he had pressed into service. The overwrought horse, accustomed to pulling a coach in tandem with his three mates, had no fondness for the ignominious task of carrying a large passenger upon his bare back.

Asada, following on a more placid fellow, towed the remaining pair behind him, one horse given the task of transporting their fallen coachman. Asada motioned to the lighted buildings seemingly nestled around a lighthouse at the tip of the flat bluff upon which they rode. "Do you know this place we ride to?"

"No," Woolfe replied grimly, "but I have a great desire to see who lives on Kingsford property."

Asada gasped, "This is your land, Woolfesan?"

"Since we left the main road."

"And now you return triumphant to claim your own."

Woolfe's answer, when it finally came, barely reached Asada's keen hearing. "Geoffrey's death brought me to this place, Asada. He was my friend as well as cousin." Woolfe's face shone hard as granite in the moonlight. His long hair, released from the leather thong he favored, blew across his face.

Asada nodded with respect. "One does not march home triumphant over the grave of his friend."

A shimmering path of moonlight flowed across the water beyond the cliffs to outline the tall mast of a cutter at anchor in the small cove and fishing boats resting upon the beach. Miles separated them, yet it seemed one only had to stretch a hand to touch the ethereal tableau in the valley below.

An amazing sight drew them forth, miragelike, toward the bluff—a sprawling, four-story edifice, out of which rose an enormous square center, perhaps another two or three stories higher, that was comprised almost entirely of brightly lit windows. From the sea the tower would be a well-lit, unmistakable landmark—a lighthouse benevolently overlooking the ocean below. On the leeward side, outbuildings stood apart, discreetly housing barns, stables, and other necessary structures.

As the weary travelers approached, two servants ran out to greet them. "Here now, what's amiss?" said a gray-bearded giant, reaching up easily to withdraw the coachman's body from the horse.

"Assaulted by thieves on the cliff road," Woolfe replied briefly as the other servant reached for the reins of Asada's string of coach horses. "We'll need our coachman prepared to be transported back to London tomorrow."

"Aye, m'lord." The huge man carried his burden across the cobbled courtyard with no more effort than if he was out for an evening stroll.

"What is this place?" Woolfe asked.

"The Heritage, sir, an inn."

Woolfe dismounted silently while the taciturn servant led the coach horses away. Asada slid easily down the side of the horse. "Woolfesan, observe these men, seamen both, who work as servants. They may not be what they seem."

"Not landsmen, with that gait," Woolfe agreed, looking off into the distance, where the cutter sat at anchor. "Still, more than one sailor has tarried upon the land or retired from the sea in the end. They were clean and willing."

Asada's suspicious rebuttal whipped away on a sudden cold sea breeze that flew through the courtyard, bending bushes and blowing dust into their eyes. With unspoken haste, they approached the inn.

Welcome heat met them as they hurried through the long, spacious hallway that led to an immense, well-lit chamber, housed in the center tower they had observed from afar. Woolfe shivered with pleasure as the warmth soaked into his chilled bones. Several long strides into the high-ceilinged room, he stopped and stared in wonder. Had he ever been blessed with an eye for trapping out a place with a visual feast at every angle, this would have been the result.

Clear glass panes marched proudly across the curved seaward wall, unobtrusively held firm with tree-high pillars, and framed a moonlit panorama of the restless ocean and the cove below. Woolfe stood transfixed.

What brilliance had bethought a curved wall of glass shaped like the side of a ship and, his eyes traveled the rest of the room, had clearly spent a grand fortune to bring the treasures of the world to this hotel.

There were magnificent rugs from India, priceless vases and ivory-inlaid screens from China, exotic spices wafting their fragrances from cloisonne bowls. A wonderful hodgepodge of diverse works of art that should have been forbidden intermingling, together, somehow, created a room of remarkable harmony. A fire roared in a huge rock-lined fireplace in, of all places, the center of the room. Emotion filled him. He suddenly longed to row out to the ship waiting at anchor and take another turn at the ports of the world, yet the room also drew him like a primeval cave, welcoming, warm with everything a man could ever want—balm for the restless soul.

"Yer Lordship?" Woolfe turned at a servant's hesitant interruption.

"Yer wishing rooms for the night?"

"Yes, two rooms on the seaward side, if you please." At the servant's nod, Woolfe added, "And ask the proprietor to attend us here."

"That's Señor Esteban, sir. Right away."

As the servant hurried away, Woolfe took another look around the room, this time forcing his bewitched senses to coldly calculate the possibilities of profit from an establishment such as this. Once having sojourned here, a traveler would certainly return, but was the owner mad? How would he lure people to this isolated area in the first place? Moreover, all the seaside attractions he had seen the world over had been near water's edge, not marooned up on a hill.

Eccentric, this Señor Esteban. Rich, but much like this room, his upper story must have an unobstructed view in all directions. Woolfe turned to Asada. "Who do you suppose—"

Asada looked past him and bowed briefly, his face guarded. A deep, strangely accented voice behind Woolfe answered, "Welcome to the Heritage, gentlemen."

Woolfe turned quickly, his curiosity in full alert. What he

saw stirred some faint warning within. Before them stood a tall man whose once-handsome visage had evidently met with the wrong end of a sword. A deep scar stretched from temple to chin, although the man's face would probably still appeal to a lusty woman of the world.

Señor Esteban met Woolfe's gaze with a faint smile and eyes that were so blue as to almost seem black. Woolfe had met Spaniards with blue eyes and even blond hair, but none had eyes as intense as this. The man's hair was long, pulled back as was the prevailing look in his country, but his beard eschewed the Vandyke image and grew naturally full with a lush mustache. Yes, Woolfe decided, mature women would love his untamed, dangerous air—and, his wealth. Especially his wealth.

Woolfe scented only the danger. He must discover if Oliver had feathered his nest by allowing this mysterious man and his crew to operate freely in Kingsford. Woolfe welcomed the challenge.

Asada spoke. "Señor Esteban?" At the older man's nod, Asada bowed once more. "I am Kyoichi Asada. My silent friend is Woolfe Burnham, Earl of Kingsford."

A sudden, almost imperceptible stillness came over Señor Esteban. So, Woolfe thought, adopting a genial expression, I am not unknown to him. Of course, he wonders how my assuming the title and estate will affect his business here, even whether he might be thrown out entirely when he must deal with me instead of Oliver.

Señor Esteban's head dipped slightly and he offered his hand. Woolfe automatically grasped it, testing the strength and temper of his host, and found the hand work-roughened and strong. Woolfe motioned to the magnificent view. "I have never seen a finer room. Was the design yours?"

A smile broke through Señor Esteban's serious expression. "Yes." he replied with quiet satisfaction, his eyes gazing around the room. Then he turned his attention to Woolfe once more. "Lord Kingsford, I'm told you met with trouble on the road. May I ask what became of the highwaymen?"

"They are dead," Woolfe replied, searching his host's face for signs of guilt or frustration, but finding only polite interest. He longed to duel wits with the man, but even as he stood talking politely, exhaustion from the day's adventures began to take its toll on his body.

"How else may I serve you, Lord Kingsford?"

"I would appreciate if you could arrange for the retrieval of the rest of our bags, and have the coach brought in and repaired. They lie along the highway about two miles toward London."

Señor Esteban nodded. "You both look like you need a good rest, gentlemen. I'll see you to your rooms."

As he climbed the broad, thickly carpeted steps, Woolfe was pleased to note the treads were generously sized, large enough for his feet to rest comfortably as he ascended—most inns had narrow steps he had to tiptoe up. A man's man, this Señor Esteban, with an eye for innovation.

After directing Asada to his room, Señor Esteban opened the adjacent door with a flourish and ushered Woolfe inside. He strode across the room, pulled the velvet burgundy drapes back, and twisted the window latch to open the window. The refreshing ocean breeze flowed in, and Woolfe smiled in satisfaction.

Esteban stooped down, resting easily on his toes before the marble hearth. He carefully lit a generous pile of kindling and logs, then rose effortlessly to his feet, revealing an amazing fitness for a man of his mature years. As Esteban moved toward the door, Woolfe's gaze followed—and stopped at a painting on the wall. His heart thudded as he recognized a distinctive Rembrandt that had always hung in the library of Kingsford Hall.

Not so innocent then, this Señor Esteban, if Oliver had been willing to put a family heirloom into his hands.

"Breakfast may be requested with a ring of your bell rope, Lord Kingsford, or you might prefer the dining room downstairs just off the large chamber you first entered," Esteban said genially. "We'll speak again tomorrow."

Woolfe followed him to the door, nodding in agreement, and waited impatiently for his host's footsteps to trail away. He stepped into the hall, strode the few feet to Asada's door, and knocked. When Asada answered, Woolfe murmured a single, terse instruction: "Lock your door."

Chapter Four

The embroidered hem of Taryn's morning dress swirled and flapped against her ankles as she turned and paced back toward the dark kitchen window. Would the day never begin so she might hurry to the vicar's?

Glaring at the still-dark eastern horizon, she brushed at the flaxen strand of hair tickling her cheek. Blast this unruly stuff, she thought, thrusting bits of renegade hair under the drooping braid already hanging lopsided upon her head. The thick mass, as usual, sought its favorite arrangement—straight down her back.

Finger-wide stripes of flour clung to her flushed cheeks, warm from her exertions of the morning. Hours before, she had risen and come down to fuel the fire left banked the night before, and to begin the soothing task of early morning baking, grateful that Claudia was not here to insist that Cook perform her usual duties—grateful, too, that her aunt's absence would spare her a morning of caustic remarks about provincials whose aspirations rose no higher than the kitchen. That she was spared complete banishment from her beloved cooking, she could credit to Oliver, who ignored his wife's complaints, saying Taryn's peculiarities saved him the cost of another skilled servant.

Jolie, the tweeney who usually slept on a pallet in the pantry and rose first to light the fires, had been allowed to crawl into bed with Cook during the night, and Taryn knew she would never awaken to start her usual morning tasks. The child, eager to be of help, had gravitated toward Cook the day before, cuddling and patting and bringing cups of tea. No one had stopped her, for it had amused Cook and distracted her from the devastating sorrow of losing her daughter.

The servants, rallying to protect one of their own, would find ways to cosset Cook over the next few days, a defense from the unpleasantness to be found in this house when Taryn's relatives were home. Claudia was a vicious mistress, much like a zealot of the Spanish Inquisition, only truly alive when she could find fault and punish. Oliver was capricious in his unpleasantness, but far more dangerous. Even Claudia seemed unable to predict whether he would support or oppose her actions.

The villagers avoided him, never even chatting, keeping every bit of personal information to themselves, including Taryn's visits and practical assistance. Whether he noticed her actions or their avoidance, no one could say, for he seldom betrayed his emotions. More often than not, he appeared quiet, withdrawn, even seemingly benign.

Over the years, though, Taryn had tracked a pattern. Two actions could result in Oliver's displeasure: any direct opposition to his will, and the simple misfortune of being within sight should his plans or prosperity have suffered in any way.

The gentry of the area, however, found the couple charming. Oliver, a younger brother of an impoverished but titled family, seemed to find favor with the less exalted members of the *ton*, who in turn came to Kingsford to enjoy the clean ocean breeze and the bountiful generosity of their host.

Taryn turned her attention back to the table and punched down the dough in the huge bowl, then rolled it over and spread a damp cloth across the whole. The fragrance of raw yeasty bread dough spread throughout the warm room, filling Taryn's senses with contentment.

Her thoughts drifted to Woolfe, as they had so many times since yesterday, when she had claimed him as her betrothed. Little did the vicar know that Woolfe, whom Geoffrey had painted as an adventurer and world traveler, would no doubt find her utterly boring.

Not that Woolfe was ever coming back, and certainly not that she wanted him to find her attractive. She fell far short of that, as her aunt so often reminded her, and was lucky to have captured Giles's affections. Here in this kitchen, Woolfe would find only an unsophisticated country girl with thick hair hanging horse-tail straight within hours after the most rigorous grooming. A girl who wore Claudia's cast-off clothing, altered with untutored skill to fit her slighter figure.

And Woolfe, how had he changed? Would he still be thin, his height outstretching any amount of food he ate? Would she still find that fierce hatred burning in his eyes, first for his tormentors, then, at the last, turning into some other, indecipherable expression for her?

She would like to see Woolfe once more and let reality dispel her unsettling memories. Perhaps then the vision she carried with her of their last moments together would cease haunting her. Perhaps then she could forget the magic of Woolfe's unforgettable farewell kiss—and finally abandon her wish that their futures had marched along in tandem, their lives linked in friendship and desire.

Foolish memories to dwell on, Taryn.

She plunged her sticky hands in a pan of warm, soapy water and washed the bits of bread dough from her fingers. As her dripping hands grasped a dry towel, her motion stopped, and she sighed in pleasure at a wonderful sight—sunlight at last glinting upon the stones of the kitchen floor. Quickly drying her hands, she turned to hurry toward the beckoning window to examine the morning's progress, smiling as the thin edges of leaves on a nearby tree glowed with the sun's dawning light. She opened the kitchen door and stepped out, quickly closing the door behind her to keep the kitchen warm. Leaning back against the dark, weathered wood, she closed her eyes and raised her face to the soft, breeze that came with the sun's rising. For a moment she enjoyed the simple pleasure, then sighed deeply. The day had begun, and it was time to forget Woolfe and plan for the real crisis before her.

How could she ensure that the burial be done quietly? She must somehow prevent it from becoming the topic of discussion among Oliver and Claudia's friends. How then could she ensure the vicar's silence when he was so determined to ingratiate himself with Oliver, who had given him the living in Kingsford? Even more complicated, how could she keep the vicar from questioning her still secret engagment to Woolfe as time passed and he never appeared to claim his inheritance—and his betrothed? When Oliver and Claudia alluded to her marriage to Giles, what would stop the vicar from revealing her deception? There were, she realized with a sigh, no easy answers—but find them she must, for she was determined that poor Martha would have a Christian burial, and that she herself would gain her freedom.

But what if her aunt and uncle were jolted from their complacency by the possibility of Woolfe returning and insisted upon an immediate marriage? That possibility was all too real. She knew she had to plan a possible escape—for without

Geoffrey's assistance, she was back where she started, completely under her relatives' control.

As soon as this crisis was over, she would think of something, for she was not going to sit here in Kingsford, sewing samplers while her aunt and uncle came home to shackle the chains of matrimony upon her.

Her life was like a stoppered teapot, ready to explode.

Up on the bluff, Woolfe woke up, swearing, "Damn it, Taryn, leave me alone!" Blast, how the Devil had Taryn insinuated herself into his dreams? After all those years swallowing insults and taking beatings for the little witch, now he was allowing her to disturb his sleep? The last thing he wanted was to start dreaming about Taryn like some bare-cheeked adolescent.

He should have ignored Elizabeth's warning about Taryn's trouble. Indeed, if Elizabeth had wanted to be of some genuine use, she might have mentioned the danger of highwaymen on the roads.

He threw back the covers and stood up just as a heavy pounding jarred the door to his room, and Asada's harsh whisper rang through the wood like a temple gong. "Woolfesan!"

"Blast, Asada," he said, donning his robe and stalking toward the sound, "why are you pounding on my door?" He turned the key and pulled the door open.

Asada's anxious gaze slid quickly over Woolfe, then sped around the room. Ignoring Woolfe's scowl, he nodded his satisfaction and intoned formally, "*Ohayo gozai masu.*"

Woolfe leaned against the door frame and shook his head. "Good morning to you too, Asada, although it would have been a better morning if you had let me sleep."

Asada raised his eyebrows. "You were not sleeping, Woolfesan, you were yelling."

"I was dreaming."

"Ah, so."

Woolfe groaned. A dream to Asada was like a juicy beefsteak to an Englishman, and Woolfe had no intention of spending the next half hour letting Asada analyze the random ramblings of his obviously overtired brain. He said firmly, "I shall meet you in the dining room in a few moments." Upon those words, he shut the door, shuddering at Asada's answering chuckle.

* * *

The morning sun, halfway to its zenith, warmed the two gentlemen exiting the inn. Across the courtyard, Señor Esteban waved to them as he slid from the back of a black stallion and handed the reins to a stableboy.

"My compliments to your cook," Woolfe said as his host approached. "I am surprised that anyone ever wishes to return home from your inn."

Señor Esteban smiled. "Actually, Lord Kingsford, we found ourselves full to the rafters on one occasion last summer."

"Congratulations, Señor Esteban. How do you attract your clientele?"

"We are very cosmopolitan here now, with your *ton* all aping royalty and wanting their holidays at the beach. Being situated not too far from the Prince Regent's watering hole at Brighton is an advantage."

Woolfe remarked, "In addition, you are a convenient distance from London." The clever devil, Woolfe thought, Señor Esteban had a prospective gold mine here, one that could only increase his revenue each year.

Woolfe mused, "I was surprised to find your inn on Kingsford property, Señor Esteban." His words dropped into the pleasant conversation like a cragged rock, fracturing the congenial mood and reverberating a wave of silence.

Finally, Esteban queried, "Richard had never mentioned it? I bought the end of the bluff and a double right-of-way—to the valley and to the public road— and we finished the Heritage a full two years ago."

Richard had sold the land? This was worse than he had anticipated. He allowed one eyebrow to lift in surprise, but his features remained unchanged. "My Uncle Richard passed on while I was away from Kingsford, and as Geoffrey and I spent only a few evenings together before his death, we did not discuss Kingsford's financial transactions. I'm sure when my man of business has conferred with Kingsford's solicitor, all will be revealed."

Señor Esteban considered him with a curious gleam in his eye, but politely let the subject die. Esteban clasped his hands behind him and began strolling toward the sea. As the others kept pace, Esteban turned to Asada. "I am curious beyond words to discover how you came to be traveling together. Indeed, considering Japan's wish to remain mysteriously isolated from the rest of us, how is it that you not only left that country, but also speak such excellent English?"

Woolfe relaxed, curious to see how Asada would respond, since he seldom discussed his background with anyone. Asada, of course, had been examining Esteban, and his reply would be a fair measure of his evaluation.

"I first traveled to the Island of Hachijo—"

"Hachijo-jima!" Esteban exclaimed, his eyes alight.

"You know the island of banishment, Señor Esteban?"

"What captain who sails in the Orient has not heard the stories?"

Asada smiled and continued. "My father was a respected and influential man in the capital, a man who collected powerful enemies. They obtained the shogun's order of banishment just at the crucial time when the spring current would take the prison ship to the island."

"Your entire family was banished?"

"No, only my father. I accompanied him to implement the unwritten custom that if the son of a prisoner of high rank goes with his father, and if the son gives his father proper filial honor, the prisoner's sentence might be reduced to fifteen or twenty years."

Asada smiled and shrugged. "I went willingly, but as to my honor, from the very beginning I urged Father to escape. My father insisted that an escape would only add shame and danger to our clan, but even so, the danger of our dying from the serious 'illness of the silken cord'—an honorable method of assassinating a noble samurai—was a constant worry." Asada's eyes grew dark, as if looking inward to some painful memory, and Woolfe was surprised when Asada chose to continue his story.

"At Miyake-jima we were detained six months, as was necessary to wait for changing winds and currents. The trustee-guards stripped us of everything, then found us employment so they could steal all we earned. Many starved, as we would have, had I not learned to move swiftly and silently at night."

"How old were you?" Esteban was as fascinated as Woolfe had been when he first heard the tale.

"I was twelve when we left, and fifteen when our enemies sent an assassin for us. I was out foraging at night. When I came home, I found my father slain, and his killers waiting for me.

"My father had taught me his samurai skills—in weapons as

well as the unarmed combat that was developed during the years when the samurai were forbidden swords—and I had traded stolen food and clothing in exchange for learning the skills of others. I wanted only to protect my father, but in the end I was not there to save him."

They waited in silence—a moment in honor of his father—before he continued his story. "I killed one of the assassins, but the other ran away—no doubt to summon help. I hurried to the home of a friend, a fisherman banished for associating with Americans who had rescued him after a storm. We had often schemed together to escape, and this seemed a most appropriate time.

"Our plan was to get into the *Kura Siwo*—Black Current—which travels northeasterly past Japan and then circles down along the northwest coast of America." Asada grinned. "We did not rescue ourselves, but a typhoon blew us below the Sea of Japan where we found an American merchant ship flying under the Dutch flag."

"Dutch?" Esteban queried.

"Yes, rather than lose their precious ships to hostile British cruisers, the Dutch East India Company chartered American ships to trade with Nagasaki."

"And you were happy to be rescued."

Asada hesitated, then spoke. "Grateful to be rescued, Señor Esteban, but full of sorrow to be so close to home, knowing we could sail only in the opposite direction." His head dipped as he said, "And so, the end of my tale."

"And you, Lord Kingsford? All Geoffrey could tell me was that you were off seeking your fortune in the world."

Woolfe shrugged his shoulders. "After Asada's exciting tale, I hesitate to bring such a paltry story to the table."

"Let us be the judge of that, young man," Esteban scolded genially.

"Very well, then," Woolfe replied, walking along the curve of the bluff. "I, of course, was born here. My father was the second son. I left home, signed on with the Indiaman, *Rowen*, and sailed down the Thames on my way to great adventure."

"Did you not find the life a hardship after being raised at Kingsford?"

Woolfe almost laughed, remembering his childhood. "I was a fairly tough boy and found the life easy to manage."

"What about your family; did they not argue against your going?"

"My Uncle Richard and cousin Geoffrey resided in London, and we did not concern ourselves with each other's lives."

Esteban frowned, and evidently finding Woolfe's sparse answers a closed door, changed the focal point of his curiosity. "And your meeting with Asada?"

"Please allow me," Asada interrupted with a slight bow, his face wreathed in a grin. "Woolfesan saved my unworthy life on the wharves of Calcutta when I was set upon by thieves. I was greatly outnumbered, and seeing my plight, Woolfesan came yelling and screaming and knocking the knaves about with his fists."

Esteban's eyes lit up, and he looked admiringly toward Woolfe. Woolfe held himself stiffly, knowing the tale was not over yet.

"They ran away," Asada said, "no doubt as terrified by the noise and fury as by this wild young man's fists, for his heart was fierce and brave."

Esteban smiled. Woolfe adopted a tolerant expression in lieu of dragging Asada off to the nearest cliff and throwing him over.

Asada's face grew solemn—as in a stage drama—the better to impress his listener with the important part of the story. "I have therefore spent my days imparting to Woolfesan the ways of a true warrior, and together we have shared many exciting adventures."

"And now," Woolfe interrupted, embarassed, "before my friend adds any more flourishes to this tale, we have a full day planned. If you would excuse us . . ."

Señor Esteban bowed slightly, obviously amused by Woolfe's discomfort. "My curiosity has kept you from your tasks."

Woolfe watched Señor Esteban's strolling retreat. "What think you, Asada? Friend or foe?"

"One is lulled by his amiability and the comfort of his inn."

"Indeed," Woolfe agreed, then turned to look down at the valley. Asada joined him in surveying the scene before them, the wind blowing into their faces and whipping Woolfe's hair in gleeful welcome. Asada issued the first criticism.

"Slothful caretakers."

"Yes," Woolfe agreed.

The land wept a lament of neglect. The roofs of the tenants' cottages sagged, and the village buildings seemed in general disrepair. The river that ran down to the sea, now clogged with encroaching vegetation, seeped into the fields. The land had no order, no clean, sharp edges. Old before its time, the land had ceased trying and allowed the marauders of weeds and wild hedges to tyrannize and subdue. An aroma of dissipation rose into the air, an elusive substantiation of absentee owners who gave nothing back.

Yet, he mused, as the rising sun lit the elegant windows of Kingsford Hall, the edifice itself appeared untouched by time. An attractive blend of Norman, Tudor, and Georgian styles, from afar it seemed only to have grown in majesty. How often had he ached to claim this house, this perfect combination of stone and glass, this place his ancestors had surely intended should be cared for and kept prosperous. Yet Richard, and Geoffrey after him, had neglected it without a second thought—and he, even more irreverently, would very likely sell it entirely. What madness possessed the Burnham blood to choose faraway pleasure over the responsibility of family and Kingsford?

"I had forgotten how magnificent the Hall is."

"You love this house," Asada observed, breaking into his reverie.

Woolfe's expression revealed nothing. "No, I hate it. But, as a child I always vowed, in my ignorance, to claim it for my own. Now, of course, I shall sell it with no regrets."

"Sell Kingsford!" Asada moaned. "I have told you, Woolfe-san, you must stay on your land and take your place here as lord."

"Asada, I have a great antipathy to becoming entangled with Kingsford. I shall leave here with no more ghosts hovering in my thoughts, completely free to have a life of my own."

Asada fell silent. Not, Woolfe knew, because he'd accepted his decision, but only to plan anew. Amused, he waited for Asada's next volley. When Asada spoke, it came from an unexpected direction.

"Taryn lives at Kingsford Hall?"

"No. Geoffrey told me Oliver and Claudia built a new house near the village. With Taryn's money, no doubt."

"Taryn has no money left?"

Woolfe laughed wryly. "No possibility of that, Asada. Her father had a way with investments—mines, shipping, and trade of all kinds. He ignored all the criticism from his peers and became personally involved in business. Taryn is a wealthy heiress."

"Why should she marry the spawn of those two when she is rich?"

Woolfe looked off into the distance, searching for The Willows, Taryn's new home. He finally identified a newer roof, then the building, a rather impressive piece of Georgian architecture. Drooping willow trees framed the house, adding grace to its symmetrical edifice.

He tried to keep the bitterness from his voice. "She marries the spawn of Oliver and Claudia because she chooses to, Asada. In fact, she stated her intentions very clearly the last time I saw her."

"What is the meaning of this name, 'Taryn'?"

"English names do not necessarily mean something, Asada. Sometimes they are a whim."

"But Taryn's name, it has a meaning?"

"Yes," Woolfe replied, grinning, "but not in the manner that you mean. Her father named her after the River Tarenig in Wales, which winds through an area where lead mining flourished in prehistoric times. Taryn's father had an almost prophetic ability to know where money could be made, and when he traveled there on his wedding journey, he purchased land nearby, saying that one day another fortune would be made there."

Seeing Asada's interest, Woolfe continued, chuckling as he concluded the story. "Taryn's mother, however, said the name sounded too much like 'pig,' so she shortened it and changed the spelling. They were an interesting couple, my father told me, always arguing but very devoted."

"An excellent name," Asada said with satisfaction, "bestowed by a prophetic father." Woolfe groaned, wishing he had never told Asada the tale. Asada stood silent for a moment, then began pacing along the crest of the hill. Woolfe watched him with unease. A pacing Asada was an Asada who was on the verge of a *pronouncement*. A pronouncement usually meant trouble, for the man was stubborn once he believed he had been inspired.

Asada marched back to his side and bowed. The *Pronouncement Bow*. Oh no, Woolfe moaned silently, what plot has Asada hatched now?

Asada's aggressive enthusiasm irritated him before the man even opened his mouth. "It is the simplest thing, Woolfesan. You have no money—"

"I am not penniless." Woolfe drew himself up and said

coldly, "I have the reward from the government for helping capture the traitor. I have my own investments—"

"Bah. You never keep any money. We live like beggars while you pour money into ships that might never return. I have often said . . . oh, never mind what I have said about your obsession with making a fortune."

"Good." Woolfe said briskly, looking toward the distant Hall. "Let's go investigate that pile of stone before us."

Asada looked up at Woolfe and shouted, "You have the intelligence of a giraffe, Woolfesan. Foolishly, you look over the tops of the trees for your future when the solution lies at your feet. It is your unworthy good luck that I have stayed with you all these years, else you might never have come home at all."

Woolfe had to admit he was curious now. He waited.

Seeing Woolfe's attention, Asada nodded and bowed again, the better to herald his news. "It is simple, Woolfesan. You must marry the heiress yourself. She is a ship that will not sail."

Chapter Five

As they walked down the winding road that led into the valley, Asada embellished his plan. "As I have said, she is perfect."

Woolfe was not sure if "she" referred to Taryn or to Asada's grand scheme. Not that it mattered—bit between his teeth, Asada was galloping toward his own triumphant conclusion.

"You have searched in all the uncivilized places in the world for your unworthy father."

"I was not searching for my father."

"So you say. You have collected a fortune and foolishly spent it all on ships—" Asada stopped and frowned. "Have your uncle and cousin spent all the money from your estate?"

Irritated at discussing the unwelcome subject, Woolfe snapped, "I suspect Geoffrey's bequest to the estate was a modest liquor supply and a large pile of IOUs from his friends. He was too softhearted to redeem them."

Asada nodded his agreement at such noble behavior. Woolfe could not resist adding, "I have arranged to collect them, of course."

Asada threw up his hands and scolded Woolfe. "If your cousin chose not to do so, Woolfesan, you must honor his wishes. Such ignoble action will bring you bad luck."

"A gentleman pays his gambling debts before his tailor, Asada. These men will not be insulted." Rather than engage Asada in further argument, Woolfe prodded him back to his previous subject. "And will marrying the heiress bring good luck?"

Asada promptly forsook his bad luck lecture and bobbed his head excitedly. "*Hai!* Yes! As I have said, there is no reason for you to roam the earth any longer, and every reason to plant your overlarge feet upon the land of your ancestors."

"Stubble it, Asada, I have no intention of *living* here."

"Of course you have. Did not the sorceress see your future here?"

"Now you choose to believe Elizabeth, when it agrees with your own plan?"

"It is obvious that she saw clearly. Very unusual for a—" Asada stopped as a wagon creaked its way toward them, distracting him from a treatise on women. The driver stared at Asada's oriental features, ignoring Woolfe completely, and directed his conveyance to the far side of the road as he passed. Asada chuckled, thoroughly enjoying the familiar reaction of Englishmen to his foreign looks.

At the bottom of the hill, the road split, the right branch leading to the shops boasting a well-used, heavily-rutted street, while the left, leading to Kingsford Hall, was crowded with vegetation that crept from both sides into the middle of the lane. Woolfe veered to the left. "We'll go to the Hall first."

Asada grew quiet as they walked through a forested region, for which Woolfe was grateful. As Woolfe passed the track leading to the cottage he had called home during his last years in Kingsford, he noted that nature had not obliterated all signs of its existence.

"Oak trees," Asada stated, motioning to the thick stand of trees bordering the lane on both sides.

"They used to cover the countryside hereabouts," Woolfe replied, "but most of the trees have been sold to fuel the foundries. A few have survived now that coal is used instead and the foundries have moved closer to the coal supply."

"And these?"Asada inquired, indicating several other trees with a different hue and shape.

"Beech and pine—they grow well on the chalky soil here." After a mile or so, the trees thinned and the ground swelled upward to the hill upon which the Hall stood.

Two small boys ran past, barefoot and rolling hoops, showing an open interest in Asada. Woolfe frowned at the ragged clothing the boys wore, but attributed it to the inherent nature of boys to prefer comfort to all else. His frown grew as they followed the lane curving around the hill. A woman pulling a cart trudged slowly past, giving them no more than a cursory glance, her expressionless face intent only upon her errand. From within a basket filled with old rags, a baby's cry issued forth, barely louder than the squawking of chickens in a neighboring crate.

Asada's glance shifted to Woolfe, a faint trace of disapproval upon his features. Woolfe forestalled Asada's remarks. "Do not even say what you are thinking, my friend." He refused to feel guilty about the state of the villagers, and wished one more time he had never come home. He would far rather be with Hawksley, matching wits with England's deadly enemies, than being forced to solve the mysteries of highwaymen, wealthy Spanish innkeepers, and the dwellers of Kingsford whom *he* had not made destitute.

As they turned off the lane to follow the road up to the Hall, they had to cross a bridge over a stagnant, vegetation-clogged stream. "Ugh," Asada moaned at the unpleasant odor. Woolfe said nothing, his dark mood deepening as he looked upstream and observed an old woman scooping the scummy water into a jug. The black Burnham temper, Asada called it, this rage that sometimes churned inside him, seemingly for no reason. He cursed it himself, for he hated violence, whether in emotions or actions—even in the midst of battle when it meant life or death. To find it overcoming him now, after all his intentions to remain indifferent and analytical while in Kingsford, only served to make it worse.

As they neared the long drive, the earlier magic of the sun-burnished windows of Kingsford Hall gave way to the reality of dirty glass panes. They halted, silently examining the building. The Tudor wing had been added to the original Norman house, and a Georgian front after that. The tower entrance, which Woolfe's willful great-grandmother had added to the edifice, was at the same time powerful and whimsical.

It drew him—and that made his illogical anger grow. Woolfe motioned Asada to go before him, and his heart began to pound. He refused to dwell on the reason.

Indeed, why entering this ancient pile of rock should give him even a moment's anxiety, he would never know. More than likely, hunger pangs had him looking forward to Cook's pastry. Cook, the feisty woman with a genius for preparing wonderful meals, had invited him into her kitchen at every opportunity. Fiercely protective of her own two young girls, she had no compunction about mothering Woolfe and Taryn, and heaven help anyone who defied her, for her skills would ensure her a welcome in any other home in the county.

He looked upward, letting his glance drift from window to window, wondering if perhaps Cook's girls were watching.

Downstairs he could see a thin woman peering out of the dining-room window. Dressed severely in black, she stood perfectly still, her pale face a study in disapproval as she surveyed the scene in the driveway. Woolfe briefly wondered who she was, but had no time for contemplation, for Asada was bounding up the steps of the Hall, incensed at the lack of attention.

"Come see to your master," he roared, "What kind of discipline is this?" He lifted his umbrella and pounded on the door.

Woolfe leapt up the steps behind Asada and reached around him to grasp the door handle. When he pushed it open, he was surprised to see the hallway empty, save for the woman in black who was rushing into the area, outrage stamped upon her face.

Instead of entering, Asada waited outside the door, his concentrated attention on the woman. After an awkward pause, he cleared his throat, turned to Woolfe, and murmured, "The English say that you must begin as you mean to go on, Woolfesan. Enter as master here, else this ugly crone will spend her days looking for your weakness." Then he entered before Woolfe and bowed low to him in a welcoming gesture of respect.

Clever devil, Woolfe thought, as he stepped forward to play his part. He removed his cloak and handed it to the surprised woman, saying, "You must be—"

"Parsons," she snapped, her face tightening into a pattern of disapproval. Two deep lines formed between her eyes, and her mouth pruned into a tiny round hole as she breathed deeply, obviously preparing to issue a scathing reply to the stranger's impertinence.

"And your position is—"

"Housekeeper!" she retorted, her gaze jumping back and forth between the newcomers. A bony woman, she was shaped like an umbrella at rest, Woolfe thought, watching her laboriously fill her lungs for the tirade she'd been denied.

Fascinated, Woolfe watched her go through the heavy breathing ceremony, then just before she reached the top, he interrupted with a hearty boom of approval, "Wonderful. Just the woman I need. We have come to inspect the Hall."

She expelled her breath in a sudden rush. "This is a house of mourning, sir, and there is no family here to greet visitors. Perhaps you have been out of the country"—she punctuated this statement with a hard stare at Asada—"and did not hear of Lord Kingsford's passing?"

Woolfe looked closely at Parsons, searching for any indication that she'd felt some emotion at Geoffrey's death; he would have welcomed finding someone who truly felt sadness for his cousin's passing. Instead, her black eyes reflected only irritation and an impatience to be rid of them.

"Parsons," he announced, "I am Woolfe Burnham, Earl of Kingsford. This is my companion, Asada."

He glanced at Asada, unsurprised to see the older man totally absorbed with studying the woman. When he turned back to Parsons, gone was the puckered mouth and tightly drawn body. Mouth open and staring in horror, wavering between disbelief and caution lest it be true, she had no words. Nor was she breathing, he noticed, something that evidently took some presence of mind with this servant.

"See to this woman," he said quietly to Asada, and strode quickly toward the back of the house. When he reached the door to the kitchen quarters, his spirits rose in anticipation. He turned the handle and opened the door, then stepped onto the smooth stone floor of the huge room. Two women were in the kitchen, neither of them his beloved Cook, Mrs. Dresden. One woman stood before the enormous fireplace, stirring something in a huge black pot hung over a small fire. The other leaned against the table in the middle of the room, cutting a half loaf of bread.

"Where is Mrs. Dresden?" he said into the cold room.

The bread-cutting servant looked blankly at him, and the older pot-stirrer frowned, then finally replied, "The Willows."

"Willows?" he mouthed without sound. Willows—Oliver and Claudia's house? Cook, the bright spot he had counted on to make this trip bearable, had deserted his Kingsford and now worked for . . . Taryn? He looked with loathing at the steam rising from the pot and inhaled the flavor of something he could not even identify.

Even as the whispering voice of reason shook its head in disgust at him, the emotional part of his brain raged—how dare they entice Cook from him? The women were staring at him now, fear in their eyes. Asada had warned him of the danger of temper governing him, and he had achieved a measure of control for which even that mentor had shown approval.

And now Kingsford reduced him in one day to frightening

women. When he spoke again, only Asada could have detected that the soft purring words were a sure indication of controlled fury. "I beg your pardon for disturbing you."

He returned to the front hall. "Prepare rooms for Asada and myself, and either instruct the kitchen staff to prepare edible meals or hire someone who is capable of doing so. Furthermore," he forestalled Parsons's obvious argumentation, "My guest and I have no intention of entering unprepared bedrooms nor tonight shall we be sleeping on cold, damp bedding in icy rooms. See that fires are laid and that clean, warmed sheets await us. In the meanwhile, Asada and I shall be in the village."

Parsons began wringing her hands and breathing deeply. "But I . . . our maid is no longer here—"

Woolfe stepped closer to the agitated woman and said softly, "Were you born full-fledged into the position of housekeeper?" She blinked and shook her head. Woolfe's voice lowered as he said, "Well then, since you must have a passing memory of maid's work, do what you must to see to our comfort. In the meantime, please attend us while we examine the Hall."

He turned and headed for the basement with Asada close behind. He lit the lantern hanging just inside the door, surprised at the neatness of the cavernous area. Down he went, the clacking of Parsons's footsteps following all the way. Woolfe tried the doors to the storerooms, but they were locked. "Parsons," he said, "please use your key here."

"I cannot," she whined, "Mr. Chastain lets no one down here."

"Give me your keys, madam, at once." He held out his hand and Parsons reluctantly placed them upon his palm. After a few tries he found the key he needed and opened the door. The smell of brandy filled the air, and Woolfe whistled. Asada and Parsons peered into the room as well.

"French," Asada said softly.

Woolfe relocked it and went to the other doors, one by one, his curious watchers close behind. They discovered a treasure of imported valuables. "Mr. Chastain conducts some very interesting business here in Kingsford, then, " Asada mused.

"Worth a small fortune," Woolfe added with a smile.

Parsons held her hand out for the keys as they ascended the basement steps, but Woolfe shook his head and pocketed them in his coat. She marched back toward the kitchen in a huff as

Woolfe loped up the stairs, a graceful panel-encased affair whose mahogany steps marched proudly upward beside the curved wall of the tower. Asada followed behind, his powerful legs soon matching Woolfe's long strides.

When they reached the top, Woolfe stopped to look downward into the now empty hallway. Gone were the remembered row of velvet-covered chairs and gleaming tables of his youth, missing were the vases of flowers that always appeared when the family made its infrequent trips home. Dust dulled the edges of the slate floor; paths of footsteps wove in one doorway and out another, like hillside tracks where children were wont to play.

The circular tower room, grand and perfect as his ancestors had built it, seemed lonely, like an old lady whom nobody visited. The powerful stairway beckoned as if its proud spirit longed once more to bear the weight of family and children and honored guests.

Somewhere in the floor above him a blustering wind wailed mournfully, and a draught of cold air drifted down to curl around his feet. Woolfe tapped his fingers impatiently against the banister, and the sound echoed in the empty tower. From a seed long buried, a strange bit of emotion stubbornly germinated in a tiny corner of Woolfe's barren heart. He ignored it and said, "Lord, I hate this place."

Woolfe opened the gate to the flint-built vicarage, wincing at the resultant screech, then grimacing at the grinding backlash as it closed. The old vicar must have gone deaf.

And lost his love for gardening, Woolfe amended, as he strolled slowly up the path through the front garden. Where were the bordering perennials, the color and wonderful aroma of roses? Roses still grew, as roses will despite neglect, but the whitish leaves curled with disease and mold while tall, barren suckers flourished, rag-tail cousins of the well-groomed plants he remembered.

Remembering his dismay at not finding Cook in his own kitchen, he prepared himself for the disappointment of an older, less energetic vicar. The door opened at his knock.

"Yes?" A surly manservant stood square in the doorway, incurious and unwelcoming. Woolfe could detect Asada's hackles rising as the seconds passed. Woolfe looked from the impassive servant to his incensed friend and decided to let the battle ensue. Let Asada be the one to draw the poisonous rage from his system.

Asada needed no more encouragement than Woolfe's silence. He threw up his chin, leaned forward on his umbrella, and announced imperiously, "The Earl of Kingsford to see the vicar."

The servant raised his eyebrows and examined Woolfe with disbelief, then turned his attention back to the oriental man before him. A faint look of disgust rippled across the servant's supercilious features.

It was a red flag to a bull.

Asada stepped forward and jabbed the man in the chest, the motion deceptively simple, but from Asada's trained hand, capable of imparting great pain, how much depending entirely upon Asada's mood. The servant staggered back and grasped a coat tree in the vestibule, staring into space as he tried to breathe.

"Where might we find the vicar?" At Asada's smooth question, the servant, who was now choking and coughing, pointed to a nearby doorway. Asada strode forward and opened the door in one swinging motion.

Woolfe walked to the door opened by Asada and looked into the parlor. He regretted the vicar missing this moment's entertainment, for the old gentleman had a wonderful sense of humor. The question was, why had he employed such a manservant?

Instead of his beloved vicar, the overweight man levering himself to his feet was a stranger. He stared at Woolfe, then let his glance roll contemptuously over his tall frame. Woolfe knew his coat had not found its way from the genius of Weston, nor had his boots spent a moment in Hoby's, but this man's brief perusal and subsequent dismissal had his blood boiling. Although he had been insulted far more expertly than this, his daily allotment of patience had long since vanished.

With a haughty pose he had once seen used by that marvelously superior Beau Brummel, he drawled, "Woolfe Burnham at your service, sir. I have come to see the vicar. Is he about?"

The man blanched and blinked fiercely. His glasses began a downward slide toward the tip of his nose. He rescued them with a shaky hand and bowed, his voice uncertain. "Woolfe Burnham, Lord Kingsford?"

Woolfe nodded, a touch of satisfaction evident. "Just so."

"Well!" The vicar was recovering and his voice gathering strength. "Well, well, we were just speaking of you."

Woolfe frowned. "The vicar? Are you waiting for his return?"

"No, no." The rotund man smiled widely. "I *am* the vicar—Reverend Sefton. The previous vicar has retired and gone to live near his family, The person with whom I was discussing you is your betrothed, Miss Taryn Burnham."

Chapter Six

Woolfe's expression stilled and he forced himself to remain absolutely calm, a maneuver he had mastered over the years, along with the smile he allowed to hover at the corners of his mouth—an artifice that deceived the recipient into thinking they shared with him some small secret. The vicar responded as expected, overjoyed at the camaraderie they were sharing.

Woolfe, remembering his manners, motioned Asada into the room. "Reverend Sefton, may I introduce my companion, Kyoichi Asada."

The vicar's eyes widened in such shock Woolfe worried he might collapse. Finally, manners won out, and he returned Asada's silent nod. Asada remained standing beside the door, a habit drilled into every samurai, resulting from a period of Japanese history when warriors were forbidden weapons. Woolfe wondered what the vicar would think if he knew that his foreign guest was even now surveying the room for weapons—a candlestick, a lamp, a marble egg on the mantel, a heavy book—not that he would need them, for his hands, feet, fan, and umbrella were lethal enough.

The vicar smiled uncertainly at him, then turned in relief to Woolfe, who carefully voiced the question that burned in his brain like an inferno. "When were you and my . . . betrothed . . . speaking?"

The vicar stilled. "She did not mention our little chat?"

It would take only a word to foul Taryn's little scheme, whatever it was, but he was beginning to relax and enjoy himself. He picked his way around the problem. "I have only just returned. I thought to speak with your predecessor on my way to see her."

The vicar seemed almost suspicious for a moment; then his face cleared and he nodded cheerfully. "I had almost forgotten. You wished to keep the betrothal a secret, did you not? You know—the awkwardness of everyone's thinking her meant for Giles, and your wishing her to be old enough to decide whether or not you are suited." He rubbed his hands together in glee as a thought obviously smote him. "You have not met with her then? She has not yet given you an answer?"

Woolfe smiled enigmatically, or what he hoped came close. What on earth had Taryn gotten herself into? Elizabeth's prophecy rang again in his mind, *"I see trouble . . . you must hurry. If you want her, she can be your future."* He came back to the present with a jolt when he heard the gate squeak. Not another visitor, he thought—he did not want this intriguing conversation thwarted when his information was so incomplete.

The vicar, seeing Woolfe start at the noise, shrugged his round shoulders, and said heartily, "Rather like a watchdog, that gate." The knocker sounded, and they waited for the servant to answer. No footsteps echoed in the hall. After a few empty seconds, the vicar walked to the parlor door and peered out, then, excusing himself, left the room, obviously intending to act as doorman himself.

Woolfe exchanged an amused look with Asada, then drifted toward the window overlooking the back garden, grateful for a moment alone to think. Had he intended to see Taryn? *No,* came his resounding denial, followed by a chortle of mocking laughter from the emotional idiot that seemed to have hopped on his shoulder and begun waging war with his common sense. That same imp who had probably instigated his dream of Taryn, and now dangled Taryn's mischief before him here in the vicarage.

His common sense argued back—that fellow who oversaw his financial portfolio and looked to his future with unflappable, farseeing calm—pointing out that every incident, no matter how outlandishly curious, had a logical solution. Even Elizabeth's prophecy, for instance. While he had every confidence in her visionary powers, even she treated those images of the future as a warning and found ways to force a change in the expected outcome. He would do the same.

However, his own plan would need some adjustment now that Taryn had embroiled him into her scheme, for he knew he couldn't resist—and why should he?—discovering what she was up to. As for letting her become part of his future, after the agony of finally dispelling her from his blood, he would fight it with all he had.

Two pairs of footsteps sounded in the hall and stopped at the parlor door. The vicar's excited voice brought him out of his own thoughts. "Lord Kingsford, imagine such a coincidence, for here is Miss Burnham!"

His heart lurched, and he swore silently. He took a second to calm himself and assume a mildly interested expression, then turned to face them.

His eyes swept directly to Taryn, and all else faded into a blank canvas around her. Damn, he thought, here was trouble.

Taryn's mouth fell open, and her throat tightened as she stared at Woolfe. She bit her lower lip to keep tears from flowing as unexpected emotion overwhelmed her. She tried to focus on him, but the room was dim and she had walked to the vicarage in the bright morning sunlight without a bonnet. Surely that was the reason he seemed a dark shadow against the window.

She looked downward, fumbling with the strings of her reticule while her thoughts went skittering around like drops of water on a hot, greased skillet. How could Woolfe stand there so casually while her life was about to explode?

Panic poured through her in a roaring flood, and she was helpless, completely unable to concentrate. She dropped her reticule onto the table, stalling for time. Gradually the feeling subsided, flowing away, leaving her mind almost at peace with the one thought that survived.

Woolfe had come home.

Had she not just wished this morning for just one more look at her dear Woolfe? She could not resist now.

She slowly raised her eyes. Seeing long, well-muscled legs, she realized he must have grown a half-dozen inches since he left. His coat stretched to the limit over vast shoulders, that hinted at powerful strength. Yet, the overall impression was that he was thin, for there was no extra flesh over that wide frame.

She forced herself to look at his face. Dear God, this was worse than she had ever imagined.

Woolfe watched her carefully, noting the flush that flooded her delicate, creamy skin and poured across her face and under the thick, tightly braided hair. He memorized every delicate curve and hollow of her face, suddenly sure he would never see anything more compelling should he roam the world twice over. Not that she was truly beautiful, for her lavender eyes were slightly slanted, her cheekbones too prominent, and her face too long to be perfect. When she bit her lower lip—that trick she used to keep from crying—he could see the front tooth that sat just a little sideways, giving her upper lip an extra fullness that had always driven him crazy. And he wanted her with every drop of blood that pounded through his veins.

He studied her as she tugged her reticule from her wrist to place it on a nearby table. He took careful note as she breathed deeply, and slowly became the person she wanted him—and the vicar?—to see. Controlled, proper, barricaded. She squared her shoulders and brought her head up, looking him over like an animal she was considering buying. He smiled at her daring effrontery.

Marvelous, Woolfe thought, alive at the pleasure of the moment. He intended to appropriate a kiss, and she knew it—and she was spitting mad—but dared not object in front of the vicar.

Taryn ran her tongue over her crooked tooth, remembering for the first time in years how the imperfection had bedeviled her as a child. Why she should think of it now as she studied Woolfe's face, she could not imagine, for she certainly had no wish to appear attractive to him. Not at all, she assured herself, with a sinking feeling, for her very worst fear over the years had come true—that he would come back and find her wanting. Judging from his amused expression, that is exactly what had happened—while he was so much more than she had ever dreamed.

He was dark—hair coal black, hanging loosely over his collar. Dark blue eyes hidden by thick Celtic lashes no man ever deserved. Dark skin, tanned like oak, drawn closely over that wonderful bone structure that had so entranced her years ago. He was not handsome, but rather something worse—dangerously attractive.

He reminded her of a caged animal she had once seen in a traveling show, a black wolf, powerful and frightening, prowling to and fro in his confinement. His dark pelt, like Woolfe's long, straight hair, had rippled as he moved, and his eyes had seemed to invade her very deepest thoughts. She had longed to let the black wolf loose, even knowing that he would likely kill her should she open the door. Like the animal, Woolfe's deeply tanned face and neck spoke of faraway places and a life she could not imagine. As for what he might do to her should she open the door of her heart, she had every assurance it would be deadly. Even knowing that, he drew her. And like the wild thing that had so mesmerized her, damn him, he knew it, and smiled to share that knowledge with her. What kind of animal had he become that he would be amused by this power?

She tried, but could not look away.

The vicar cleared his throat as the moment stretched. Woolfe moved first, crossing the room to place himself between her and the vicar. Without releasing her gaze, he lifted her hand to his lips. His warm mouth lingered, then he lifted his head and his hypnotic eyes examined her face at leisure.

He was going to kiss her. It was in his eyes and in the heated air between them. She must stop him, of course. It was unseemly in front of the vicar, and a mockery to the true status between them.

Releasing her hand, he lifted her chin. She stared into his eyes, dark eyes that studied her mouth with unmistakable intent. She did not want the kiss, she told herself, ignoring the times she had cursed her weakness in aching for just one more touch of his lips.

Taryn ceased breathing as his hand curved to cradle her chin and his thumb touched her lower lip. His hand was warm and dry, and the pad of his thumb rough as it slid slowly across her mouth. Her face softening in wonder, she let his marauding caress roam across her lips, his thumb stopping to rest at her crooked tooth.

Taryn came to with a vengeance. He was making fun of her, entrancing her with his experienced ways, then showing his contempt of her by targeting her imperfection. She snapped her teeth closed, nipping his wayward thumb to show her contempt. He jerked his hand back and glared at her.

She lifted her chin and glared back.

He recovered first. He grinned and murmured softly, "Does this mean our betrothal is over?"

She closed her eyes and swayed. Oh, no! The vicar had told Woolfe of their supposed engagement, and he had only been playing with her. What had she done? How could she have forgotten her purpose in coming here? What would the vicar do now that her story had fallen apart as he stood and watched the two of them together?

An arm wound round her waist and, startled, she opened her

eyes to find Woolfe beside her, steadying her. He turned them both to face the vicar and said aloud, "Why are you here, dearest? I was on my way to you."

Was he going to help her after all? She smiled faintly at him and said, "I've come to make arrangements for a burial in the church cemetery." Her thoughts steadied as she spoke. "Today as we agreed, Reverend Sefton."

The vicar looked surprised, then looking at Woolfe's blank expression, his own expression changed to annoyance. Obviously, the arrival of a Man of Authority relegated her back to the status of Useless Female, and her anxiety became Hysteria. As she thought of the consequences of the vicar changing his mind, she began to tremble. Cook's heart was not strong enough to see Martha buried at the crossroads.

Woolfe felt her body shake against his arm and wondered at the feelings it aroused in him. The old protective fury rose at the thought of Taryn being threatened, and he began to search for the culprit. What had caused her to be so upset? What had she said . . . she had come to arrange for a burial? And then what had happened? Ah, yes. The vicar had frowned.

Taryn's voice quivered as she spoke, and Woolfe watched the vicar closely. "But, Reverend Sefton, last night you agreed to let her be buried in the cemetery. We want only a quiet prayer for the family, and it will be over."

The vicar gave her a condescending look and turned to Woolfe to speak man-to-man. "What say you, Lord Kingsford?"

Woolfe felt Taryn lean against him as her trembling increased. He wanted to throttle the vicar for causing such anxiety in Taryn, but at the same time, the request seemed so simple.

"Why are you questioning Miss Burnham's request at all, Reverend Sefton? It seems an easy matter to me."

The vicar hesitated, and the suspicious expression returned. He looked at each of them in turn, then his face suddenly cleared and a fatuous smile appeared. "I keep forgetting you two have not had time together before now." He seemed to be enjoying himself and said heartily, "I have forgotten my manners and left us all standing. I shall ring for tea, and we'll all sit down and have a comfortable coze." He pulled the bell rope and waved them toward the furniture grouped around the unlit fireplace. Woolfe doubted the tea would be coming any time in the near future.

Taryn seemed to gain a measure of control, and when she made a move to leave his side, Woolfe subtly directed her to a well-worn, comfortable settee and sat beside her. As his arm settled down around her again, she leaned forward slightly, her back perfectly straight.

Woolfe's arm fell easily upon the curved back of the furniture, and he studied her as she hid her fear and became a proper young lady making an expected, formal visit—head erect, hands folded neatly on her lap, feet tucked under her skirts. Had he not felt her tremble against him, he would have been completely fooled by this performance. Even her smile for the vicar was a parody of the way a confident woman might look at a person whom she greatly admired. "Reverend Sefton, you have only to order it done, and we can have it all behind us. There is no need for a man of your importance to be troubled unduly by such a simple matter."

The vicar lapped it up, as she intended, but then, stubbornly, turned to Woolfe. "Since you have not spoken together, you cannot know the details of the girl's death. She was found by servants underneath an upstairs window, obviously having jumped."

"Or fallen, Reverend Sefton," Taryn interjected, an edge to her voice.

"Hmmm." The vicar humored Taryn, then turned to Woolfe with his story. "I questioned Parsons—"

Woolfe interrupted. "She fell at Kingsford Hall?"

"Yes, indeed. As I said, I questioned Parsons, and she explained that the maid, being overly excitable, had no doubt succumbed to shame over a reprimand and threat of dismissal she had received that day."

The vicar, leaning one hand on the arm of a sturdy, overstuffed chair, let his bulk settle heavily into the seat. He looked from Woolfe to Taryn and back again. His confidence seemed a little strained, but he continued, "With that information, I could not give her burial in hallowed ground." The vicar sat back, clearly satisfied with his story.

Woolfe turned to question Taryn. Her face, still frozen in the sweet smile, told him nothing, but her trembling had begun anew. Woolfe looked at the vicar, sitting so self-complacently as Taryn feigned calmness while shaking like a leaf.

Woolfe's next question was dangerously soft. "When was the girl found?"

"The Kingsford servants brought her to The Willows the next morning. I had been visiting Miss Burnham as I do weekly, discussing some improving tracts, when we heard a scream in the kitchen. I observed the entire scene."

"The girl died the night before and was found the next morning?"

"It would seem so, Lord Kingsford."

"Then Parsons knew the girl had taken her own life the evening before, yet she went to bed, leaving the girl to lie outside all night?"

The vicar sputtered, "It couldn't have been like that, sir. No one would be so uncaring—"

"Then what part of the story seems wrong to you, Reverend? Did Parsons actually see the girl jump or not?"

"Well . . . she did not say anyone actually saw it happen."

"But still she knew of the girl's reason."

The vicar, clearly on the defense now, argued, "Parsons is a righteous, God-fearing woman . . . "

Taryn's hands had grasped the fabric of her dress, squeezing it into a wrinkled ball in her fist. Looking at Taryn, at the pulse beating frantically at her throat, at her expression still as marble, Woolfe realized he still lacked the full story.

"What interest have you in this girl, Taryn, this maid for Kingsford?"

She did not look at him then, her eyes filled with unshed tears. "It's Martha, Woolfe. Cook's daughter."

"Martha, little Martha? Oh, my God." He stood slowly and stepped forward to stand before the vicar. "Reverend Sefton, you will immediately arrange for her burial. In the church cemetery. Miss Burnham will leave now to bring Mrs. Dresden and her other daughter, Alyce, back. She will return in . . . " He looked for Taryn for instructions.

"Two hours," she answered. The tears now ran freely down her face, and as she stood to leave the room, she stopped short at the sight of Asada.

"May I present my companion, Kyoichi Asada?" Woolfe said smoothly, noting Asada's fatuous smile. "Miss Taryn Burnham."

Asada bowed low, as if to a princess. She nodded graciously at Asada and sailed out of the parlor.

"Until then." Woolfe said. "And, Reverend Sefton? I expect to hear only loving, comforting words about Martha, else you will be looking for a living elsewhere."

Chapter Seven

The sound of a door opening startled Taryn out of the light sleep into which she'd fallen. She opened her eyes to see Alyce slipping quietly into her bedroom. Oh dear, Taryn thought, sitting up in a motion that made her dizzy, she had only meant to lie quietly for a moment, but the strain of the last two days had taken its toll.

She had hurried home from the vicarage to tell Cook and Alyce of the vicar's acquiescence, hoping this would put a quiet end to the tragedy. By the time she arranged for the traditional wool burial shroud and the cart for transporting poor Martha, the numbers of mourners from The Willows had swelled to include the other servants, all wanting to pay their last respects, and she hadn't the heart to say them nay.

When their little cavalcade had arrived at the cemetery, Woolfe was there, waiting with the vicar, along with—to Taryn's dismay—what seemed to be the entire village. Cook had wept tears of gratitude at such clear evidence of love for her dear daughter, and Taryn had felt like an ogre for selfishly wishing for a quiet affair.

And now, she thought, smiling at Alyce, she must hurry below, for Cook's friends would be dropping by with offerings of food and personal words of comfort, while here she sat half-asleep upon her bed, still wearing her cloak. "Has anyone arrived yet?"

Alyce nodded. "Yes . . . rather more than we expected."

"That's nice," Taryn said absently, standing to slide the dark cloak off her shoulders. She glanced into the mirror and groaned. "Oh Alyce, I look terrible." She plucked at the black dress she had purloined from her aunt's closet for the graveside service. On her aunt's fuller figure, the dress was stylish, but it only served to make Taryn look lanky and shapeless.

Alyce stepped forward and looked over Taryn's shoulder. Her pert nose wrinkled, and she nodded. "It's true that mirror has seen better sights, Miss Taryn, but since you ignore it most days, why all the fuss now?" She lifted Taryn's cloak off the chair where it had fallen and carried it to the wardrobe. As she leaned into the cabinet to hang the garment up, she continued, her words echoing against the fragrant cedar. "Would the new Lord Kingsford have anything to do with your concern?"

Taryn ran her brush through her hair and tied it back with a ribbon at the neck. Images flashed through her mind—Woolfe's rough thumb across her lips, his eyes *laughing* at her. "Certainly not. I hope never to see the man again. I hope he has gone home to Kingsford Hall—or better yet, gone away entirely."

"In that case," Alyce said, briskly closing the wardrobe door, "you needn't worry over what you're wearing after all."

Taryn bit back a caustic reply. She was fatigued to the bone and unreasonably irritated. Surely that was the reason for the overpowering urge to run shrieking through Kingsford, committing mayhem upon the vicar and Woolfe and anyone in between—especially those who had the temerity to stop her and exclaim one more time how exciting it was that Woolfe was home.

"Strapping fellow," and "Seems to know his way about," comprised the flavor of most of the conversation, the villagers' eyes alight with an emotion she had not seen in their eyes before . . . *Hope*. Oh, dear heaven, she thought, please don't let them think a Burnham means to stay and rescue them. No, Woolfe had outdone them all, for once he had made his escape, even London hadn't been far enough away—he'd had to completely disappear for years at a time.

She glanced at Alyce's teasing expression. Even Alyce had not been able to resist crediting Woolfe's presence with more meaning than it merited. Taking a deep breath, Taryn said gently, "Go down and sit with your mother, and I shall be there in a moment."

"She sent me after you, Miss Taryn. Come away now." Alyce put her arms around Taryn and said softly, "Thank you for what you did for Martha. I don't know how you got round the vicar, but Mum is peaceful for the first time since it happened. Her heart stopped skipping around, and already she's feeling better."

She stepped back and added, "And so many people there to honor our Martha. My own heart was bursting at the sight." She pulled Taryn toward the door.

Taryn looked back over her shoulder at the mirror, wishing that she did not look so pitiful. She wished it all the way across the hall and at each step down the staircase. She wished Woolfe had not discovered her lie about claiming him as her betrothed, for now, not only might he tell the story, but it also had given him something to laugh about. She wished he had not grown so attractive, replacing her fading memories of an intense, solitary boy with an attractive, virile male.

Halfway down the stairs she glanced out of the landing window, and stopped in amazement.

Outside under the willow trees the hedge-enclosed lawn was littered with people. Chairs and small tables from the house had been moved out, along with the large kitchen table that stood covered with food and drink. Children sat on rugs or played hide-and-seek in the hedges. Taryn groped for Alyce's sleeve. "What on earth?"

"Mum's friends came to the kitchen, but your aunt's friends turned up at the front door, all excited to see his lordship." Alyce shrugged her shoulders. "Mum wouldn't budge from the kitchen, and the gentry stayed put in the parlor—so Lord Kingsford moved everyone outside." Alyce grinned. "He's a clever man, quick to fix a problem, you can see that."

"Clever, indeed." Taryn murmured. She nudged Alyce away from her. "Go to your mother while I see what needs to be done." She hurried outside and searched through the crowd for Woolfe. She finally found him, sitting beside Cook, the two of them on chairs filched from the parlor. Judging by Cook's expression, Woolfe had captivated her as well as the vicar, who sat nearby, looking disgustingly cheerful.

Woolfe stood as she approached and came to meet her. Before she could protest, he appropriated her elbow and pulled her along toward Cook, smiling that we-know-a-secret smile she was beginning to detest.

Cook looked up at her nervously. "Miss Taryn, we shouldn't be"— she waved her hand at the mixed crowd— "like this. I tried to tell the boy"—nodding at Woolfe—"but he just ignored me and invited everyone out together."

Taryn looked around at the guests, a little nervous herself. It was rather like a sedate fair, with servants from other houses mingling freely with merchants from the village, while scattered among them were a few friends of Oliver and Claudia. Although this was commonplace among public gatherings,

Claudia would never have tolerated this breakdown of the social strata upon her own grounds.

"Nonsense," Woolfe assured Cook, watching Taryn closely. "After all this is Taryn's home, and she is free to invite whomever she wishes."

Taryn leaned over and kissed Cook's cheek and said, "Don't be silly, Cook. You are the heart of this home, and everyone knows it."

Assuming her usual serene demeanor, she continued, "Do you mind if I steal Lord Kingsford away for a moment?" Without waiting for a response she tugged on his arm. "Come let me reacquaint you with your neighbors." He went tamely enough and seemed content to greet folk as they moved across the grass, and a little hope rose that she might be able to manage him.

"Woolfe," she said in an undertone, "please do not mention our supposed betrothal to anyone."

"Wouldn't dream of it," he returned smoothly, with a casual indifference that reassured—and irritated—her. She took a deep breath and began to hope they might squeak through this after all.

She turned her attention back to the guests, and her heart sunk, for just entering the entrance to the garden was Mrs. Johns, who had leased a summer home in the village, and her two daughters, Cynthia and Julie. And, she noted with the sudden feeling that she was living a nightmare, trotting closely behind them was Mrs. Johns's bosom beau, Lady Islington, with her daughter, Iris.

Why were they here? Neither of them would attend a wake for a simple maid. They visited often when Claudia and Oliver were at home, but they never came to visit her alone. Even more confusing, the Season wouldn't be releasing the *ton* from its round of parties until July.

"Lord Kingsford!" Lady Islington gushed as the ladies moved toward them en masse. Then Taryn realized, slow top that she was today, the real reason for their appearance, indeed, probably the reason they had eschewed the Season and hared down to Kingsford. They had between them three lovely, *marriageable* daughters.

"We met at Lady Crowper's ball, where you so distinguished yourself. Do you not remember?" Lady Islington's voice quivered in excitement as she stretched forth her gloved hand.

Woolfe's expression, the enigmatic, closed look that so epitomized him, did not change as he observed the tall, thin woman. He bowed over her hand, though, and said, "I never forget a beautiful woman, dear lady, but my brain is hopeless with names. You must rescue me."

Why, the smooth devil, Taryn thought, as the woman simpered and brought her daughter forward. "I am Lady Islington, and this is my daughter, Iris." Iris, dressed in icy blue, looked straight at Woolfe, then lowered her eyes in a parody of innocence. As he bowed over the voluptuous blonde's fingers and his hooded gaze moving appreciatively over her form, Taryn fought back the strangest feeling, one that reminded her, ever so slightly, of jealousy.

Mrs. Johns brought her daughters forward as Lady Islington made the introductions. The two stunning brunettes made their bows, clearly in awe of the unsmiling earl. After the introductions, Julie smiled at Taryn, an open, friendly expression. "How wonderful to see you again, Taryn. How are you?"

As they exchanged courtesies, Taryn noted Iris whispering to Cynthia behind her fan. Cynthia seemed shocked and then looked at Taryn with sympathy. Nevertheless, she greeted Taryn pleasantly and stood aside as Iris came forward, a smirk on her face. "I was just thinking of you a few evenings ago, dear Taryn, when Giles and I were dancing."

"How kind of you." Taryn forced a smile, knowing from experience that Iris had not finished with her. Iris moved closer to Woolfe as if to denote a united front as she spoke to Taryn. "You certainly have more confidence in your beau than I would, for I see him everywhere. Why just the other night at Vauxhall's . . ." She broke off as if she had misspoken. She gazed up at Woolfe, the picture of innocence. "Taryn is such a sweet girl who never fusses over his naughtiness or loses her temper. She will be a perfect wife for Giles."

Taryn ignored Iris, but couldn't resist looking at Woolfe to gauge his reaction. The dark look had changed, but only for the worse. She thought he might be angry with Iris for her spiteful tongue, but his gaze pivoted directly to her, just as if she were responsible for Giles's behavior. Well, she did not care; she had more to worry about than what Iris and Woolfe thought of Giles—or her.

Having disposed neatly of Taryn, Iris and Cynthia deftly culled Woolfe from the crowd, talking loudly about the latest *on dits,* isolating him effectively from the country folk in the garden. The two mothers beamed their approval as he politely parried their questions with extravagant compliments.

Julie gave her sister a scolding look and turned to Taryn. "I am sorry about Martha's death, Taryn. I know you grew up with her and must be heartbroken about the tragedy." Such kindness in the wake of Iris's deliberate cruelty only intensified the grief that had underlined every moment since yesterday. She touched Julie's arm and said, "Come say hello to Cook and Alyce." She drew her friend along with her, leaving Woolfe to deal with the hopeful mamas and their offspring.

"I'm sorry about Iris, Taryn," Julie murmured. "I hate it when she comes calling, for she overpowers Cynthia and then I do not like either one of them."

Taryn murmured, "So nice of her to come today, though, don't you think?" Julie bit back a gurgle of laughter as they moved across the grass.

Woolfe watched Taryn escape, irritated that she had slipped out of his grasp. When she had suggested they mingle, he intended to force a private moment to conduct a thorough interrogation into the mystery surrounding their supposed betrothal. If bullying the vicar into a proper burial for poor Martha was the extent of her "trouble," and he had come rushing to her rescue for nothing, he might have a few pithy words for Elizabeth and her over-anxious idea of "danger."

His eyes turned to Asada, who stood stiffly near the garden entrance, like a guard on duty, a habit he clung to no matter how Woolfe tried to convince him to do otherwise. Asada's expressive scowl reprimanded Woolfe across the expanse of the garden, telling him that he was trading dross for gold in not getting on with his courting of The Heiress, *the ship that would not sail*, instead of wasting his time with these chattering girls. Asada's current brainstorm nudged Woolfe's sense of humor, and a smile quivered at the corners of his mouth.

Iris evidently took this for a sign of encouragement and moved closer to him, "accidentally" turning so her impressive bosom leaned against his arm. He was not a monk, and the motion stirred an automatic bodily response. Neither was he a fool who would miss the trap being set for him. He was not in the market for a wife such as Iris, whose virtue would not endure past the obligatory heir, if indeed that commodity of virtue still existed. It was time to rid himself of these clinging women.

"Well, ladies," he said, glancing from the girls to their

mothers, "have you time to greet the bereaved family?" The older women glanced guiltily toward the crowd gathered around Cook and broke into a flurry of conflicting excuses. Their resultant rush to leave afforded him an additional moment of dark humor. Mrs. Johns yodeled over to Julie in a manner that brought a bright red flush to her daughter's face, but Julie obediently came to heel at her mother's side. The group left, loosely joined together like a ten-legged creature, avoiding the commoners with ease as the crowd indifferently opened a wide path straight out of the garden.

"Lord Kingsford," a rough voice tugged at his attention. He turned to the speaker, a plainly dressed man with a fringe of thin gray hair, ears like pot handles, and blue eyes trying to hide his eagerness. "I am Rolf, Eugene Rolf, proprietor of the Flying Goose. Here's m'son, George, home from the mills."

"I'm happy to see you again," Woolfe said to them both, vaguely recalling the innkeeper. Age had not been good to him, he thought, and even less to his son, whose pasty complexion and undernourished frame verified stories of mill workers' ill-health. Rolf cleared his throat nervously and forged ahead with what was clearly on his mind. "We're all looking forward to having you home," and before the words left his lips, other villagers moved in to crowd around Woolfe as Rolf continued, "if you're looking for a strong lad to work in Kingsford now you're home, George's your boy. He's good with horses and can cut wood in the forest—or anything else you have a need for." George had barely looked at Woolfe, and an aura of resentment emanated from the boy.

Woolfe studied the sullen young man more closely, recognizing something of himself in the youth—ashamed of his dependent situation and too proud to like his father's importunities on his behalf.

Not to be outdone, another man reached out to touch his coat, then pulled it back in alarm. Woolfe found an anger rising at the man's fear, a feeling that had often plagued him in Kingsford. Tamping it down, he turned politely to the new petitioner, an old fellow dressed in patched and faded homespun. "You'll be wanting someone to put things to rights. I can work a twelve-hour day and more if you want."

Woolfe held out his hand. "John Spaulding, my father's assistant." Woolfe wondered how old the man was now, for his hands were age-spotted and the skin beneath his chin hung in thin, whiskery folds. His shoulders drooped with age. Broad though, Woolfe had to admit, and the fellow was alert and his manner firm.

A woman pushed forward, pulling away from the detaining hand of a man beside her. Her chin rose, her eyes desperate but brave. "You don't remember me, my lord, but I used to work as a kitchen maid at Kingsford. My name is Rose—Widow Simpson now. This is my brother, Tom." Her brother jostled her, and the glass of ale he held in his hand spilled on her hem and onto her worn shoes. Someone tittered—a well-dressed woman who looked amused. Woolfe's anger rose another notch, and Rose's eyes widened as she stared at him. Her courage faltered, and she fell quiet.

He studied her downcast face, lined with worry and blotchy from the sun. Mentally, he compared her with the two ladies who had accosted him with such confidence as they presented their daughters. He wanted to strangle someone, but the overwhelming emotion came from out of the thin air, with no reason he could tie down. Rose winced as her brother drained his glass and pushed his way back out of the circle, and she turned to follow him.

"Rose," he called, "I *do* remember you." Her head lifted, and she turned back, letting her brother weave unsteadily through the crowd without her. "Weren't you the girl who created the most delicious pastries in our kitchen?" She blushed and nodded, but did not speak. He wanted to detain her, to offer her something, but he was floundering in this unaccustomed role. As she curtsied and hurried away, he swore under his breath, reinforced in his belief that he was no more suited to manage Kingsford than the rest of his clan. He was making the right decision to sell and leave. In fact, he vowed, the sooner, the better.

Taryn watched Woolfe from her vantage point near Cook. The ladies had finally gone, trailing invitations to Woolfe behind them. The villagers and tenants were eager to bring themselves forward, though, and she wondered what they were saying. Eager, that was the word. Woolfe meant hope, as surely as he stood there, his solemn face giving nothing away. Did he hate it? Was he laughing at them—scorning them? Or worse yet, charming them and raising their hopes even higher, when he would only leave as he had before? She must know—now.

She squeezed Cook's shoulder and moved away slowly, drifting invisibly through the guests. Automatically, her gaze moved to the food-laden table to check on the level of refreshments. Housewives were manning the table, and the rest of the guests moved in like waves at low tide, filling a plate or glass, then drifting out again to visit with their neighbors in quiet voices. She swept her tongue over dry lips, wishing she could stop for a glass of water. Maybe after this was all over, she would take up the bottle like poor Rose's brother, and hibernate for a month while her nerves settled down.

Her steps slowed as she walked toward Woolfe. How was she to manage a private conversation in this crowd without blatantly drawing him away from the others? She raised her head, intending to catch his eye, only to gasp, for straight ahead was more trouble. Evidently, all her sins had decided to stand up and say hello at once.

The vicar had drifted over to stand beside Woolfe, his round face brightening as she approached. He opened his mouth to speak, and her heart started pumping away in pure fright. A knowing nudge to his new hero, Lord Kingsford, told Taryn what the vicar was going to blurt out. She raised an imploring entreaty to Woolfe, but not in time, though, for the vicar began, "Why, Lord Kingsford, look who is coming to join us, your—"

Woolfe's hand moved so fast she couldn't believe it. He clamped his tanned fingers on the vicar's arm and his knuckles turned white as they tightened upon that stout appendage. Woolfe murmured words in the vicar's ear, squeezed tighter, then lifted his hand.

The vicar blinked and gulped and blinked again. Sweat broke out on his face, and his glasses began their downward slide. Woolfe excused himself from the group, turning his back on them before they could detain him. Then Woolfe started toward her, moving with a determined manner that stopped her like a transfixed rabbit. When he reached her, he grasped her hand and turned her to walk beside him without breaking stride, without even a pleasant word or a by-your-leave.

Luckily, she was tall and her aunt's gown was full-skirted, for keeping up with him with some semblance of grace required a long-legged stride of her own. Her heart was still pounding, but now it took on a different rhythm—a touch of alarm, a warmth that spread out from his firm clasp, and a feeling of inevitability.

As they moved through the back exit of the garden, she looked up at him, conscious of the grim lines surrounding his mouth, entranced by the way the setting sun's rays burnished his tanned skin. Suddenly aware that she had no control whatsoever over this new Woolfe, she wondered if this was just a dream, and she was being led away by a stranger while everybody watched helplessly. She left them all behind, fading like ghostly figures, and let herself be conveyed through the formal topiary and statues, past the thick veil of willows, to the edge of the small knoll upon which the house stood.

He turned her toward him, grasping her shoulders with both hands. It didn't matter that his manner was not intimate. She was helplessly lost in a stream of pure emotion, roaring toward something she could not define.

His arms tightened, and he pulled her closer. She could feel the heat from his wide, towering body, and she knew that his dark eyes were measuring her mouth for the same kiss that he had intended in the vicarage. The moment grew, then, roughly, he wove his fingers in her hair and assaulted her mouth with his own.

A wild inferno roared through her as her eyes closed and she melted against him, powerless to think of anything except the heat of his mouth and the strength of his arms as they pulled her tightly against him. His hands moved, one tipping her head to give him better access to her mouth, the other roving, leaving heated tendrils of pleasure behind as it moved slowly down her back, sensitizing her skin to an aching pitch.

Woolfe . . . oh, Lord, what was he doing to her? She had wished for a tender kiss. Instead his mouth was bruising, seeking, demanding—and still it was not enough. She had wished to see him once again, thinking to put to rest the memory of his sweet farewell embrace, only to find herself whirling in a conflagration of desire.

His mouth lifted, and she tried to open her eyes, but the powerful elixir flowing through her veins held her captive, pliant. "Taryn," he whispered, his breath warm against her parted lips. Then he kissed her lightly once more, the scent of his skin familiar and dear.

His hand drew tenderly around to caress her cheek. She looked at him then, and found his face wary and bemused at the same time. He held her at arm's length and broke the spell at last.

"Taryn," he rasped, "what in the hell kind of trouble are you in?"

Chapter Eight

Trouble?" she whispered, latching on to the one word that penetrated the fog in her brain. For a moment while she had been in his arms, she'd wondered if he still loved her, had come back to claim her. But now, examining his expression, she could see this rude inquisitor was not a man with affection in mind. Those eyes were serious—definitely not romantic.

Why had he kissed her?

She pulled her hands free and took a step backward. The rough bark of a tree grated against her shoulders through the silk of her aunt's dress. Keeping her gaze safely upon the buttons of his waistcoat, she stalled. "What trouble?"

"Don't waste my time telling me you're not in trouble, Taryn. I know you better than that."

Her head snapped up. "Nonsense. You no longer know me at all."

He raised a dark eyebrow. "If I recall correctly, at our first meeting you were single-handedly defying Oliver, Claudia, Quinn . . . and his whip. Your hot little temper got you into trouble on a regular basis after that, a fact that I have good reason to recall. Then," he continued before she could remind him how she had finally subdued her temper, "when I left Kingsford, you were promised to Giles, but now I find that you are betrothed to me—secretly, of course—which suggests that you are now betrothed to two men at the same time. I do not think 'trouble' is too strong a word to use where you are concerned."

"You refer to what happened at the vicarage?"

"A nice beginning," he said dryly.

"Well," she breathed with relief, "it's a simple matter. I told the vicar I was betrothed to you because I needed to borrow your . . . umm . . . new authority to coerce him into a proper burial for Martha." Her impish smiled invited him to share the humor.

He smiled briefly, then shook his head. "It won't fadge, Taryn. All day you've been hopping about like a nervous cricket. I'd like to know why."

When she didn't reply, he prodded, "Well?"

"Let me think, Woolfe," she said, slipping sideways against the tree to escape. She winced at the sound of ripping silk, but walked briskly away from him. If only she had a clue why he was here, what his plans were, if only she could trust him with her delicate situation—*If only she knew why he kissed her.*

"Take your time," he taunted, following her along the ridge of the knoll. "The longer you have, the better story you can concoct."

She stopped at a stone bench nestled between two trees and sank gratefully to its rough surface. "I think I should be allowed a case of nerves at a time like this, Woolfe—first Geoffrey's death, and now Martha."

He nodded soberly, his features softening as he looked out toward the sea. After a moment, he seemed to draw himself up, away from his somber thoughts. A man of great self-control, she remembered, and not one to show emotion.

He ran a hand through his thick hair, obviously recalling himself to the matter at hand. "And your . . . relatives?" The aroma of something spoiled hovered around the word. "Where are they?"

"My . . . relatives," she echoed his caustic tone, "are in London—Claudia and Giles for the Season, and Oliver went to the city yesterday after hearing of Geoffrey's death."

"Oliver rushing to pay his respects?" Woolfe scoffed, the unlikely picture clearly igniting his temper. "No doubt he hoped to discover I had drowned at sea so that you would inherit Kingsford." She gasped at his animosity, but he wasn't finished. "Why are you not in London as well, Taryn, keeping Giles out of mischief at Vauxhall? And," he added, staring at her ringless hands, "why are you not married by now? You're, let's see, almost twenty-one. Can you not entice Giles into marriage?"

She closed her eyes while the aftermath of his fury sizzled in the air between them. Grasping the rough edges of the bench so hard her fingers hurt, she reminded herself that she had endured far worse with Claudia. Her voice shaking, she looked him straight in the eye. "Why did you come home, Woolfe? For revenge?"

Woolfe's face flushed. "I am sorry, Taryn. That was ill-done of me."

"Just answer my question, Woolfe." Her voice was hard and unforgiving.

"Very well, then," he said, answering in kind. "I have come to assess the value of the estate, sell it, and return to my own life."

She stood slowly and walked away from him a bit, gathering her composure about her. It was not easy, for his bald announcement had, surprisingly, taken her breath away. She had expected him to leave again, thought she was prepared for it, but to hear him say it aloud was like a physical blow. Perhaps her reaction was so strong because this was so like the last time he walked away—without looking back, without another thought for her, leaving her entirely on her own at the mercy of her relatives.

At that moment, she felt more lost than ever before. Part of her had hoped, she admitted, that Woolfe would come home and rescue her—that foolish dreaming girl who never quite believed him when he said he would never return. But he hadn't lied. *Her* Woolfe had not returned—rather, a cruel, cynical adventurer had come in his place.

No matter, she scolded herself, this was no time for revisiting the past. Her entire future hung in the balance, and she must decide how far she could trust this new, harsher Woolfe, what she dared tell him, and how he would react.

A moment ago, she might have confessed her intention to evade marriage with Giles, but now she doubted the wisdom of that, for no matter why he had come home, one fact was plain. He had come home full of anger, obviously looking for revenge, a revenge from which she was not exempt. If she should confess her plan *not* to marry Giles, he would delight in throwing that little tidbit in the faces of her aunt and uncle, might even throw in the story of her "secret betrothal"—and let the broken pieces of her life fall where they may.

Yet, in order to extricate herself from the web Oliver had woven around her inheritance, she still needed Woolfe's help. She would start with that.

She turned back to him, her hands held tightly at her waist. "In February, at Uncle Richard's funeral, I asked Geoffrey to examine my father's will so I might understand what my status truly is in regard to his plans for me. Did Geoffrey ever mention this to you?"

He was immediately suspicious. "I gather that you do not entirely trust your relatives to see to your welfare?"

Ignoring his query, she took a deep breath, then plunged into the heart of the matter. "I shall reach my majority in a few weeks. Before then I need to know what he had learned. Since you will now be privy to whatever investigations he made, will you examine his papers and speak to the solicitor if necessary, to see what actions he might have taken on my behalf?"

"You will not confide in me, then?"

"Is your help contingent on my doing so?"

He shrugged his shoulders in defeat and bowed graciously. "I shall send a messenger to London in the morning. Is there any other task I may do for you?"

She hesitated, her mind churning furiously. What about Kingsford? He could sell it to anyone. He could leave it in its present condition and hand it over to another absentee landlord who would not lift a hand to help the people.

There must be some way to stop him, to make him change his mind. Perhaps . . . perhaps she could find some way to get him to take a good look at Kingsford, and it would touch his heart—if he still had a heart. Perhaps his youthful dreams of rebuilding Kingsford could be rekindled. An idea took shape . . .

"In return for your favor, let me be of service to you, Woolfe. Things have changed here, and not for the better. Would you like me to take you around to meet the people and see for yourself the condition of the estate?"

She smiled at him, her finest artless smile, the one she practiced in the mirror for hiding her true thoughts from Claudia. Innocently, she explained, "It would keep you from hurting their feelings when you do not remember their names."

Woolfe watched her clever little charade, wishing he could discern her true thoughts—and fighting the impulse to hop on a horse and ride straight to London to ferret out Taryn's secret.

One day in Kingsford, and already he was losing his mind.

He had lost control of his emotions so badly that they had fallen from his wayward tongue without the courtesy of consulting his mind. Of course, he might not have lost control and spoken to Taryn like that had she not shaken off his hands, and pulled herself into that tight facade of dignity. He had felt her respond to his kiss, only to have her turn and walk coldly away on the ridiculous excuse that she needed to think. He had tried to tease her, to strike some spark of warmth, but she had only retreated into a harder shell.

Then she had asked him *why he had come home,* making him feel like an interloper once more in Kingsford.

As for showing him around the estate, though, the idea had merit on her argument alone, for he had experienced one very uncomfortable taste of speaking with the tenants back in the garden, and had no wish to shame any more of them by not remembering their names.

He smiled, intending to accept her offer. She smiled sweetly—then enraged him further with her words. "That way you can go right back to . . . your own life."

He looked away, not trusting himself to speak. His intention *was* to do just that, make an evaluation and go quickly—but he didn't like being *pushed* out. Lord, the woman had the touch of a drunken tooth drawer, prodding in all the most sensitive spots. How did she do it?

And, where on earth had all this *emotion* come from?

No doubt from the same source that had unleashed the idiocy of kissing her. Some *old* business he couldn't get out of his mind, no doubt, for he certainly felt nothing for her now except an abnormal dose of lust. That lust alone should have sped him galloping out of Kingsford without spending another moment with her.

But no, he was not leaving yet. Nor would he let Taryn orchestrate his actions, either by the practical advantages of her offered help, or the enticement of her kissable mouth. As for hurrying out of Kingsford, he would stay until he *chose* to go—and the rules governing that event changed with each new mystery unveiled, not the least of which was the mystery of Taryn's chameleonlike behavior.

The one satisfying facet of the puzzle, he thought with an admitted smirk of male ego, was Taryn's transparent response to him—her enthralled face when his gaze captured hers at the vicarage, and her warm response to that kiss moments ago. No man could resist enjoying the fact that a woman who once rejected him now found him appealing, nor could he help being amused by her surprise and dismay at that telltale response.

And enjoying her discomfiture was a harmless exercise, almost medicinal, he insisted when his conscience popped up, blinking its eyes against the sudden light. It soothed him and loosened the tight knot in his chest. He banished his conscience, telling himself that enjoying Taryn's flattering reaction to him was better than a bottle, but with no morning headache. In the meantime, she was here beside him, soft and fragrant, and mad as a hornet. It gladdened his heart.

"I would be honored to have your escort around Kingsford, Taryn. I shall call for you early tomorrow morning."

Then he smiled hesitantly, an apologetic plea for mercy. "Is there any other way I may serve you to make amends for my harsh words? Grovel, perhaps? Bring you my head on a platter?" When she didn't smile at his nonsense, he added, "Please note, Taryn, that even though you have dangled a most curious matter before me, I have given up my interrogation." He gave her a hopeful look. "You may even interrogate me in return if you wish; no question will be turned away without a truthful answer."

She blinked in surprise, and he could see her softening finally as she considered his playful offer. She lifted her adorable chin and said, "Very well then, Woolfe . . . why did you kiss me?"

He grinned, a mischievous grin that he knew was going to put him back in hot water—but he couldn't resist. "The truth is, Taryn, that I never turn down the invitation for a kiss in a woman's eyes."

She glared at him, lifted her skirt, indignant anger squaring her shoulders, and marched back to the house. He followed, determined to tease her back to good humor once more. He found her standing near Asada on the edge of the garden, her face chalky white. A great clamor of horses and carriages had everyone's attention riveted toward the front driveway.

"Dear God," Taryn whispered. "They've come home."

Chapter Nine

It was almost humorous, Woolfe mused, keeping one eye on the stricken Taryn, the way the mood of the crowd turned from genial and relaxed to stiff and wary. As if polarized, the guests separated, each social strata withdrawing from the one above, as if the family's noisy entrance had suddenly awakened them to how improperly they had been behaving.

Alyce assisted Cook from her chair, and the pair hurried from the garden. Asada murmured, "I have always had to draw my sword to elicit such a reaction."

"Bringing a skunk into the Hall is the closest I've ever come to scattering a crowd like this."

"Ah." Asada laughed softly. "I bow to your ingenuity and withdraw from the contest."

Woolfe moved closer to Taryn, sure she had not taken a breath since her frightened exclamation. He touched her back gently, and she turned to him, gasping as if suddenly remembering he was there. She looked out at the driveway where Claudia and Oliver were being assisted down from their carriage, then looked up at him, her eyes imploring. "You won't make trouble, will you, Woolfe?"

"You mean I must not reveal our secret betrothal?"

"Be quiet about *everything* we have ever discussed," she hissed, looking toward the lawn where the guests were delaying Claudia and Oliver. "You remember how . . . delicately I must handle Claudia, Woolfe. She will be furious enough at this gathering at her home." She reached out blindly, her fingers resting on his sleeve. "Please."

"Well, Cuz," a lazy voice slurred beside them, "I see the prodigal son has returned and is already running tame in my garden."

Woolfe couldn't resist appropriating Taryn's hand just as she turned at Giles's snide remark. She hurriedly snatched her hand away, but Giles noted the action and raised his quizzing glass to study their faces, one after the other. His rheumy gray eyes glazed over, and he let the glass fall dangling from its chain, glaring at Woolfe with a territorial snarl.

Giles was obviously drunk, and slovenly as well. His coat and pants were wrinkled from traveling, and upon his yellow satin waistcoat sat the menu from his last meal. He swiveled his entire body to look around the garden, an unnecessary maneuver, for his high collar had lost its starch and no longer presented a danger to his vision. He swiveled back to look at them, his body swaying dangerously to the starboard side before he finally caught his balance.

"Having a party?" he asked, his eyes brightening.

"No, Giles," Taryn began, while Giles's young friends drifted toward them through the hedged entrance to the garden. "Martha died, and we buried her today. Our guests have come to express their condolences."

"Martha?" A deep line appeared between Giles's vague eyes. "Cook's girl?" At Taryn's nod, he mumbled, "Damned shame." Mollified, Taryn nodded, but Woolfe saw the lack of true feeling in Giles's words. Geoffrey had warned Woolfe how dissolute Giles had become, but seeing it in person made him wish he had dragged Taryn away with him years ago; it would have been the greatest service he could have rendered her.

Curious, Woolfe quickly assessed Giles's friends as they drew near. He recognized the two women, widowed sisters who had both outlived older husbands and were enjoying their freedom. The gentlemen with them were a strange mix—Sir Lionel, a whip of some renown and handsome as a painting, and two of Geoffrey's close friends.

Giles waved them closer. "Brought guests, Cuz, and they'll need to fre—freshen up." He smiled casually toward the others while his searching gaze found what he wanted, the table where food and drink awaited. He turned and walked carefully in a straight line toward the refreshments. "C'mon, Lionel," he threw over his shoulder. "Told you m'cuz managed a ready household."

Lionel watched Giles weave his way through the thinning crowd of mourners, an indulgent expression on his convivial features. Lionel directed his attention back to Taryn. "Miss Burnham, you must forgive your cousin. The trip was delayed at an inn when one of our coaches broke an axle, and I fear our boredom mingled with the excellent liquid fare to be found. Giles will be right and tight by tomorrow."

Nodding, she dipped a small curtsy. "How are you? Sir Lionel. Have you made the acquaintance of Lord Kingsford?"

"Lionel," Woolfe said briefly, extending his hand in response to Sir Lionel's outstretched hand.

"Wondered if we might find you here already, Lord Kingsford. My condolences upon the death of your cousin. He was a fine man, more amiable than most, and a true gentleman."

Woolfe's stern expression softened. "Thank you."

Sir Lionel stepped back and brought the others forward. "May I present Mrs. Nancy Tristin and her sister Mrs. Georgia Lawnsdale." The ladies were lovely blondes, dressed in vibrant colors and low necklines. They greeted Taryn, then bestowed flirtatious eyes upon Woolfe as Sir Lionel introduced the other two gentlemen.

"Please meet Mr. George Humbolt and Paul Tanner, Viscount Lodges." The young men fairly fell over each other in charming Taryn. She smiled tiredly at their antics, nervously watching Oliver and Claudia move slowly through the crowded garden.

Viscount Lodges beamed at meeting Woolfe. "Afraid we tagged along after Giles, my lord, in hopes of meeting you. We're friends of Geoffrey's and would like to speak with you soon, if you're willing. Matter of some importance, you know." His silly grin excused his impertinence, and Woolfe nodded his acquiescence.

Taryn thought her heart was going to burst, it was pounding so loudly as Oliver and Claudia came toward her, graciously greeting the few remaining guests. A few curious country folk remained, but the rest were mostly Claudia's friends. Their voices thundered against Taryn's eardrums. "Oh yes, we heard that Lord Kingsford had organized a wake for your priceless Cook's daughter and had to come and make our condolences . . . My dear, such a *strange* occurrence . . . So like your sweet Taryn to honor even the servants in your house . . . "

Claudia sent Taryn a promise of retribution across the distance, even as she answered the speaker. "Yes, one must always show kindness to the lower orders . . . We have always taught Taryn the proper way of things."

Taryn shifted her attention to Oliver, even more fearful of the impending confrontation between him and Woolfe. Oliver's glance brushed past Taryn, pausing only briefly on its way to Woolfe. Cold, expressionless Oliver, Taryn thought, and she wondered what he was thinking as he approached Woolfe.

Woolfe made no effort to greet Oliver, but stood relaxed beside Asada as if he were the host and Oliver the interloper. Even as Oliver stopped directly in front of him, he waited for his old enemy to make the first move.

Curiosity, like a softly falling mist, silenced the garden.

"Woolfe," Oliver said, the single word filled with polite loathing.

"Oliver," Woolfe returned. He looked toward Asada. "May I present Miss Burnham's uncle, Mr. Chastain? And her aunt, Mrs. Chastain," he added as Claudia joined her husband. "My friend, Kyoichi Asada, from Japan," he explained. Then Woolfe once more waited for Oliver to speak.

Oliver's eyes narrowed at the insult of being presented as if the foreigner was of higher rank. He nodded at Asada without actually looking at him, and Claudia's nostrils flared in distaste.

Oliver spit out the expected greeting. "How are you finding Kingsford, Woolfe?"

"Well, Oliver," drawled Woolfe, "so far I have found the incidence of crime higher and the standard of living lower. But then, I have been here only two days. I am sure there are much more interesting tidbits to be unearthed as each stone is turned over. Nasty little things, overturned stones."

Like a game of battlecock, all eyes turned to Oliver.

Smoldering, Oliver opened his mouth to retaliate, but Woolfe continued in the same bored tone, "And while I cannot commend you on your stewardship of Kingsford, I must congratulate you wholeheartedly on the noble pantry you've stocked for me in the basement of Kingsford Hall."

Oliver's eyes spit fire. "Those stores are mine!"

"Oh dear, what a shame," Woolfe replied with a moue of regret. "If that's the case, then, just show your receipts to my man, Asada, and come pick them up."

"I have no receipts; it is a private transaction. No one has ever questioned my word here."

"Your word as steward for Kingsford?"

"Of course," Oliver said arrogantly.

"Well, now that you mention it, that is another matter that should be discussed. As of this moment, you are relieved of those duties."

Oliver's face turned choleric, and fairly sputtering, he waved his hand in the air. "Get off of my property!"

"Yours?" The word dripped derision.

"What do you mean by that?"

"Since this land belonged to Kingsford when last I stood here, The Willows' ownership is just one of those stones whose bottom side must be examined, Oliver."

"Speak with Mr. Fletcher. He will set you straight."

"You know, I thought about doing that, but decided instead to use my friend's solicitor—he serves the Marquess of Hawksley. A veritable bloodhound, that lawyer. A devout man, I believe, with a penchant for strict accounting and severe penalties for any havey-cavey transactions. Oh, by the way," he said, glancing briefly at Taryn, "I shall direct him to examine Taryn's estate as well, just to see that you truly have safeguarded her interests—such a large inheritance might inspire all manner of financial shenanigans and pressure on the girl, such as marrying your son against her will."

Oliver's fury was so fierce he could not speak. Taryn wondered if he might not die of apoplexy right before them all. But Woolfe wasn't through with them.

"However, before all this comes about," Woolfe expounded, "I have need to examine the estate, and since you are relieved of your duties, I shall need someone to show me around tomorrow. I believe Taryn would certainly be the most knowledgeable. Who knows, perhaps she can convince me that all is well, and then all those questionable stones will simply become a matter for tallying."

He paused to look at Claudia. "Since the girl will need her aunt's continuing chaperonage and loving care, you all may remain in the house with my blessings until matters are settled." He smiled to see that lady's expression match that of her husband.

"Taryn," Woolfe said in a conversational tone, "I shall call for you at eight in the morning."

She nodded automatically, grateful beyond words that she had not confided the whole of her secret to Woolfe. Even though he had not revealed the matter of her "secret betrothal," he was too dangerous to be trusted.

Into the pregnant silence came Giles's intoxicated demand from the food table: "Taryn, darlin', come here and fill my plate."

Taryn jumped at the interruption, and for some reason,

looked at Woolfe for his reaction to Giles's rude directive. Gone was the amused cynic who had baited Oliver; instead, looking back at her was a watchful Woolfe, a Woolfe who waited for her to step into his trap as had Oliver. Her heart sank. She had been right—he had truly come back as an enemy.

Chapter Ten

Woolfe's eyebrow lifted as he looked directly at Taryn, challenging her to defy Giles's arrogant demand. Challenged and accused and condemned.

Taryn's anger smoldered. One more insult from this overbearing, judgmental barbarian, and she would pick up the nearest object and hurl it at him. Very deliberately, she curtsied to him, insultingly low. "Good evening, Lord Kingsford." She turned her back on him and walked angrily toward Giles, ignoring the sounds of Woolfe's leisurely departure.

She was furious with Giles as well. How dare he, even though in his cups, adopt this arrogant, lordly manner with her? She joined him with a honeyed smile—and promptly managed to pour a glass of punch down his embroidered waistcoat. Apologizing sweetly, she turned to Giles's guests. Like a whirlwind, she rushed them through their refreshments and saw them settled for the night with a skill and efficiency that even the most experienced London hostess might have envied.

When she glimpsed herself in the parlor mirror after dealing with all her guests, she winced at the sunken eyes she saw there, the bluish circles beneath them reminding her of a weary raccoon. With visions of crawling in bed and indulging in an enthusiastic bout of tears, she turned toward the stairs.

"Taryn, you stupid girl," Claudia said from the parlor door, "everyone is talking about you." Claudia stepped back with a clear command for Taryn to present herself within. Taryn stiffened her spine and obeyed, preparing herself for one more distasteful scene with Claudia, only to find herself being examined by two more pairs of eyes, those of Giles and Oliver.

Taryn looked at Claudia, automatically starting to apologize, but stopped herself, for she wasn't sure how many of her sins Claudia had discovered. Claudia went on, her voice increasingly strident as she whipped up her own anger. "First you invited the entire county to run wild through my garden—stripping my home of furniture to do so—and then you included that miserable Woolfe Burnham. You know very well how that boy used to sniff around your ankles just to make Giles jealous. How do you think Giles felt seeing Woolfe with you, you ungrateful girl?"

Her voice moved up a notch. "When I heard that poor Geoffrey had passed on, do you know what I thought? I thought I would forgive Woolfe everything, and was perfectly prepared to welcome him home, hoping that he had become more civilized. But what was the first thing he did? Come lording it over us and threatening to throw us out of our own home! He was a horrid boy, and has turned into a monster just as I have always predicted."

She moved closer to Taryn, glaring at her just as she always did in the middle of her tantrums, reminding Taryn of how animals intimidate each other in battle. Logic wasn't a necessary part of Claudia's diatribes; they were impassioned orgies that seemed to give her pleasure, especially if they ended with Taryn taking the blame for whatever had stirred Claudia up in the first place.

"And that dress, Taryn. You look ridiculous wearing mourning for a servant. And wearing my own gown without permission, and reducing it to tatters—" She rolled her eyes to the ceiling, working herself into a fine tantrum. "And another thing, what have you done to entice Woolfe to spend tomorrow with him, a betrothed girl—"

"What's this?" Giles growled, sobered somewhat by the hearty victuals he had consumed. "Has he been making overtures to you, Taryn?"

Taryn shook her head to deny the charge, just as Claudia turned to Oliver, now that she had catalogued Taryn's sins, to obtain his approval. "You see how inept the girl is, Oliver. She cannot even manage in our absence for the least time."

Oliver stood silently, his head cocked to the side as he considered Claudia's outburst. "You are correct, my dear. Your niece has quite forgotten her place. By offering her hospitality to Woolfe without deferring the matter to me, she has exhibited a willfulness I have not seen since she came here as an undisciplined child. As for her accompanying Woolfe around the estate, however, I wish the girl to go with him in order to discover what he is about, and to keep him busy—we need more time before he acts."

Taryn stared at Oliver, shocked at his complaisance. Even Claudia and Giles sputtered their protests. Oliver turned his soulless eyes upon Taryn and murmured, "Unless you have any objections?"

"None," she said meekly.

Giles was still growling his objections when Claudia turned her fury upon Taryn. "Now see what you have done. Go to bed and contemplate how miserably you mismanaged the freedom you have enjoyed in this home."

Taryn walked slowly out of the room and started up the stairs toward her room, relief vibrating through her. Thank heavens Claudia was not going to make trouble over Martha's burial. At least in this Woolfe had done her a favor, having Claudia's friends trap her with their compliments for her compassion.

Taryn washed and readied for bed in a daze, too tired to even contemplate anything, least of all how "mismanaged" her last two days had been. Bewitched was more like it, cursed certainly—and possibly a nightmare of gigantic proportions. Upon that fervent hope, she closed her eyes.

Upon awakening, Taryn took hopeful stock, only to mournfully admit that every moment of the previous day glared brightly in her memory—she had not dreamed that Woolfe was home and on the rampage.

She hurried out of bed, not sure what to do with him. How in the space of the last two days could her life have wrought such turmoil? She rushed through her morning ablutions, anxious to get downstairs, for guests in the house meant extra work for Cook and Alyce. She reached for her faded gray dress, her most comfortable for working in the kitchen. Almost of its own accord, her hand strayed past the gray to a soft pink gown, the one Cook called her "roses in the cheeks" dress, for it gave a glow to her creamy skin. Should she? Why not, she defended herself, for she could do whatever she pleased, never mind what Woolfe thought.

She grabbed it and hurriedly put it on before she could examine her motives more closely. There was nothing wrong in looking nice to go visiting the tenants. Remembering that Woolfe had last seen her in Claudia's too-large black gown had nothing to do with it.

Leaving her room, she dodged hurrying servants on her way to the kitchen. Oliver, penny-pinching as always, refused to pay the extra staff to live in The Willows when he was gone, but took them with him to London, paying them the lower country wages. Now they were home, and the house was swarming with maids and housemen scurrying to keep their master happy.

Cook smiled at her entrance. "Young Woolfe said he would come over this morning to collect you, so I've fixed his favorite pastries."

"And," Alyce added, "Giles has asked for a picnic lunch for this afternoon. He wants crab puffs and champagne."

"How dare he do this to you," Taryn fumed, donning her apron. "He knows very well how difficult it is for anyone to see to unexpected guests even under normal circumstances." She slammed the baked ham down on the scarred kitchen table and reached for the carving knife.

"Young Giles has ever been a thoughtless lad," Cook responded, adding a decorative sprig of parsley to the plate of sliced tongue. "You've never seemed to mind before, and I hope it's not on my account now, for I cannot lie upon my bed, crying another minute. Work's what's good for a body in trying times." She handed the plate to Jolie to take to the dining-room sideboard, and the child darted away like a little hummingbird.

"Oh, Giles," Taryn said. "Never mind him, he doesn't mean anything by it; he's always been spoiled. It's the other one who's wreaking havoc."

Alyce sipped a tasting spoonful of chocolate and added a bit of sugar to the pan. Stirring with a long-handled wooden spoon, she joined the conversation. "Who can she be talking about, then, Mum?"

"Don't be pert, Alyce," Taryn warned her friend, "you know very well I mean the thorn in my side, Woolfe Burnham."

"Young Woolfe?" Cook placed her hands on her rounded hips and looked incensed. "After what he did for our Martha, I hope I won't be hearing anything bad about him in my kitchen, miss."

"Taryn's the one who faced down the vicar, Mum."

Cook looked thoughtful. "The vicar told me yesterday that Woolfe convinced him to bring Martha into hallowed ground."

She gazed at Taryn, who looked down, feigning a deep interest in the thinness of her ham slices.

"Let's have it, Miss Taryn," Cook said, sitting herself down on the bench.

Alyce grinned, a touch of triumph in her voice. "Yes, Taryn, let's have the story, for you know Mum will never rest until she's got all the facts."

Taryn groaned and shook her head. "You don't want to hear this, truly you don't."

"Hah!" Alyce declared, amused at Taryn's discomfort.

The sound of footsteps on the gravel path made Taryn jump, and the women turned apprehensively toward the door. The handle rattled and in walked Woolfe, smiling grandly at them all. He kissed Cook on the cheek and roughed up Alyce's hair as if she were a five-year-old. Sniffing appreciatively at the aroma in the room, he declared, "I'm in love."

He sat down beside Taryn and snitched a piece of ham off her stack, grinning at her incensed expression. Cook twisted on the bench to rise, but Alyce jumped up, pressing her hand against her mother's shoulder. "Don't get up, Mum. I'll get Lord Kingsford's tea and pastries."

Woolfe frowned. "For heaven's sake, Alyce, if anyone in this room calls me anything but Woolfe, I'll fire you all."

"You can't fire them, Woolfe," Taryn bit out. "They work for The Willows."

"Ah," he said cheerfully, "but I came here to beg them to come cook at the Hall." Taryn's mouth dropped open, and her eyes spit fire. Woolfe grinned and continued on without waiting for her to speak. "Very well then, I shall marry Cook and adopt Alyce." Everyone smiled but Taryn.

Alyce placed his food before him and said, "Mum was just grilling our Taryn about how you two changed the vicar's mind about Martha." She sat down at the table without any reverence for his title or position, waiting for him to speak.

While Woolfe raised a pastry to his mouth, Taryn blurted out a few brisk words. "I simply warned the vicar about how fond the new Lord Kingsford was of Cook; Woolfe then scowled at the poor vicar like a dragon—and the deed was done." She cut the last slice of ham and began arranging the slices on a clean platter.

Woolfe's eyebrows arched at her story, and Alyce said. "Now let's hear the long version."

He took a sip of tea and answered with an innocent air, "I

daren't utter another word, for I promised Taryn I wouldn't tell."

The interior door opened, and Jolie walked in. Her eyes widened at the sight of Woolfe at the kitchen table, and she hurried to Cook's side and leaned against her, not taking her eyes from Woolfe the entire time. Cook hugged her and said, "Jolie, run up to my room and bring down my shawl." She patted her and smiled as the little girl scampered out of the room. "Now, young lady," she ordered Taryn, "what mischief have you been up to for our sake?"

Taryn stopped fussing with the meat and, letting her elbows rest on the table, cradled her chin in her upraised hands. "You cannot tell."

Cook nodded, waiting with all the patience in the world. Woolfe grinned. "I didn't know Woolfe was coming home," Taryn explained.

Cook nodded, waiting for the rest.

"The vicar wouldn't listen to me. He was in this exalted mood, acting like a maniac with some grand purpose no one else understood." Taryn paused, her cheeks warm with embarrassment. "So I told him I was secretly betrothed to Woolfe."

"You didn't!" Alyce whispered in awe.

Cook smiled and nodded, looking at their heads so close together. "And about time, I say."

The chocolate boiled over and foamed down the side of the pan. Alyce jumped up and pulled it off the stove. Her clucking over the mess was the only sound in the room. Cook looked at the two silent people staring at her. "I've always said what I thought, and I'm not taking back my words."

Finally, Woolfe winked at Cook and finished his pastries without speaking, his attention solely upon Taryn's red face, deliberately letting the onus of responding to Cook roll entirely in Taryn's direction.

Taryn reached across the table and gave Cook's hand a quick squeeze. "I am not offended, dear." Cook looked a little embarrassed, but not repentant in the least.

Taryn raised her chin and looked up at Woolfe. "I think it a very nice compliment to Woolfe that you think he is good enough for me." Then, to the sound of Alyce's soft chortle, she rose and said sweetly, "I offered to reacquaint you with the village, Woolfe. Shall we go?"

She turned away, and Woolfe said silkily behind her, for he had risen as well, "Will you be needing your apron, Taryn?"

She stopped, stiff as a board. Woolfe tugged at the ties in the back and pulled one strap off her shoulder, lightly caressing as he went. Taryn burst into action, finished removing the white garment, and tossed it on a chair. Without a word, she walked regally from the room.

She truly hated the wretched man.

"Lovely as a flower," Asada said, bowing as Taryn and Woolfe approached the carriage. With the reins in one hand, he assisted her into The Heritage's new curricle, a shiny green two-seater with two black horses abreast, one that she had admired from afar.

"Good morning, Mr. Asada," she said sweetly. Asada handed Woolfe the reins, then raised the leather hood to grant Woolfe and Taryn privacy. Grinning triumphantly at Woolfe, he scurried around behind to ride between the springs as tiger.

Woolfe settled in beside her, holding the reins easily in one hand. She could feel the heat from his large body, and felt a traitorous longing creep insidiously through her. When he didn't start the horses, she looked up at his face, only to find him as uneasy over the situation as she. She cleared her throat, determined to say something to ease their day together, but Woolfe broke the silence instead. "Taryn, a lot of things were said yesterday, some harsher than you approve of, but waiting all these years to be voiced." He paused. "No doubt we have other matters to discuss . . ."

She opened her mouth to argue, not about to answer any more questions, but he shook his head and placed his finger over her lips. ". . . but not today, Taryn. Today, let's cry truce and be friends again." He grinned down at her, melting the edges of her anger. "After a few days, when I have recovered, we'll have at it again. Fair enough?"

What could she say? She was relieved and frustrated all at once, and hated it that he was so charming. On the other hand, noticing what a splendid day it was, the prospect of some time with Woolfe—friends again—beckoned like a sweet song.

He held out his hand. "Truce?" She hesitated, then laid her hand in his. The wretch lifted it for a kiss, never taking his eyes from her face. Starting the horses, he kept her hand in his and leaned against the back of the seat, smiling at some private thought in his devious mind.

She leaned back as well, noting with pleasure the poppies blooming along the meadow at the bottom of the knoll. So he wanted to coldly view his kingdom and leave it without a qualm of conscience, did he? Well, let's just see about that!

Taryn brought him to Rose Simpson's cottage first, venomously happy to shock him with one of the worst. "Rose's husband drowned before the birth of their last child, and now she lives here with her brother." Rose came to the door, along with her children. She curtsied as well as she could with the two young ones clinging to her like sweet little limpets. Her older girl stood beside her, awed at their arrival as well.

"Lord Kingsford," Rose said breathlessly, that wretched hope that broke Taryn's heart glowing from her tired eyes. "I told my brother you'd be seeing to us." Then, almost as an afterthought, she dipped again. "Hello, Miss Taryn, would you like to see the baby?"

Taryn nodded, hesitating a little in order to give Woolfe time to finish surveying the surrounding grounds. "Let me go in while you show Lord Kingsford your plot, if you don't mind."

The two-room cottage was ruthlessly clean, Taryn noted, amazed at Rose's fierce pride. Of course their possessions were so few that they weren't likely to be cluttering up the place. The infant was lying awake in the baby bed, looking a little lost in the ornate piece of furniture that Taryn had confiscated from Kingsford Hall.

Taryn ran a finger over the child's cheek and smiled when she turned her face frantically toward the caress, her mouth working to find sustenance. The sound of Woolfe's chuckle brought her head up, and a hot flush of embarrassment ran up her neck. She lifted the sweet bundle from the bed and buried her face in the folds of the baby's neck, inhaling the clean infant aroma.

Let him laugh, she thought, deciding she deserved a little revenge. She stood and handed him the baby, moving so fast that he had no time to protest. In a second, the baby was on his shoulder and his hands had automatically clutched her tight—just as Rose and the children trooped in behind him. Rose gasped, then beamed at the picture, probably emblazoning the scene in her memory to tell her grandchildren.

Woolfe turned his head to see the child's face, and she latched onto the edge of his chin, suckling with noisy gusto. Then she screamed her rage at such a trick being played on her, and Woolfe hastily handed the crying child to Rose.

"Well now, my sweet," Rose crooned, expertly settling her

into the crook of her arm and inserting a knuckle into the tiny mouth, "you've been cuddled by Lord Kingsford, so don't show him your bad manners." She smiled at the two visitors and asked, "Would you like some elderberry wine and biscuits?"

Taryn shook her head, but Woolfe nodded. "Just what we need," he said. Taryn glared at his thoughtlessness, for Rose barely had enough for the children between what she grew in the garden and stored each year, and what Cook and Taryn could manage to spare from their own kitchen.

After Rose served them, Woolfe shocked her again with his insensitivity, asking questions that were far beyond the bounds of good taste. "How do you make your living here, Rose? I see you have a garden and a cow, but how else do you feed the children? What does your brother do?" Taryn felt sorry for Rose and wanted to drag Woolfe out of the cottage with great violence.

"Our Tom fishes," Rose replied, a little uneasily, taking the questions from last to first. "Miss Taryn brings us extra from time to time. And," she added proudly, "I sell a little wine to the Flying Goose."

"I believe I remember this farm being larger when I was a youth, when it was farmed by Old Tom Simpson. You and your brother now farm the property?"

"Yes," Rose said, frowning as she thought about Woolfe's question, "but Mr. Oliver has given over a lot of the land for sheep, so young Tom has turned to the sea."

"Does he make a good living?"

Rose was flustered by his question, but Woolfe waited without offering her any relief from answering. "Our Tom likes his pint," she said, "and he's gone a lot, you understand."

Woolfe left Rose with glowing compliments for her wine and for the beauty of her children. Asada came from around the house to join them at the carriage, shaking his head at Woolfe. "The thatch roof needs replacing and the cow is drying up. The garden is healthy, though, and hasn't a weed in sight."

"And her brother runs with the local smugglers," Woolfe replied. As they took their places in the curricle and trotted back to the lane, Woolfe turned to Taryn. "You look ready to explode, my girl. Start talking before you die of apoplexy."

Taryn needed no encouragement. "How could you have let her feed us, Woolfe? She barely has enough for the children, and we could have done without. And those questions! How do you think that made her feel?"

"She wanted to talk, Taryn, and courtesy and pride demanded that she feed us. Leave it alone."

"That's your apology?"

"I am not apologizing, just explaining," he said calmly. "Where to next?"

"To Solly's pig farm," she snarled. "If you behave, I'll let you kiss one of those, too." He smiled at her and chuckled, not a cozy smile, but one of indulgence. She spent the next leg of the trip daydreaming of ways to inflict pain on an overbearing, unfeeling man.

The pig smell bid them hello long before the rock house came into view. The pens sprawled almost entirely around the house, and patched fences barely held the inhabitants in captivity. Solly came to the door, scowling, but when he saw Woolfe, his long face broke into a smile. "Lord Kingsford," he bellowed. "You've made me a happy man and a pint richer at the Goose, for after I saw you at the wake, I bet you'd be along to see what's what." He took off his old cloth hat and beat it against his leg, practically dancing in glee. "Come along in," he insisted, and Taryn squirmed in her seat when Woolfe smiled and agreed.

Much as she would have liked to, she couldn't very well hold her hanky to her nose to ward off the acrid odor, for then she would be behaving worse than Woolfe had at Rose's. She'd always sent Solly's share of her quarterly allowance along with the stableboy when Cook ordered their pork from him. Solly cured and smoked his own and supplied the village entirely, small as it was. She moaned aloud.

"Leave off, Taryn," Woolfe ordered quietly. "I've smelled worse in India, and that on the main street. They revere the cows there, and the blasted beasts roam the entire country, doing as they please." She nodded bravely as she stepped out on the weed-strewn front yard, breathing too shallowly to talk. "And," he elaborated with a smile at her horrified expression, "you should have been in Portugal a few days after a battle—hell, even parts of London smell to high heaven."

He was a crude barbarian, Taryn thought as she passed her hand over her nose as if rubbing that appendage. Just listen to his language and the disagreeable things he talks about to a lady! She walked steadily along with him, though, determined to give him no reason to criticize her.

"I've home-grown gooseberry wine and imported brandy without a tax, Lord Kingsford," Solly said. "I'm sure Miss Taryn would like the wine, but what about a little brandy for you?" Woolfe agreed without asking her, and she found herself sipping the wine gratefully, for it eased her discomfort.

Woolfe grilled Solly about his financial status, and it was even more uncomfortable for Taryn than at Rose's, since Solly had never discussed his troubles with her, and she felt rude just to be sitting there hearing such intimate details.

"I get by," Solly said, rubbing a dirty hand along his stubbled chin. "Now and then the pigs get sick, and we have to quarantine, but Miss Taryn sends her bit over regular. When m'wife was alive, she was an angel, Miss Taryn was, but now I'm a bachelor, and I don't need much." He leaned back against the wall, for he'd taken the bench and left the dirty settee for them.

"Thank ye for coming, Miss Taryn," he said slyly, a mischievous gleam in his eye, "I hear tell young Giles is home with a crowd from the city."

"Yes," she said, all too aware that she had deserted Cook, "we always enjoy company." Solly looked from Woolfe to her and back again, grinning at his own thoughts.

Thankfully, Woolfe was brisk about leaving, and as they gained the country lane once more, she concentrated on breathing in and out as if the air were ambrosia. "You're a good sport, Taryn," was all Woolfe said.

They went to the Bittersby farm next, and the crop of that place was clearly children. John Spaulding, the old steward's assistant from Kingsford Hall, sat on the porch with a crying grandchild on his lap. After conducting his inquisition of John Spaulding's daughter inside the house, Woolfe parked himself outside with Mr. Spaulding, whom he remembered very well. They danced around each other verbally for a while, then Spaulding surprised her by offering his advice. "Kingsford is a victim of neglect," he announced, "and you need someone to put it to rights. Not just the grounds, mind you, but also to see to overall planning of the estate itself. I'd like to volunteer for the job."

Taryn looked at the old man, furious once more that Woolfe's questions had spurred Spaulding to such an impossible dream. Surely Woolfe would not accept the offer when here the dear old man was comfortably sitting out his years on a porch.

What surprised her was the serious answer Woolfe gave the petitioner. "I haven't made any definite decisions about my plans for the estate, Spaulding, but there are a few things that are immediately needful. Give me a few days to look over the estate, then come up to the Hall and I'll hear what you have to say."

Asada, prowling around the farm as was his usual task, had stopped to listen to the conversation, beaming at Woolfe as though he had just accomplished a great feat. When they walked to the carriage, parked some distance away, Taryn couldn't keep her thoughts to herself. "Woolfe, you would kill him in a week with all that work. Then how will you feel?"

Asada, grinning broadly, needled his friend. "Woolfesan, this would not be an economical judgment, for if you would hire a younger man, it would be done faster and perhaps for a lesser sum."

"You are always preaching respect for one's elders, Asada," Woolfe retorted.

"Ah." Asada winked at Taryn. "Be careful then, else coming home may make a wise man of you yet."

Taryn shook her head. They were both incomprehensible!

They visited more tenants, all with the same result. Woolfe questioned and nosed around their land. Asada did his own snooping and gave a succinct report at the end of each visit. Taryn cringed at Woolfe's brusqueness, but behaved as if she wasn't shocked at all.

Taryn's feelings toward Woolfe were ambiguous. A vast longing for him to stay; impatience for him to leave so she might not gather too many memories of Woolfe as an adult. Amazement that his blunt manner won his tenants' respect, disgust that he intended to sell Kingsford—and them—for profit. Horror at his taking their precious food and drink; surprised that it seemed to please them so. Pride that he had become such a decisive, aggressive person; dismay that he would not stay and use those abilities to develop Kingsford and enrich his own life.

Most of all, she felt helpless before the forceful, authoritative Lord Kingsford that Woolfe had become. He was beyond her influence, and she could only watch as he rolled through their lives like a giant boulder, gathering power as he moved relentlessly to gain his own objective.

The last place they visited was pitiful indeed. Their former housekeeper at Kingsford Hall, ousted by Claudia when her age slowed her down, lived at the bottom of the hill below the Hall. The building had been the dower house so long ago that it no longer held that distinction. Damp from a leaking roof and missing window panes had driven Mrs. Maloney into the kitchen—cot, clothes, and all. Blackened by a smoking fireplace, the room was dark and smelly. Mrs. Maloney was reduced to drawing her water from the brackish stream that dribbled past the house, and Taryn constantly worried over her health.

When no one answered the front door, they ventured in, calling as they went. After a moment, Mrs. Maloney appeared at the kitchen door, inviting them into her kitchen just as if she were handing out dance cards at a ball, her dignity undiminished by her lamentable circumstances. "Lord Kingsford, I've had a dozen neighbors drop by this day to herald the grand news. Sit you down and our Miss Taryn as well." She might have been old and slow, but her mind was sharp as a nettle.

Woolfe asked his usual, intrusive questions: what did she do all day, how far could she walk, what kind of meals did she prepare for herself, could she read, and who her relatives were. And yes, they would love some currant wine.

By the time they returned to The Willows, Taryn was tipsy on the wine and her knees felt like pudding. She sailed from the curricle—well, to be truthful, wobbled from the curricle—brushing off Woolfe's offer of help with a snarling hiccough, overcome as she was with elderberries, gooseberries, and currants.

She left one parting, inebriated shot with Woolfe. "Now that you have seen the lowly condition of the estate, perhaps you will consider your responsibility to these people." She pointed a shaky finger at him to punctuate her slurred words. "And before you turn away from them, ask yourself honestly if you care how any buyer might treat them, or if you care only about your precious gold."

She paused, pleased to see surprise ripple across his features, then delivered her final blow. *"If all you want is to profit from Kingsford, no matter the cost to the people, why then, you are no different from Oliver."*

She left him openmouthed and speechless, with just the horrified look she had wanted to see on the barbarian's handsome face. She marched up to her room, crawled onto her bed, and promptly fell asleep to the sounds of a tipsy little snore. She awoke hours later when Alyce tiptoed into the room, whispering in a voice that chimed in her head like church bells at a fire: "Claudia's in the parlor and she wants you."

Chapter Eleven

Taryn sat up, frantic at Alyce's words, then promptly wished she had never moved. Alyce frowned. "Are you sick, then?"

"Visiting tenants," Taryn whispered. "Berry wine." Alyce giggled. Taryn waved her away, vowing never to touch the vile stuff again. She gingerly slid off the bed and shuffled to the wash basin. The cold water felt wonderful as she washed, almost making her feel human again. She donned a fresh dress and made her way carefully to the parlor.

Claudia waited, along with Giles and Oliver.

"Where did you go?" Claudia began.

"To the farms," Taryn said quietly. She selected a chair in the darkest part of the room.

"Did he touch you?" Giles wanted to know, a scowl on his face.

Taryn sighed. "We fought all day. The man is a barbarian."

"What are his intentions?" Oliver interrupted in an insistent voice.

"He asked them questions—to see what needs to be done to make Kingsford into a profitable estate so he can sell it." Oliver nodded, his face clearing.

"Did he talk about us?" Claudia asked. "About our home? What is he going to do with us?"

"He's waiting to hear from the solicitor."

Giles stood and began prowling back and forth. "You're not to go with him again, Taryn."

"Be quiet, Giles," Oliver interjected. "The girl's not going to fall in love with him. You heard her; he's a savage."

Giles stopped pacing and faced his father. "I don't like it."

Claudia agreed—Taryn could see that from the look on her face—but she gave in to Oliver. "Do what your father says, Giles."

Giles scowled and held his hand out to Taryn. "Come on

then, Taryn. Cook has a basket fixed, and we're taking our guests on a picnic this afternoon."

Oliver paced back and forth beneath the oak tree, ten steps forward and ten steps back, his once-gleaming Hessians wearing a path atop the dead leaves and dry acorns beneath his feet. Every tenth trip he pulled his fob watch from its pocket, checked the time, swore, and carefully returned the watch to its allotted place. Damp half moons grew beneath his armpits, and deep lines formed between his cold eyes. At the sound of a coach coming down the road, he swore once more and stalked out toward the noise. Oliver stood without flinching as four horses rushed to a snorting halt only a few feet away.

"Fletcher," he called angrily as the lawyer opened the coach door, "I've been waiting here for twenty-five minutes. Where have you been?"

"You try changing horses in a hurry when every inn is filled with Prinny's gang on their way to Brighton." Fletcher stepped down into the swirling dust kicked up by the horses. "Your note said you had important news you could not put in writing."

"Woolfe has managed to reach Kingsford . . . alive. And that's not all, Fletcher. He's hired the Marquess of Hawksley's attorney—"

"Hawksley's lawyer? Blast it all!" Fletcher walked away from the coach, wringing his hands as he went. "I wish you had warned me that such a prospective heir stood in the background," he grumbled. "I've thought of nothing else since hearing about him."

"What do you mean?" Oliver asked, his voice lowering to a snarl.

"Kingsford's a walking menace. He and the Marquess of Hawksley recently smoked out a spy who has been peddling war secrets to France for a dozen years. Not only that, he was recently set on by thieves in London—armed with knives and clubs, mind you—and he left them lying in the street with a batch of broken bones, and he did it with only his handy fives and his walking cane." Fletcher turned to face Oliver, his face pasty white. "Are you sure you want to tangle with him?"

"I am not worried about him for the present. He intends to sell the estate, so I've got my niece distracting him, encouraging him to stick his nose in every corner of Kingsford, which will give you time to do your part. All you need to worry about is getting my records in order, Fletcher. Now get back to London and get to work."

"As you will," Fletcher said in a sullen voice. He climbed back into his coach and slammed the door. As the coach turned in the road and headed back to the City, Fletcher grimly considered his position. He pushed aside a traveling bag and leaned back against the squabs, his hand shaking as he procured a large white handkerchief from his pocket and wiped his perspiring face.

Long moments passed before he turned to a rough-visaged fellow sitting silently across from him with a gun resting across his knees. "Well, at least you didn't have to use that, for he still thinks I can bail him out. The poor sod—he hasn't a clue how hopeless it is. As for us, I believe we shall take a little vacation, Jones. If we drive all day and night, we can catch a boat tomorrow morning."

Taryn rose early the next morning, deliberately donned her faded gray gown, and braided her hair tight enough for a strong wind. Thoughts of Woolfe had plagued her throughout the night, and she had found herself dreaming of him, concocting scenarios of them together that were so far-fetched, so impossible, that she was determined to put an end to such nonsense at once.

Today she would conduct their tour in a businesslike manner and endeavor to open his eyes even further to the condition of Kingsford. Then, if she could convince him to stay, and obtain his help to achieve her own independence, her life would reach some semblance of serenity. That's all she wanted—a quiet, independent life for her and Cook and Alyce—one where no one told her what to do.

"Where are we going today?" Woolfe asked, seating her on the bench. Cook placed a full plate before her, then joined the others at table, all waiting for her answer.

"The countryside," she blurted, naming the first place that popped into her mind where there were no tenants eager to ply her with homemade beverages. Cook and Alyce exchanged confused looks, and Woolfe bit back a knowing smile, the first of the morning. She hated that canny way he had of reading her mind.

She glared at him and quickly improvised, determined that he would take her seriously. "The forest, for one, has been neglected and mismanaged." His face lit with a real interest, and she tried to think of some other valid *outdoor* places. "The dew pond and the river and . . . the spring on the cliff."

Cook jumped up from the table. "You'll need a lunch."

"What's wrong with the spring?" Alyce asked, joining her mother at the sideboard. "Ouch . . . " she moaned as her mother gave her a warning nudge in the ribs.

Taryn ignored Alyce and ate quickly, letting the conversation go on about her. Minutes later, she was marching out to the curricle and sliding in without any help from anyone.

Woolfe took his place and sat quietly staring at her. "I've done something wrong?" His arm lay across the back of the seat, and as he adjusted her shawl, his lingering fingers sent shivers down her arm.

She looked up at him just as she had done the morning before, and was flooded with the same unexpected yearning that had smitten her yesterday. It had no name or logical reason for existence, but it surged through her veins, dissolving the fine anger she had gathered around her like armor.

He wanted to know if something was wrong—and she wanted to scramble out of the curricle, lest she find herself rubbing up against him like a purring kitten. In answer to his question, she shook her head—and trembled as Woolfe's fingers tucked an escaping tendril of hair behind her ear.

"No, I'm not angry with you."

"Then what is wrong?" he persisted. "Your relatives?" He clicked the reins and started them on their way. "I suppose they hated your coming with me?" He drove with his arm still draped across the back of the seat, his head tipped slightly to see both the road and her face. His warm fingers rested lightly on her shoulder, their tips absently caressing her neck.

"Yes," she whispered, trying to ignore how his touch fogged up her mind, "my relatives."

He smiled with a cozy understanding, encouraging her to continue. Grateful for a distraction, she elaborated. "Claudia is worried about her home . . . Oliver wants to know what you're up to and wants me to distract you . . . and Giles is jealous."

"Jealous?" Woolfe chuckled. "What did you tell him?"

"I told him you hadn't changed a bit"—Woolfe looked smug at that—"and that you were the same barbarian you had always been, so he didn't have to worry at all."

"Barbarian!" The curricle swerved. "You little vixen!" Then he chuckled again and said, "What did you tell Oliver?"

"I told him you were grilling the tenants, looking for a way to make more money out of them." She could see he wasn't happy about that rendition, but she couldn't resist adding, "He understood perfectly."

He gave her a strange look, grasped the back of her neck with his long fingers, and gave her a little shake. "Are you sure you aren't angry with me, Taryn?"

It was her turn to grin. "I'm feeling more cheerful every minute, my lord."

They saw John Spaulding coming out of the woods, blunderbuss over his shoulder and a string of rabbits dangling from one hand. Taryn gasped, and Woolfe quickly looked at her. "What is it?"

"The rabbits," she whispered, leaning forward, a hand pressed to her heart. "Oliver will . . ."

Woolfe looked from her to Spaulding and back again. He stopped the curricle and turned to her. "Oliver regulates the hunting in the woods?"

"No, he forbids it, except to his friends." Then she leaned back with a sigh of relief. "But he's no longer steward, is he?" She looked toward Spaulding, coming cheerfully toward them. "What will you do?"

He gave her a dark look. "I could hang him, I suppose." He stepped out of the vehicle and drew her out after him, murmuring, "What do you think, shooting or hanging?" To Spaulding he bellowed, "Good hunting this morning?"

"Good to have Lord Kingsford in his rightful place," the old gentleman bellowed back, dipping his head as the best greeting he could manage, hampered as he was by gun and rabbits. "It's like a swarming zoo in there, m'lord; they'll be starving this winter and that's a sad fact."

"Tarry with us, Spaulding, and give us some advice. Miss Burnham and I have come to study the problem." Spaulding flashed a huge grin and hung his catch over a shaded branch.

Woolfe's hand spread across Taryn's back and guided her forward with Asada strolling along behind them. "Miss Burnham has informed me that the forest is badly mismanaged. I've come to listen to her ideas."

Spaulding nodded politely, giving Woolfe a sidelong glance of man-to-man understanding. They strolled into the cool tangle of greenery, following a path that led them curving through the trees. Taryn felt like a fool, but hated to admit it. She pointed to the ground covered by rotting logs almost hidden beneath thick ferns. It looked very untidy. "This for example."

Spaulding bobbed his head. "It's like fertilizer, Miss Taryn; normally, it's a fine thing, unless it's so thick that seedlings can't take root."

She nodded, hoping she looked wise and thoughtful. "And these," she said, pointing to thick clusters of trees, young and old growing snug against each other, "they seem so *crowded*."

Asada and Spaulding smiled approvingly. She looked quickly at Woolfe, but his face held only a thoughtful expression. "I am not a woodsman, Woolfe, but what I see is all this *firewood*"—she pointed to the floor of the forest—"and think of how it would help the villagers." She threw him an imploring look. "Can you not give it to them?"

He frowned and shook his head. Her heart dipped. For a few moments she had hoped that his heart was softening.

He strolled a few feet, the two men following, and looked around the forest, his keen eyes inspecting every facet, up and down. "What do you think men? Mark some of the good, mature trees for lumber and mark the dead ones for firewood? And as Taryn says, give the young trees room to grow." His voice gathered enthusiasm as he spoke. "We'll want it done with saws, not by hook or crook pulling down what they can reach. I don't want broken branches and a lot of crippled trees."

He looked across the way to where Taryn stood in a patch of dappled sunlight, feeling a bit unnecessary. "We'll let Miss Burnham advise us how we might combine the villagers' needs with the necessity of getting this job done in a profitable manner."

Spaulding shuffled his feet and shifted his gun to the other arm, obviously not in favor of putting such a decision in the hands of a woman. Asada grinned at Woolfe like a doting father.

Taryn gulped. Was Woolfe serious? She searched his dark eyes for a trace of condescension or mockery. Not a drop of humor shone back. He meant it.

"Profitable." She frowned, stalling for time. "What does that mean? You're going to sell off the forest?"

"Gainful," Woolfe retorted impatiently, "fruitful, beneficial, worthwhile. Think, Taryn, for it's your decision."

"Well then," she began briskly, stung by his harsh tone, "hire the villagers—" She stopped at Woolfe's sharply upraised eyebrow.

"*Hire* them to do the work," she insisted, "and *pay* them

with the firewood." Her eyes slewed to Spaulding's rabbits. "And give them access to the game in the woods."

Up came Woolfe's eyebrow, so she haggled the point. "Supervised, of course, just to thin it out so there will be game next year." Woolfe's face broke into an approving grin. She smiled back as a sweet link of memory rose between them. "Just like your fish story when we were children, Woolfe. I haven't forgotten."

A sudden thought smote her, confusing, but very, very strong as he strode toward her. He had the strength and decisiveness to get things done, had so much to offer Kingsford. Perhaps it was good that he had gone away, she admitted reluctantly, for it had turned all his rebellious energy into this *constructive* force. Like her father had been, Woolfe was a Burnham with a fierce zeal for expansion and growth. Now, if someone could only teach him some manners and knock off the rough edges, he might learn to not demolish everything in his path.

"Come see me about this, Spaulding," Woolfe threw over his shoulder at the old man. "We'll work out a plan. We're off to inspect the spring."

"There was nothing wrong with the spring," Woolfe said later, laughing as they walked away from the cliffside waterfall. "You were just flinging ideas at me to keep away from—"

"It's not the spring, exactly, Woolfe," she said stubbornly, continuing the argument that had been raging for several moments. She hated him laughing at her. "It's what happens to it as it runs into the streams."

"Oh, now we are going to examine the streams, are we? Is this another ruse on your part to keep me away from the people?"

"Certainly not. I'm just giving you a broad view of the entire waterway system that's clogged in several places. Not only that, but you've left poor Asada back with the horses."

"Poor Asada is getting exactly what he wants, Taryn. He's probably taking a comfortable nap right now. Don't worry about him."

"Is he tired? Should we take him home?"

Woolfe laughed. "Heavens no, Taryn, and don't start your mothering routine on Asada. I mean that he has this scheme brewing in his head to make me stay in Kingsford and—"

"And what?" Her heart fluttered at the thought. If she could not convince him to stay, perhaps Asada could. "What else?"

Woolfe hesitated. "He's decided that I should marry an heiress to rescue Kingsford, and that I should plant myself upon the land of my ancestors and rule my people. Very feudal."

Taryn kicked at a rock with her half boot and said casually, "He's found an heiress . . . in London, perhaps?" She ventured a peek up at his face.

He glanced down at her and, she knew, noted her burning curiosity. "No, actually, he's decided that someone like you would be the perfect heiress." She caught her breath, and her mouth fell open while he grinned at her surprise. "He's even more convinced after seeing you mother-henning all those people yesterday."

"Hmm," she mumbled, quickly studying the dusty track at her feet. Her face was flaming, and she couldn't remember what they were arguing about.

"Impossible, I told him, for you are betrothed, and I intend to sell Kingsford." Woolfe sighed. "But Asada sees obstacles as challenges and won't give up until I've convinced him by finally selling Kingsford and dragging him off to make our fortune."

She stopped at the bend of the road, dismayed by his offhand attitude. Choosing the safest of his two arguments, she challenged him. "Why must you leave, Woolfe? It's your estate now, and after Oliver and Claudia leave, your bad memories will surely leave as well."

He turned to face her. "I need the money to invest. The John Company's charter is coming up for renewal this year, and after their reckless spending, the merchants and manufacturers are all lobbying Parliament to open the India trade to all comers. If that happens, the opportunities are endless to a man with money."

"Take some money from the estate."

Woolfe shook his head. "There is no money left in the estate, Taryn, and all my own money is invested in Country Ships out of India, collecting merchandise in the small ports and carrying it out to the East Indiamen."

"But all those ideas you had for Kingsford—"

"Kingsford will need years to heal, Taryn. I can begin making changes, but it's going to take hard work and endless time before Kingsford will support itself, much less rend a profit. I need the cash now. My man of business is already looking for buyers. As it is, it may take too much time."

She stepped closer to him, desperate now. "You seemed so enthusiastic this morning, Woolfe. And yesterday, talking to the tenants, you asked so many questions . . ."

He clasped her hands. "That doesn't mean I will be able to implement all my ideas, Taryn, that's just how I think. Everywhere I turn, I can see ways of making things *work*—like your father. He was brilliant; just look at the fortune he amassed. You wouldn't be in the position you are today if not for him."

"I know." Dear Lord, how she knew.

"Woolfe," she said quietly, "you are remembering only one side of my father. He was responsible, and neither his tenants nor his family suffered his neglect. He could have never turned his back on the sorry plight of people such as you have seen here in Kingsford. Woolfe," she implored, tightening her fingers on his, "think about it."

Suddenly aware of what she was doing, she tugged to free her hands, but he held her fast. Around the bend came Tom Simpson, glancing quickly at them, but hurrying past with his eyes averted. Woolfe ignored the man, released Taryn's hands, and lifted her chin with his fingers to search her face. She couldn't bear looking at him and stared across the meadow.

"I've upset you, Taryn, and I am sorry for it, but I've told you the truth from the beginning. Let me take you to the village. I'll buy you a nice lunch and we will talk about it."

"I'd like to go home. My head aches." In truth, it was beginning to pound. She had no idea how strongly she had counted on his changing his mind and staying in Kingsford, and now to see clearly that he never would—the disappointment was altogether too painful, and she needed time alone to absorb the blow. Why on earth did she keep tormenting herself with hopeless causes?

If she were made of sterner stuff, she would go with him to further argue her cause over lunch. She might even be so lacking in pride as to tell him of her plan for independence, that she had no intention of marrying Giles, and offer herself and her fortune as a sacrifice for Kingsford. But after hearing Asada's plan of finding an heiress, Woolfe might think she was fickle and opportunistic, looking to marry an earl. Could she face his rejection? No, she hadn't the strength to combat all that today.

"We'll talk tomorrow, Woolfe."

He threw his arm over her shoulder, and they strolled on. "I'll take you home then. Tomorrow you can beat me about the ears and make yourself feel better. Don't worry; we have plenty of time for that."

She leaned against him as they walked alone upon the path, soaking up his warmth while she could.

Taryn was grateful to discover Giles and his friends absent from The Willows when she returned home. She went directly to Cook to beg a headache powder and found herself pouring out her disappointment into Cook's sympathetic ear.

"I suppose he cannot help it, Cook," she said, closing her eyes and gulping down the bitter medicine, "for he's a wandering Burnham after all."

"Nonsense. He's nothing like his Uncle Richard, or Geoffrey either, God rest his soul." Cook broke two eggs into a large crockery bowl and beat them with a fork.

"I cannot see the difference, Cook. Perhaps he doesn't have the gambling fever, but he's possessed by the lure of riches; it's the same thing."

"He's just like his father, if you ask me, and there never was a finer man than that."

"Justin, the pirate? My goodness, Cook, he must be the worst of the lot."

"I'm talking about Justin before he disappeared—and if you ask me, there was something havey-cavey about that, him just disappearing one night without a word." She poured a cup of milk into her mixture and measured out a portion of sugar. "He loved his son. He would have never left him. And if he could have seen how it broke the little lad's heart, he'd be rolling over in his grave, which is where the dear man must be, for I don't believe all that nonsense about him being a pirate." Her hands fairly flew as she added ingredients to the bowl and beat them furiously.

"Cook! I believe you were sweet on the man."

Cook blushed. "Admiration is what I felt, missy, and plenty of that. And after having a man like that for a father, taking Woolfe along everywhere he went like a little shadow, how could Woolfe not love the land? The problem is that after his father left, he decided to hate his father for his betrayal, especially after Oliver got control of him. I could see him growing hard and making plans to never let anyone hurt him again. I suppose to him, that meant getting rich."

Cook poured the mixture into an oblong pan and slid it into her shiny Rumford oven. "You were the only one he ever let himself love, my girl." She wiped a tear away with her sleeve and sat down on the bench. "I thought the two of you together would be the healing of him."

She gave Taryn an intent look. "And don't tell me that you don't care for him, missy, for as hard as you're fighting it, it's clear to me."

Taryn stared at Cook's hands, clasped tightly together as she waited for Taryn's reply. A dozen times she had started to tell Cook of her plan for independence, but it was too precarious, and if things went badly, she didn't want her beloved Cook involved. Once more she fought back the impulse to confide in her, and instead concentrated on Cook's words.

Love Woolfe? She barely knew him now. He was a stranger. A rough, ambitious man without a smidgen of softer feelings, always laughing at her. Always touching her.

She propped her elbows on the table and tucked her chin into her cupped hands. What would it be like to love him—to have him love her back? A little picture formed itself in her mind. She and Woolfe. Arguing, of course, as they had today in the forest.

A curling tendril of warmth shivered up her back. She'd liked it—the arguing. She'd liked scolding him the day before as well, when he rode roughshod over the tenants. She'd liked how they had admired him. She'd been torn between being proud of how powerful and decisive he had grown, and angry at how he'd lost the gentleness of his youth.

You can't have both, Taryn. He's a man now, not the boy who kissed you good-bye.

He's more than you expected, and it frightens you. He touches you and sends all your thoughts flying—while your body wants to twine with his until there is only one complete, exalted soul.

No matter how she tried to tell herself she didn't care, it was not true. Just having him near watered and nourished the tiny kernel of love that had never really died. Oh, yes, she could love him—if he'd let her. The challenge beckoned, like a great adventure that would last all her life. Perhaps, if he ever offered again, she might have him this time.

And pigs might fly.

He might have loved her when he left, but a man who cared would have found some way to see how his love was, to see if she was safe, to see if she was happy—to see if she might change her mind.

If he loved her now, even the tiniest bit, he would be delighted to see her still unmarried, would be mouthing sweet love words, finding some way to entice her away from Giles.

No, he didn't love her, but her feelings for him—unworthy wretch that he had become—were growing at an alarming rate. But she was no whining heroine in a novel, crying while life *happened* to her. She'd tried to entice him into loving Kingsford by softening his heart, and that hadn't worked. So now, she would do the next best thing—send him on his way with his heart's desire, and do it quickly.

She looked at Cook and gave her a crooked smile. "I have an idea that might rescue Kingsford, but it will only free Woolfe to leave. Will you send Alyce with a note to Woolfe?"

Cook nodded, and while Taryn rooted through the kitchen for pencil and paper, she stood and walked to the open kitchen door. "The only problem with life, my girl, is that we have no say over other people. Not our children, not our sweethearts, and not our enemies. We can only fight for what we want, make the best of what comes our way, and pray about the rest."

She turned, waiting for Taryn to hand her the paper, then said, "Go put your head on your pillow and let those headache powders work."

"I'll kill him," Giles raged, beating his hand against the mantel.

"Calm down, Giles." Oliver leaned back against the settee and waved a manicured hand at his son. "Tom said they were standing in the middle of the lane, and looked like they were arguing."

Claudia crossed the room to stand before her husband, her voice hard. "They must be separated, Oliver. Taryn always had a weakness for Woolfe—I've told you that all along. It's only a matter of time before he has her thinking his way."

Oliver considered this for a moment, then nodded. "Pack immediately. We'll take her to London; Giles can fuss over her, turn her up sweet. And you, Claudia," he said coldly, "cease tormenting her for a while. It doesn't help our situation a bit."

Claudia's eyes flashed with anger, but she nodded her assent. "How soon can we leave?"

"Tonight, if you like."

"Be reasonable, Oliver," Claudia sputtered, while Giles stepped forward to add his objections.

"My friends would think we are out of our minds—"

Oliver shrugged. "Very well, then, tomorrow morning—early. In the meantime," his voice purred on smugly, as he uttered the coup that silenced them both, "we'll have the vicar call the first banns immediately."

Claudia was the first to respond. "Oliver," she protested, "we need more time to plan a wedding than three weeks. I need at least three months." Giles merely looked stunned.

"Next Sunday," Oliver said flatly. "I don't want Woolfe interfering."

Claudia was furious. "You have to give the vicar notice, two weeks at least—it's the law. Do you want everyone questioning your motives?"

"Very well," he conceded, "we will do everything properly, but I do not want you telling anyone—including Taryn—until he reads the first banns. Tomorrow we will send the vicar a note, and five weeks from this Sunday, Taryn and Giles will be married."

Giles laughed. "You're far out if you think you can keep this secret. That blathering vicar will have it all over town in two minutes."

"I believe I can convince him to remain silent," Oliver said with an unpleasant smile as he strolled from the room. "Perhaps I shall deliver my note in person."

As Oliver walked briskly toward the vicarage, his thoughts all quite in harmony with one another, the mood in the master bedroom of Kingsford Hall was not so tranquil.

Woolfe threw back the bedclothes and sat up with an oath, sending the covers spinning onto the floor. He snapped up Taryn's note from the bedside table and read it once more. *"I'll buy Kingsford from you. We'll discuss it tomorrow."*

He was worn out and needed his sleep tonight, but damn his mind, it was going mile-a-minute and wouldn't shut off. Rather, he thought bitterly, his mind was playing host to all sorts of irrational notions as it kept chewing over Taryn's offer and the events of the past two days. If his mind must fight off idiotic, *emotional* considerations, let it do it as he slept, and let him wake up to its usual practical, common sense solution.

On two occasions he had ignored his common sense and

acted upon emotion—when he'd jumped between Quinn's whip and Taryn, and when he'd let himself hope Taryn loved him—and both occasions had handed him back a full serving of pain.

He had returned to Kingsford simply to measure the value of the estate, not to engage in foolish fantasies about Kingsford and Taryn and his future. He had depended on the strength and practicality of his mental facilities to set at rest any uninvited ghosts of the past, and to see him calmly back on his chosen road.

How could his mind betray him now, when he needed it most?

Or was this, he wondered, suddenly alert, *one of those times when his watchdog mind was warning him that he was on the wrong road?* How many times had he avoided danger because, while he was wandering into trouble, his vigilant intellect was waving its arms in alarm?

Time to pay attention, Woolfe.

He reached for his robe at the foot of the bed, pulled it on, and padded barefoot to the fireplace where embers glowed cheerily as if pleased to see him up at last. Sinking into an old, tattered chair, he leaned forward and began building up the fire. Then he relinquished control of his thoughts and sat back to *listen.*

His mind led him, not to the battle at hand, but rather to contemplation of the panorama of his life.

Solitary. That basically described the core of his being.

When as a child, his father had disappeared so suddenly, Woolfe had gone from being the center of his father's attention to being a forgotten, unimportant piece of flotsam rattling around the Hall. And how he had rebelled at the injustice of it, how hard he'd tried to make everyone's life as miserable as his own. Finally, he had been removed to the cottage in the woods to give them all a little peace.

Then Richard and Geoffrey had moved to London, patting him on the head as they left, and giving him over to Oliver to subdue. His unhappiness turned into a nightmare where his only thought was to escape the pain of Quinn's whip. He had run away, of course, but Oliver always dragged him back, making him pay a higher price each time.

He had withdrawn inside himself and found a friend—his free, untrammeled mind—an entity that Quinn's whip could not touch.

How they had soared, his mind and he. Across the ocean with ships, into the hills on snorting stallions, up to the sky with the mighty hawks. They had rebelled, become mutineers together. They had taken over the Hall with swords and spilt blood everywhere, had imprisoned Richard and Geoffrey in the Hall, and taken themselves off to London to enjoy its wonders for themselves.

And through the years, how his mind had kept loneliness at bay—in idle hours atop the rigging of a ship, in a lonely bunk at night, in low company when he found himself unable to sink into the mire with his companions.

His friend, his mind, had come to his rescue and given him back his life—had been his steadfast friend over the years, even as it had given him the labels "solitary" and "dreamer" when in company.

Always on the move, Woolfe usually ended up invoking the ire of his companions, who sarcastically proclaimed it "normal to rest upon occasion." Those same critics found that a Woolfe with a book in hand was a dead bore. The only thing worse, they declared, were the times he went off in a deep trance, beyond their entreaties for conversation.

Nor did he want to share with them his thoughts, for those thoughts were as furiously paced as his actions. Every situation, every new person he met, every business he observed, gave him endless thoughts of how to catapult it into a fortune. Despite Asada's complaints, he had acquired a measure of wealth. He had little money at the present time, only because a wise man did not let even his shillings sit idly doing nothing. Rather, he put them to work, investing them back into schemes for greater riches.

And now the greatest opportunity in years beckoned, the culmination of years of planning—his scheme to sail up the river of gold—free trade with the East Indies. And for that he needed cash. All he had to do was say yes to Taryn, and it would be his.

But his mind wouldn't let him do it. Instead, flags were waving in alarm, whistles were blowing, and church bells were ringing a warning.

Time to pay attention, indeed—and this time to the present.

The first thought that assailed him was Taryn's accusation—that *he was just like Oliver.* All night her words had rolled through his mind, charging him with the unspeakable crime, and he'd been appalled to realize there might be a grain of truth in what she'd said. Yes, he was going to sell Kingsford. And no, her father—whom she admired—would never have done such a thing.

Woolfe moved restlessly in the chair, shifting to find a more comfortable position, and arguing furiously with himself. Of course he was going to sell Kingsford. Why should he sink his life into a losing proposition when everyone knew that the only sensible commodity was money?

Indeed, it was the same battle he had waged the last two days, trying to hang on to his common sense as emotion pricked at him—the fury he felt as he came upon poverty and criminal neglect, the plans for change that fury had sparked as he and Taryn had gone from farm to farm and seen the wasted forest.

His common sense had mocked him, insisting any plan for bringing prosperity back to Kingsford would take far too long to turn a profit.

But the challenge! When he pushed aside his common sense and looked deep into his heart, the simple act of plunking down gold coins for the East India project and watching them quickly multiply failed to inspire him. Even though the odds against reviving Kingsford were overwhelming, how soul-deep would be the satisfaction of changing the lives of his people.

Sensible or emotional? Go or stay? Sell or build? Desert or rescue? Could he, indeed, do it? Leave Kingsford to the further mercies of Oliver, even under the guise of selling it to Taryn?

No, he could not.

His mind, his friend, had not deserted him this night by insisting he make a decision of the heart. No, having led him safely to adulthood, it had brought his reigning common sense and his renegade emotions into harmony; simply, it had joined forces with his heart.

The difference between Oliver and myself, he realized with a surge of satisfaction, is that Oliver destroys, while I have never done so. Nor shall I do so to Kingsford. I shall stay and lay claim to my own—and build.

He took a deep breath, freed at last by that admission. He gazed into the flames, brighter now than a moment before, and felt that surge of pure energy that preceded all his successful endeavors.

He stood and hurried to Asada's bedchamber, fervor deep

within him. Asada woke in an instant as he always did, on his feet and ready for combat, but equally willing to listen to Woolfe's new schemes. "Please," Woolfe said with a grin and an upraised hand to ward off a lengthy lecture, "do not remark on how many times you have told me so, but I have reached a decision, old friend. I am staying in Kingsford. I shall claim my birthright and plant my overlarge feet upon the land of my ancestors."

Asada returned the grin, clearly proud to share the significant moment. *"Mateba kanro no hiyori ari*—waiting brings a happy day." He dipped his head in a bow of respect. "You have lived up to the promise I saw in you when first we met—a mighty warrior who would protect his kingdom with honor."

When Woolfe finally returned to his room, he did so knowing he had won Asada's approving benediction—although he was rather jarred by the thought that after all the years of Asada's sound advice, it had taken Taryn's accusation to prod him toward embracing that truth.

Woolfe put himself to sleep that night thinking how he would meet with Taryn the next day and change her accusation into admiration. Ignoring the fact that they had twice parted with daggers drawn, he saw them together, laughing at the antics of their day.

Chapter Twelve

Woolfe and Asada rose before dawn to make plans, full of resolve to make Kingsford stand on its own two feet. They reconnoitered the unfamiliar kitchen and secured mugs of hot coffee. Grateful for the steaming drink that warmed their chilled hands, they soon walked the entire perimeter of the Hall's sloping hill.

"Spaulding will need a crew of workmen just to beat back this jungle," Asada said, watching the old man under discussion trudging up the road toward the Hall. "The house is surprisingly solid considering its neglect. The north wing needs a new roof and the windows on that side need to be reset. We'll need fires in all the rooms to dry them out."

"In the library we'll have to throw out the carpet," Woolfe said bitterly, turning to look back at the Hall, "and the ruined books as well. And," he added, "we'll have to see about the flooring." He thought for a moment and said slowly, "My mother always had roses climbing there by the library window so she could smell them in the parlor above. Funny that I should remember that, for she died when I was only seven."

"One's entire life is captured like a tapestry in the mind, Woolfesan. It only takes the meditation of a peaceful moment to release it like a bird freed from its cage."

"I must remember to avoid that particular exercise, Asada," Woolfe replied dryly. "The future is always so much easier to contemplate." He pointed down the road. "The stream at the bottom of the hill needs dredging, and eventually portions of the river itself, don't you think?"

Asada, delighted at Woolfe's farseeing plans, couldn't resist adding, "In my country, one courts good luck by furnishing each town with two rivers, not just one."

"Then," Woolfe replied, walking toward the back of the house, "I shall put you in charge of the waterways of Kingsford. Of course," he said with a smile, "you will have to negotiate with Taryn." He opened the kitchen door. "Ah, Parsons, just the woman I need. Please make a mental list. First I shall need fires burning in all the rooms to dry out the Hall . . . arrange for the carpet in the library to be discarded . . . and I shall personally be working in there, deciding which books are too badly damaged to be saved."

"My lord," she objected, steadying herself against the kitchen table as Asada came in behind Woolfe, "as I explained yesterday—"

"I know, you cannot do it all yourself. However, John Spaulding is joining us momentarily to head the staff as steward—"

"Old John Spaulding? Surely, you don't expect me to take orders from that senile old man?"

Ignoring her complaint, Woolfe resumed his instructions. "Tell him how many servants you need, and he will recruit them. In the meantime, please prepare our breakfast and start the fires."

A knock at the door heralded Spaulding's arrival, and he soon joined the little group. "Spaulding, just in time," Woolfe said. "Parsons, please bring breakfast for three into the dining room. Come along man. Leave your bags in the hall, and you can select a room for yourself later."

Parsons screeched, pointing to the Scottish cairn terrier trotting behind Spaulding. "Get that dog out of here. No house of mine will be insulted by a rat catcher."

"Why then," Spaulding replied with a distinctive, gravelly challenge as he followed Woolfe through the door, "the house won't take any insult from my dog at all, will it?" He closed the door behind him.

Seating them around the table, Spaulding took off his cloth hat, stuffed it into his pocket, and took over the meeting. "First of all, Mrs. Dresden, the cook at The Willows, sent a message to you, m'lord. She said Miss Taryn wanted you to know that Oliver's taking the family to London this morning, and she will see you when they return."

Oblivious to his employer's ominous expression, Spaulding blithely continued, "I began calculating yesterday afternoon after you left, m'lord, and the first thing we need is to repair the broken windows . . ."

Hours later, after hearing Spaulding's plans and authorizing all proposed changes, Woolfe sat in the study, the sun's noontime rays resting on his face. He had done battle with his warring emotions and assured himself that it would be far more satisfying to present—and amaze—Taryn with what miracles he could accomplish while she was gone, rather than surprise her with a simple announcement of intent. With that, he had turned his thoughts firmly in a forward direction.

To that end, he now found himself in the midst of a most entertaining interview. Quill pen in hand and his amusement held tightly in check, he observed the two men—friends of his cousin, Geoffrey—whom Lionel had introduced at the wake.

"So you see, Lord Kingsford, we have been sent as emissaries from the gentlemen whose IOUs you hold. You being Geoffrey's cousin, we all figured you for a right 'un, likely to understand. Not"—Viscount Lodges gulped with a glance at George Humbolt—"not that we won't honor our vowels, but between us all, there won't be enough to go around right at this moment."

"Let me get this straight. You and Geoffrey, and all the rest—in order to give the illusion of men-about-town with plenty of blunt, have been gambling with your own select group, just passing the same monies about between you?"

"We started it in school," George said, wanting to show the innocence of youth, "and when we got to London, we began losing our allowances before the quarter was up. Our fathers were making noises about putting us on an even shorter leash, so we drifted back into the habit, don't you see?"

They sat like penitents at the gates of heaven, and Woolfe wanted to howl with laughter. What a grand farce they had played upon society, these young aristocrats, with their resourceful system to keep out of the River Tick.

Woolfe had played the stern lord with them, never letting them know how he stood in respectful awe of their ingenuity. They made him feel a hundred years old, and after the last few days, getting older by the second. They were waiting for his decision, shaking in their boots for fear he would blow the lid off their secret.

"Come back tomorrow, gentlemen," Woolfe said solemnly, "when I have had time to think about it." The two young men stood and bowed, hurrying out as if Woolfe had set their coat tails on fire.

After time enough had passed to let them get out of hearing, Woolfe turned to Asada and they burst into laughter. "I cannot think what to do, Asada," Woolfe gasped. "I can't put gentlemen to work dredging the river or pulling fish out of the sea."

"Let them go home and forget their childish trick."

"Nonsense, Asada, I have been counting on that money. If I can't make this place pay for itself very soon, I might as well leave now."

"Very well. If we are to find some way to prosper from this situation, first we must discover what activities will flourish at the seaside. What do they do in Brighton that is profitable? What does it take to attract your rich society?"

Woolfe sat forward in his chair. "Outside of having parties and admiring the Prince Regent, they race horses and bathe in the sea and have a place where they drink vile water and cure themselves. Indoor baths and shops and libraries . . . the usual round of entertainment."

"And your young gamblers, what else do *they* do for fun?"

"Hmm," Woolfe speculated, "they love gambling and racing, of course, but lately driving coaches is all the crack with them. They bribe the drivers to let them take over and are a menace on the road."

"Interesting," Asada said with a telling smile that caught Woolfe's attention, "and here we are without a race ground nearby or a coaching inn anywhere along your stretch of highway."

Woolfe grinned in reply. "I think it's time we let Señor Esteban make himself useful to Kingsford."

An hour later they were at the Heritage, and Señor Esteban was laughing heartily. "Imagine the bald-faced nerve of those young scamps. I swear, my hat's off to them." He leaned back in the chair, took several deep breaths, and chuckled again. "So, Kingsford, you have to find some way to get Geoffrey's money out of the youngsters without disclosing their game or damaging their pride." He paused, then said, "I see a look in your eye that says you have a reason for telling me this."

Pleased at his host's perception, Woolfe explained. "I have indeed, Señor Esteban. Your own innovative methods tell me you'll be interested in my plan. I've a proposition to make to you concerning our young gamblers."

Esteban raised an interested eyebrow, and Woolfe plunged into the plan that had been growing on the way up to the Heritage. "You need more visitors to make a go of this inn, and Kingsford needs an influx of cash. I propose we lure both here by introducing a sport that has flourished in Brighton. Young bloods come from all around to gamble and horse owners bring their racing stock in, hoping to make their fortunes as well. The folk who make the real money, though are the—"

"Race track owners and hotels," Esteban interjected with relish.

"And the merchants in town," Asada finished.

Woolfe got down to terms. "I propose we build a race ground near your inn on the bluff. You furnish the cash, and I'll furnish the land and labor. We split the profits down the middle."

His host blinked in surprise, but nodded cautiously. "If I agreed, we could send someone over to hire the men who designed the Brighton grounds, if they're still around."

"And I would send my young men back to London to get their friends to spread the word. I guarantee they'll be coming here en masse."

Asada turned to face Woolfe. "You have said that all your young Englishmen are crazy for coaching. We should find a way to profit from that as well." The conversation stopped while the idea took root, then resumed more furiously as ideas flew through the air.

That topic finally ran its course, and another was introduced. "In addition, I know you are buying from our local smugglers," Woolfe said, grinning at Esteban's surprise, "and I have discovered a large cache of imported goods in the Hall for which no one seems to have a receipt. I suggest that I now sell your usual supply to you at a slight discount. What I cannot sell to you, I shall sell in the shops we open to cater to our expected influx of visitors." By now Esteban's astonishment had rendered him speechless.

As the customary rush of excitement flowed through Woolfe, he wondered what Taryn would think of this, wishing against all reason that she were here. He could picture her before them, brimming with indignation. And as for his next proposal, he thought with a smile, that too would no doubt make her fighting mad.

"My tenants are yet another matter. Oliver has the farms squeezed down to little more than garden plots, and has given over the rest to sheep. Mutton from the South Downs is a favorite all over England—the result of the sheep grazing on thyme, my shepherds are quick to tell me. So you see I would be a fool to halt that enterprise. However, these tenants need to be paying Kingsford decent rent, or they're just a drain on the estate. That may be where you come in, Señor Esteban." Woolfe grinned at the older man's caution. "Just how much of your provisions do you buy from Kingsford?"

Esteban looked wary, but his eyes revealed his willingness to spar with Woolfe. "Not much, I'll admit, for the people are poor, as you say, and the shops are sparsely furnished."

"Exactly," Woolfe said. "But did you know that every household in Kingsford has a store of berry wines that would sink your cutter out there? And the berries are local, grown back along the banks of the small streams."

"You don't say?" Esteban leaned forward, rubbing his hands together.

"We've a pig farmer whose animals have spread all over his property, and he slaughters and cures his own meat. Trouble is, he has no place to sell it. And," Woolfe said, warming to his subject, "on any commodities my people supply, I'll match your present supplier's price. Of course, you will realize a discount if we become your sole supplier."

"Quite an enterprise," Esteban said, his eyes alight with what Woolfe hoped was interest. "I might consider this, but what guarantee do I have that if you sell Kingsford, whoever buys Kingsford will honor your contracts?"

"I should have mentioned it at once, Señor Esteban. I'm not selling. I shall stay here and run Kingsford myself."

Woolfe watched his host's reaction, for reaction there was as he eased back in his chair. What that surge of color meant, he could not determine, but he was not surprised to hear him say, "Well then, let's get down to business."

Hours later, after invigorating negotiations with Esteban, Woolfe dropped Asada at the Hall to begin planning the waterways with Spaulding and took the curricle down the hill to the old dower house. He knocked on the front door, but knowing Mrs. Maloney couldn't hear from her kitchen retreat, he didn't wait for her answer. The wind was making its afternoon pass up the valley, and it had stopped to pester the poor old house on its way, rattling and howling as Woolfe strode toward the back.

Woolfe knocked again on the kitchen door and waited for her to answer before entering. Mrs. Maloney stood at his entrance and curtsied with a dignity that touched him. Her cap sat squarely on her head, starched and poufy as it should be, and her manner wasn't at all cowed by his presence. She knew her own worth and couldn't help it if no one else did.

"I've come to take you up to the Hall, Mrs. Maloney."

"And about time," she stated.

"Yes, ma'am," he answered, hiding his grin. "Shall I send someone for your things, or do you want to pack them now?"

"I'm packed," she replied testily, pointing to a trunk beside her chair. "I've been waiting all day for you to come."

"Fine," Woolfe said, his smile finally getting the better of him. He hefted the trunk up on one shoulder and offered her his arm with a flourish. She grabbed hold and held on tightly as they maneuvered out of the maze of furniture packed into the kitchen.

They arrived at the Hall a few minutes later, and he ushered her in through the front door. "Parsons?" he yelled, but there was no answer. Moments later, Asada came down the hall, shaking his head. "You'd better come to the kitchen and calm the old witch down."

"Shall we?" Woolfe said to Mrs. Maloney, and she nodded with relish. They found Parsons standing beside several bags, huffing for air. The terrier lay before her in adoration, his paws guarding a large rodent offering.

"I shall leave, sir," Parsons fumed, "if you don't get rid of Spaulding and his dog."

"Well," Mrs. Maloney replied in a sharp voice, "don't just talk about it, my dear. Take your bags and get your complaining arse out of my kitchen."

Taryn looked into the mirror and slowly turned, peering over her shoulder to see the back of her ice blue slip with its silver tissue overdress. She sighed with pleasure, for London was almost everything she had ever dreamed London would be. She loved shopping—shopping for shoes, hats, feathers, gloves, lovely underthings. She even liked the fittings, seeing dresses materialize as she watched, transforming her along with them.

And the new Taryn . . . was someone she rather liked.

For instance, she was, she thought with a grin, quite simply—lovely. She wasn't sure if it was the clever cut of her thick, heavy hair, now soft around her face and shortened from her waist to the edge of her shoulder blades. Perhaps it was the colors she wore—the lovely, soft shades that made her skin all roses and cream. Or the cut of the gowns, created by a sharp-tongued French woman who hated Claudia on sight, and superseded her every caustic, condescending recommendation for Taryn's clothing with her own brilliant designs.

Claudia's unguarded, venomous glances were not the only measure that told her that her looks had improved, or the shock she herself received when peeking happily in the pier glass.

No, for the first time in her life, men stared.

Stared in the streets, stared when she entered the room, stared at her with an intensity that unnerved her. Young men grew speechless and fumbled during introductions, and experienced rakes took their seducing seriously. Oh my, it was so much fun!

And it was driving Giles truly crazy, which was rather good for her ego, she was ashamed to admit. Not the synthetic manners he had adopted on this trip, but honest-to-goodness jealousy. For no other reason than curiosity, of course, she could hardly wait to get back to Kingsford and see Woolfe's mouth drop open in shock. She wondered if Woolfe would fall into the category of speechless youth, or if his thoughts would turn to seduction. She was simply dying to find out—and ignore it in a charming, ladylike manner, of course.

She drew on her gloves, smiling at the thought that here she was, Taryn Burnham, on her way down to dinner and then the theater with Giles and his friends, not even dreading it no matter how many people would be there. All she had to do was smile and curtsy and listen, for, as she'd discovered, London forgave a lovely woman almost everything.

And dinner conversation was the simplest thing—one only had to memorize the gossip one had already heard, and repeat it in the most ingenuous way possible. Or else talk about clothes, the theater, the balls. Just don't, she thought with a qualm, mention the bookstore.

Qualms—of course, there were a few, she had to admit. Not that she intended to let it bother her, but any nodcock would have to see through the nonsensical charade her family was enacting. However, she had decided to enjoy it while it lasted. This must be their London manners, this act of theirs that was . . . just a little bit off step.

Claudia—the new Claudia—had become everything Taryn had ever wished for as a grieving orphan. Claudia's sweet smile no longer heralded some new cruelty; indeed, as Taryn fumbled through the strict London manners and mores, Claudia had been solicitous and helpful. At social events, Claudia no longer relished the image of the inept little heiress trotting along like a pet dog behind her, but instead introduced her as her sister's dear child. She even had insisted Giles take Taryn to see the sights she'd previously been denied. Taryn could almost believe Claudia had changed into her very own fairy godmother. Almost.

The new Giles, as opposed to the casual, take-her-for-granted Giles she was accustomed to, was beginning to grate on her nerves. His newfound affection only made her compare his attentions to those of Woolfe, whose simple touch could set her heart pounding. It wasn't that she didn't like Giles. Indeed, although often exasperated with him as a child, she had always felt great affection for him, especially after Woolfe left and Giles began interceding with Claudia on Taryn's behalf. She'd always known that Giles needed her—in fact, had found his dependence on her somewhat gratifying—whereas Woolfe had always brushed away her sympathy, preferring to stand apart and suffer in private.

Oliver, too, had come with them to London, and even though he went off with Quinn at night, he gave Claudia carte blanche in spending money for Taryn's wardrobe. Remarkable changes, indeed.

Had any of them once before exhibited such noble attributes, Taryn would not be so wary, suspicious, and skeptical. For to balance it all, they smothered her, making her long for solitary moments, the extended season when they were gone and she could wander through Kingsford alone.

She'd slipped away from her maid one day and taken a hackney to Mr. Fletcher's office, but she had been advised that the solicitor had not been in his office for several days. Confused and uneasy, she had assured herself that Woolfe was taking care of it, and would advise her when next she saw him. She felt even more uneasy when she realized how very busy her relatives kept her, so busy that she had no time to daydream, or question, or even plan. And she suspected that she was taking the coward's way out in letting them do it.

When random thoughts did break through, however, she found herself wondering what Woolfe was up to, what hornet's nest he had stirred up now, how many casualties of his abuse were littered about Kingsford, and if he might have sold Kingsford to someone else in her absence.

What truly upset her, however, was that her fine anger toward Woolfe had begun to dissipate. She was itching to go home and whip up her fury once more, to remind herself of all his sins—for maybe then she could find the strength to put him out of her mind once and for all.

Much had happened back in Kingsford, for Woolfe was in his element, stirring up the inhabitants to a fine froth of activity.

On the bluff, Señor Esteban had thrown his immense wealth and impressive organizational abilities into building the race ground. Woolfe's crew of young gamblers provided the word-of-mouth advertising and wild enthusiasm. Each day more coach-mad youths came to join in the practice races.

Down in the valley, a newly organized village council headed by Rolf, the proprietor of the Flying Goose, was fast in pursuit of attracting the up-hill visitors, who had money to spend and only the Heritage in which to spend it.

Whole families, importing their relatives from neighboring towns for help, marched into the green and put their minds to work. Empty shops were rudely awakened by zealous villagers with unearthed saws and hammers, mops and brooms, brushes and paint. Children swept stones and cobbles; and ferried supplies in their dog carts. Nor did the green itself escape the marauding merchants-in-training, for hadn't fairs and booths been held there in other towns, in other times?

Woolfe was everywhere, uphill and downhill, the spark that fired and refired the explosive energy that was fast turning Kingsford into a talked-about sensation. News traveled outward to Brighton and London and everywhere in between. People came to gawk and join in, and hand over their coins for the privilege of doing so.

And this was just the beginning, Woolfe thought as he stepped out of the curricle that he pulled to a stop in front of the vicarage, something he did every morning on his way about town. For he was engaged in an ongoing mission, a noble mission to make the vicar a productive, serving member of the community.

Asada stood beside the curricle, stretching. "A wondrous sight," he yawned, looking at the enormous tree that dominated the churchyard.

"A yew tree," Woolfe explained, "possibly a thousand years old. English tradition has it that it was once against the law to cut down a yew." Asada's interest was instantly caught, and his face, normally taciturn, was alight with questions.

Woolfe explained. "Some say they were officially planted to ensure an unending supply of wood for the longbow, which makes sense considering that it used to be the ultimate weapon at one time."

Asada nodded appreciatively. "Have we not seen this tree in other churchyards?"

"Ah yes, you might like that part of the legend. The ancient Druids, a very superstitious people who used to live here, revered the yew trees and planted them in sacred places. When the Christians came along, they were smart enough to build their churches upon ground already considered sacred—where the yew tree grew."

"Ah, so. Such is the cunning of my people."

"Hallo!" They turned to see the vicar hurrying out to greet them.

Asada returned the greeting. "Good morning. We are admiring your sacred tree, Reverend Sefton."

"My sacred tree?"

Woolfe interrupted, not willing to listen to the conversation that might erupt from that controversial beginning. "Asada has been supervising our uphill workers, and I am about to show him our progress down here. As a member of the council, you will be able to help explain things to him."

Woolfe really had to smile at the poor man, for he stepped backward, as if he'd been asked to do manual labor, which might not be a bad idea for a man in his shape.

"Well, after yesterday's activities, I really am weary . . ."

Woolfe studied the vicar, deciding that although he had been putting him through an exhausting schedule, the man was not exactly at death's door yet. "I really am a busy man, Reverend Sefton, and this would fit my schedule. Unless you are on your way to tend the sick?"

The vicar blanched. "The sick? No," he protested, "I have a very delicate constitution and cannot—"

"Splendid, then, let's be off." Woolfe started off toward the shops, his long stride keeping the others trotting along at double-step time. Fighting a niggle of shame for giving the vicar a good bit of exercise, he appeased his conscience by reminding himself that the heavens should be grateful to him, considering the vicar's health.

The vicar looked nervously at Woolfe, as if something lay heavily on his mind. "You seem cheerful, your lordship. I trust all is well between you and Miss Burnham?"

"Things are taking their course; why do you ask?" Woolfe replied, not at all amused at the vicar's anxious interrogation. He was still fighting his own frustration over Taryn's haring off to London with her family, no doubt happy to avoid his own presence.

The vicar wiped his glasses and smiled weakly. "I thought with her gone to London that perhaps . . . you'd broken off the betrothal?"

Since Taryn hadn't given him the benefit of her latest story to the vicar, Woolfe could only dissemble and stall until she returned home. "I'm waiting for her to make her decision, Reverend. You know how the ladies are, they like to have the last say."

"Will you be attending church on Sunday?"

Woolfe nodded automatically, wondering if the old church could withstand the shock of his long-overdue presence within its walls. "We'll visit the Flying Goose now and collect Rolf," Woolfe said, indicating the inn, strangely enough, the establishment often found closest to the church.

"Black and White," the vicar told Asada, pointing to the inn and proudly cataloging the architecture of the building. Asada nodded, following the vicar into the courtyard around which bedchambers were constructed, gallery above gallery, two stories high. A few coaches were present, Woolfe noted, and the building seemed solid and capable of servicing a larger number of patrons.

The vicar huffed his way along behind them as they trooped into the inn. The announcing sound of bells on the door brought hurried footsteps that heralded the arrival of their host. "I'm touring the shops today, Rolf," Woolfe said easily, still uncomfortable with the way the village folk bowed, actually pulling at their forelocks like ancient serfs.

Rolf, practically dancing with eagerness, was clearly proud of his efforts. "I'll show you what we're doing to the Goose first." He led the way to a doorway that opened onto the newly decorated ladies' parlor. "You must bring Miss Taryn," Rolf said to Woolfe. "We have a special punch we serve to the ladies, and this is a fine place for courting."

Woolfe nodded, just as if Rolf's pointed remark wasn't the echo of ones he heard everywhere he went. Clearly, Taryn was everyone's sweetheart, and he had been chosen as a mate noble enough to carry her banner. He was heartily sick of it, but he had more sense than to incur the entire village's displeasure by saying so.

Just ahead, Asada had stopped to wonder at a large room near the back that had a stage. "Haven't seen this before," Woolfe mused, wondering how he had missed it.

"Been using it for storage, m'lord, but now we'll be holding sing-songs in here, and I've hired traveling players to perform while the races are going on this summer. I used to be a fine chairman in the old days," he said, his face glowing with past glory. "We're planning to renew the contests and exhibitions we once had here."

"I've seen inns where they used the room for orating politicians," Woolfe reflected, "and debating societies. A room full of drinkers makes a fine audience." As Rolf led the way to the next room, Woolfe asked, "What else are you licensed for, Rolf?"

"Well, billiards and bagatelle, of course, and we have cards and dominoes, although we aren't actually licensed for that. Mr. Oliver never much cared about the laws as long as we could provide the rent."

They passed one door without investigating, and Asada stopped and rattled the door handle. "What have you in here?"

"Used to be a printing and publishing office," Rolf explained, producing a ring of keys from his pocket. "Has its own front door to the road. A long time has passed since anyone worked it, been empty for years." He opened the door and a chilled flow of air hit them. The vicar stepped back, and Asada slipped quickly inside the room, curiosity leading him by the nose.

"Is the equipment still working?" Asada asked, snooping through the room like a hound after the fox. "You could produce your handbills here, Woolfesan, without having to send to London for advertisement." Asada's eyes gleamed with enthusiasm.

"A timely idea," Reverend Sefton answered, proud to have something to add. "The printer retired and went to Wilmington to live with his son, but the council could send for him to come back."

"Excellent," Woolfe replied, pleased that the vicar had made the next suggestion. "Let's show Asada our progress next door." As they began moving back toward the front of the inn, Woolfe cornered the innkeeper. "Tell me about your boy, George. Does he work with you?"

"Well, he . . ." Rolf faltered, "he spends his time down in the cove." He was having trouble meeting Woolfe's eye and clearly wishing the subject of his son's whereabouts had not been included in the conversation. "The truth is that he doesn't much want to listen to me these days, m'lord."

"Direct him to me Monday morning, Rolf."

Rolf stopped short at Woolfe's terse command, staring uneasily at him for a moment. "He'll be all right, I promise you." Woolfe said. Rolf's face crumpled and nodded at Woolfe, then, squaring his shoulders, he led the way to the tea shop.

Rolf pointed to the colorful sign and read, "Polson & Simpson Tea and Pastry Shop, serving baked goods." To Asada he explained, "The Widow Polson used to close most days because of the rheumatiz, but now we've installed Rose Simpson to help out, and they are not only open every day, but also are supplying the Heritage."

They entered the tea shop, where Woolfe found himself missing Taryn's fury as he questioned Mrs. Polson and Rose. "How many customers do you have a day? Is the bakery cart coming on time? Has Señor Esteban been paying you regularly? Is your stove good enough, or do you need a better one?"

When his questions had been answered, Woolfe looked carefully at Mrs. Polson, wondering, as Taryn would have argued, if he had been too hard on her—only to find the lady beaming with happiness and ready with a few remarks of her own. "Thank you so much for bringing Rose to live with me. I'm not surprised Miss Taryn talked you into this wonderful idea, bless her kind heart."

Rose added her bit. "And to think that it all came about because Miss Taryn brought you out to see me."

Woolfe smiled and nodded, mainly because he couldn't think how to respond to their outrageously misplaced gratitude. If Taryn had her way, both ladies would be sitting on comfortable chairs, with chocolates on a flower-bedecked table beside them, and a maid waiting on them hand and foot. A smile crept forth as he contemplated the glorious argument he and Taryn could have over this situation.

Rose offered one last comment as Woolfe turned to leave: "Bring Miss Taryn by when she comes home—nothing like a dish of tea and a plate of biscuits to turn a girl up sweet."

He hurriedly collected a beaming vicar just finishing a hot cross bun. "Reverend Sefton, I want you to watch over these ladies. See that their suppliers are not taking advantage of them, and that the Heritage is paying them fairly. Tell me if they are working too hard and need help—and hire another girl to help with the children." The vicar's eyes bulged, and he choked on his food. Woolfe pounded his back and said, "Come along."

Woolfe gathered his group out on the pathway. "Rolf, you and the vicar show Asada the rest of the shops. I have an errand to run."

Nowhere, Woolfe thought, as he bid them good day, had he seen Taryn, nor heard mention of her return. How long did her family intend to keep her away? The more he thought about Oliver's true nature, the less he liked everything about the situation here. He didn't like playing this defensive game with his old nemesis, and he wished his solicitor would finish his investigations so he could quickly oust Oliver from Kingsford.

And Taryn, was she also to be ousted?

He needed to clear his mind over the matter of Taryn as well, for all the pieces of the puzzle that was Taryn didn't match. In the back of his mind he had mulled over the incongruity of her being betrothed to Giles, but shivering with pleasure when Woolfe touched her. The memory of their parting kiss so many years ago blended with the raw passion that they had shared only days ago. She was innocent enough to simply be confused by it, he knew, but knowing Taryn, her response meant far more. The longer he analyzed it from a distance, the more confusing the puzzle became.

In addition, he found himself reviewing every bitter thought he had about her all these years, how he'd told himself she wasn't worth it, how she wasn't any better than her family. Yet with every glowing description he heard of her goodness, the more his own accusations seemed false.

He'd been led by his anger and affronted by her rejection of him, and in instant judgment, had condemned her. Presumptuous indeed, he admitted, to waltz back into town after six years and presume—despite her obvious innocence—to stubbornly find guilty his only true love.

He looked around, realizing that he was striding through the woods like a man demented. As he got his bearings, he discovered he was on his way to The Willows. He smiled. Of course—he was on his way to find out the truth from the one person who knew the truth, Cook.

Well, he couldn't just storm in. He must remain calm and

casual, lest Cook know how vital her answers were. He must be clever with his questions and give nothing away. Just to pass the time and keep his excitement down, he surveyed the house and grounds as he came toward them. He studied the willow trees, calculating how long it would take to grow the brown and buff and white withies—they would make fine baskets for wealthy ladies' pampered dogs.

If they cut branches from these willow trees and pushed them into the damp ground, it would take only three years before they could begin cutting them down to stools. After that, they could be harvested every year. It wouldn't be an instant accomplishment, but basket making was a project children could help with, and baskets were always in demand—bottle carriers and carriage umbrellas and fish traps. He wondered if some enterprising villager was already doing it, but just didn't know how to sell them in quantity. He took a deep breath. He was in his element, dreaming up ways to make money.

He came to the kitchen at the right time, for Cook was alone. "Lord Kingsford," she said with a curtsy just to annoy him. Then as if she'd read his mind, she added, "Oliver's sent a note—they'll be home Friday night."

"All right, you mind-reading gypsy," he laughed, "I've come to ask about Taryn."

"And about time," she said, nudging him to the table like a recalcitrant child. She reached into the cupboard and pulled forth a plate of cakes. Setting it on the tabletop before him, she carried a pot of tea and two cups over to join the plate, and sat down cornerwise beside him. "Sit you down and get things straight before the two of you waste any more time."

Two enlightening hours later, he wandered back past the willow trees, his mind full of Taryn and as far away from making money as it had ever been.

The fog flowed like a river along St. James's Street. On a night like this, no one sat in the two-year-old bow window to ogle the passersby, and the street was clear of the young bloods who typically strolled along it, looking for trouble. As Oliver Chastain exited the front door of White's, however, he found trouble anyway.

His name was Quinn, and his looks had changed somewhat during the years that Woolfe had been away. His hair had receded to a low crown of dull brown, and his eyebrows now met in the middle. He slumped lower, reminding observers of a large ape, and the look in his eyes gave even the flash-coves pause. Oliver's fists clenched at the brute's defeated stance, and he motioned him to walk away from the lighted doorway. "Well?"

"We finally found a servant who would talk."

"Try using more than one sentence at a time, you cretin."

"Yes, m'lord," Quinn said, knowing the value of giving Oliver a title in times like this. "Well," he said, shuffling his feet, "it's like this. We got hold of a stable boy who we had to pour a half-dozen pints into to loosen him up, and it seems Mr. Fletcher's gone abroad. Left over a week ago. The boy said he went to Kingsford one day and never came back."

Oliver didn't move, didn't blink, didn't breathe for a long moment. "Set a torch to Fletcher's office," he snapped.

"I'll do it if you want, but they moved all your records to Hawksley's attorney's office, and there's not a chance of getting near that place."

"Damn, is there no end to this?"

Quinn stood mute while Oliver stalked back and forth along the footpath. "We cannot wait any longer. We've been one step behind the bastard up to now, and it's time to put an end to his interference. Get your men together immediately and storm the Hall at night. Get back my stores and kill Woolfe and his man. Leave some evidence to show it was smugglers. I'll be back in town on Friday next, and I'll meet you near the beach to hear your report that night."

He stopped and took a deep breath. "I need some sport now." He stormed into the coach and slammed the door. Quinn crawled up to the high driver's seat and flicked his whip expertly over the heads of the horses. He drove through the streets at a steady pace, turning here and there without peering at street signs, stopping finally in front of a house whose number had long since fallen off.

A voluptuous woman with hair the improbable color of golden yellow met Oliver at the door, smiling—until she looked into his eyes. Her animated features fell into a mutinous scowl. "I haven't anyone under the age of twelve, m'lord."

Oliver's hand opened, and the clinking of coins drew her attention. Her mouth worked as she counted, and her hand reached out, palm up. "If she can't work afterward, you'll pay double before you leave."

Chapter Thirteen

Woolfe waited for two days before allowing himself to make the journey to his old cottage, giving himself time to steady his thoughts. "She'd go to your old cottage," Cook had said. "Sometimes she'd seem so lonely, and then she would go and stay for hours. Never talked about it, just went by herself."

He walked slowly through the woods, his ambling steps bringing him to the low rock cottage huddled like a hermit in the trees. The valley rang with the sounds of industry, and progress on the race ground up on the bluff sent a fog of dust floating everywhere.

He kicked away leaves and branches blown against the door from the wind the night before and pushed it open. It wasn't a mess as he'd expected; instead it was clean, with a cushion on the rocker and the remnants of a recent fire. Snug too, he remembered as he walked through the small rooms, a good place for an old couple to live in or a single man. He moved through the house, opening cupboards, checking for nesting animals and rotting wood, and found none.

He opened a drawer and stopped to stare.

There, carefully preserved, he discovered a nostalgic collection of little bits and pieces from his own childhood—and a trailing length of faded lavender ribbon, wrapped in a yellowing monogrammed handkerchief.

He picked the ribbon up and slid it through his fingers, wandering out onto the front step to sit and ponder. The early morning sun beat down on his head and shoulders while a cool breeze blew his hair into a tangle across his neck.

Taryn, he thought as he laid the small treasure across his knee and smoothed it like a precious piece of silk. Everywhere he'd been the last few days, the villagers praised her kindness, the way she portioned out her allowance just as if they were her family, how she went along meek as a mouse—until the old besom, Claudia, forbade her to help with the sick or a new mother, and then that chin came out and off she'd go with her help and offerings, taking her punishment without a word.

The villagers hadn't been unaware either of how she was included in social events when the family's friends came from London, but never quite got caught up in the *fun* of it. Or how Giles and Claudia let her be the brunt of pitying whispers by the younger set, or just simply overlooked her.

He'd been thinking over the things he had accused her of, and the way she came back at him, spitting fire. The thought brought a smile to his face, and he leaned back against the warm side of the cottage, letting the sun soak into his face and chest.

What had gotten into him to be so angry with her—and what had happened to make her so fierce? *Fire and ice* they were now, fighting as they had never done before. She'd hurt him with her accusation that he meant harm to the people of Kingsford and her eagerness for him to leave. And he'd hurt her by threatening her relatives, and by stirring up her emotions just to feed his own ego. The list went on and on, back and forth. And the wild attraction that sparked between them made it worse—for both of them.

Did it matter that she didn't love him, did she deserve to go on living with her relatives in penance? Did she deserve a life with Giles? Hadn't she been the only kindness in his life all those years, the sweetest thing he'd ever known? And just because she didn't want him, should he then feel justified in deserting her?

He'd left her once, stripping her out of his heart with the same ruthlessness he had turned loose on his father's memory. Could he heartlessly leave her behind now in any of those places he'd seen her—lying to the vicar to help Cook; taking insults from Giles's women friends; so afraid when her family arrived at the wake that she had quit breathing; waiting on drunken, demanding Giles without a single complaint?

When had he ever seen her happy? With Rose's baby, not even her own; in Cook's kitchen with Alyce, laughing; for a tiny second when he had touched her in the vicarage; and in his arms during the most memorable kiss he had ever experienced.

He'd made a resolution about the villagers, unable to leave them without a helping hand. He sure as hell was not going to do less for Taryn. He had left her once, turned his heart and mind from her with the fury of rejected youth. But now . . .

He made himself a promise, an unwavering vow, that he would save her from Giles if he had to dump her over his shoulder and carry her away from her greedy aunt and uncle. She didn't deserve them, and they certainly didn't deserve her. By God, he'd see to it that they had given her the last measure of pain and had taken from her the last parcel of goodness that they were going to get.

Meanwhile, in London, Taryn, the rebel, who in her youth had turned in her sword and shield for Woolfe's sake, was on her way out of confinement.

Oh, she was not waging a full-scale revolt—yet. Instead she was observing and reevaluating, testing the air for whiffs of freedom, daintily dipping her toe into the waters of insurrection.

Sometimes she couldn't believe that she once had feared and envied Giles's friends for their sophisticated ways. Now, she had done it all—dances, breakfasts in the afternoon, evenings of music and poetry, the opera, plays, and Almack's—and had learned a few things. Not everyone was as ignorant as Giles and his friends—yes, ignorant; some Londoners were well-read and knowledgeable about the terrible war and the poor British soldiers who were dying while society kept right on playing.

Taryn had picked up a few other tidbits about London these last two weeks. It was fun to shop—if you could make your own choices. It was wonderful to attend the theater—if only you could hear the play over the noise of the unmannerly patrons. It was always exhilarating to dance—even if you had to make inane conversation and didn't mind your partners ogling the low cut of your gown. It was miserable to pass a bookstore knowing you were not allowed to enter—at least not yet—but she was working on it.

Another thing she had discovered, quite a disconcerting matter, was that the men of Giles's set in London . . . bored her. They had no depth, no strength, no *muscles*. Like Giles, their valets poured them into their clothes, terrorizing them into obeying the most ridiculous fashions. They lounged, they drooped, they lifted their quizzing glasses as if it was the most exhausting thing in the world. They offered the most fulsome compliments without consulting their minds, then went off to the card rooms where they lost all their money. Heaven help them should anyone ask them to *earn* their living, for it simply wasn't done. In fact, heaven help anyone whose relatives worked for a living, for they *smelled of the shop*.

Oh, she was full of judgment, she supposed, and was not so blind that she didn't realize she was comparing all of them to Woolfe, to his vibrant energy, his keen mind—even the incessant questions he asked. Just the sound of his name in her mind gave her shivers these days. Just remembering those muscled legs and broad chest, the tanned skin and strong hands, the rough thumb across her lips—all were part of the grand rebellion inside her, this sensuous longing for Woolfe and her impatience with the wilting-lily men of London.

She was so brave these days, seeing the world from a different branch in the tree—for after all these years of being treated so badly, it had taken the longed-for kindness of her family to break the shell of submission into which she had crawled. And in just the smallest of ways, she was getting a bit of revenge on them, pushing them to the limits of their patience, forcing them to cling to their allotted role of sweetness while she did all the things that drove them mad. It wasn't only revenge, she assured herself, but a show of strength she would need if she was to hold her own with them in the years ahead as an independent woman.

Tonight, for instance, she intended to carry the dinner conversation into troubled waters. Although Claudia had invited Sir Lionel and his good friends, Mrs. Tristin and Mrs. Lawnsdale to join them, this night seemed as good as any to forge ahead with her plans. She smiled at Giles as he seated her at the table and forgave herself for the misery she intended to cause him, for it was in his own best interests, as well as her own. She valued his friendship, but had no intention of letting him bully her forever as had his mother, and he might just as well know it now.

Taking a deep breath, she said calmly, "Sir Lionel tells me that Woolfe and Señor Esteban are building a race ground in Kingsford to compete with Brighton."

Ah, she thought, that's more like it.

Claudia scowled at her as if she were a traitor, Oliver looked murderous, and Giles's face turned red. The pleasure of watching them try to smother their true feelings under the guise of affability was every bit as good as the turtle soup the excellent chef had prepared for dinner. She enjoyed both thoroughly as she lifted her spoon—their exercise in control and the soup.

The widows, oblivious to the undercurrents, grew vociferous upon the subject of Lord Kingsford. Sir Lionel in turn grew verbose on the subject of horses, adding, "Geoffrey's old friends are spreading the word all over London. They've dragged the race course, but they've barely started the spectator areas. Doesn't seem to bother the crowd though; they've come to watch the building. I've heard Woolfe has hired a coachman to start a coachmen's school, and the Heritage looks like an academy for demented young men, with hordes of them driving up and down the bluff like the devil was after them." He chuckled. "Have a mind to give it a go myself."

Claudia interrupted. "Taryn, dear, let us not allow these gentlemen to turn our dinner table into a gentleman's club. Do change the subject."

Time for a bit of inanity, Taryn thought, falling back on the easiest polite dinner conversation she knew. "The weather was lovely this morning," she began, "you could see blue skies for the first time in days." Surely no one could find fault with that.

Georgia Lawnsdale smiled at her, but her sister, Nancy, offered a caustic, subtly critical comment that suggested *proper* ladies didn't keep such early hours: "We didn't rise until afternoon, Miss Burnham, and by then it was foggy."

Now, Taryn had been willing to be nice, but Nancy had thrown down the gauntlet, so she threw a little bluestocking flavor back into the conversation. "I enjoy the fog, though, don't you? I love to sit by the fire and read."

Nancy just looked at her as if she had spoken in a foreign language, but sweet-hearted Georgia took pity. "What book are you reading?"

So delighted to be handed a wonderfully irritating subject, Taryn admitted the truth. "I haven't had time lately to indulge, so today I spent hours getting caught up on the newspapers."

Giles, still angry over the mention of Woolfe, reverted to his old personality and rolled his eyes heavenward in exasperation, while Nancy looked down at her plate to keep from laughing. Sir Lionel frowned at the two and tried to keep the conversation running smoothly. "I admire your effort to keep up with the news. It seems you only have to be out of touch a day or two and you're behind before you know it."

"Yes, exactly," Taryn enthused with a touch of innocence. "And even then it's hard to find what you are looking for. For instance, have you heard anything about the seven-week armistice Napoleon agreed to at the conference in Plestwitz? One paper said it might be extended, but I haven't read anything more—"

"Taryn dear," Claudia said sweetly, choking on her anger, "What kind of dinner conversation is that?" Claudia was livid, and with good reason, Taryn thought, for ladies did not follow the war news, and she had embarrassed Giles in front of his friends. All-in-all, she was enjoying herself exceedingly, and was willing now to pull back her claws as Georgia turned the conversation. "The gentlemen have promised to take us to the shops in Kingsford on Saturday, shall we all go together?"

Claudia shuddered, but smiled sweetly. "No thank you, I shall be too busy, but you all go without me."

The mention of Kingsford gave Taryn shivers again, and Woolfe's face hovered in view. Taryn hadn't intended to let her attraction to Woolfe get past the rebellious dreaming stage, but the sudden thought that she would see Woolfe somewhere in the days ahead, filled her with excitement. Much as she wished it otherwise, the truth was, she could hardly wait.

Chapter Fourteen

The leader of the Kingsford smugglers and Asada, should they ever have met in friendly circumstances, would have had a lot in common. His name was Fische, George Fische, actually George Fische IV, if you didn't mind pronouncing it, and if you were to consult his mum who believed that a name meant a lot—and since England was working on their fourth George as king—it must mean good luck. Like Asada, George Fische IV was a great believer in luck and the favor of the gods.

And tonight he had a bad feeling about the whole enterprise they were engaged in. He had been in the throes of making a decision, leaning heavily toward telling Quinn to do his own dirty work, when Quinn mentioned a large reward for reclaiming the stores in old Kingsford Hall.

Now, a large sum of money was a subject he and George IV—Prince Regent for the present time—both understood. It tended to balance out things like decisions, and who got to do the ordering.

So here he was, coming in the back way—the secret back way—to the cellar, and so far, so good. Quinn had gone up the cellar stairs into the house to watch for awakening dwellers. George's men hadn't made enough noise to awaken the inhabitants, who, in his estimation, couldn't have been much of a threat even if they did wake up, for Quinn said he would take care of them if necessary, and Quinn's word was good on the subject of subduing enemies.

Moreover, what trouble could the two of them be? A foreign man and a Burnham—and you knew what that meant. Burnhams spent their days gambling at their clubs and their nights dancing and gambling at their balls. Should they even decide to fight, the foreign man was *short* and the Burnham was *skinny*.

The first indication that something was wrong was the empty storeroom where the cloth and fancy work were supposed to be.

The second was the great clamor that arose when they opened the door to the room where the liquor was stored—or should have been. Upon opening that door, the heavens opened up and fell clanging upon their heads—large, noisy things that broke when they hit the floor, and metal things that sounded like church bells on Sunday. Things that banged their heads and shoulders and made George IV consider once again the value of a large reward.

The third was the dog. Even Royal George IV wouldn't have wanted to go up against old Molly, John Spaulding's cairn terrier, for it was a fleet guarding canine, fully willing to fend off anyone coming into its territory uninvited. The flying, nipping little monster, making up in speed and violence what she lacked in size, had his three men screaming and running out the back way when common smuggler George IV remembered he was supposed to leave something to show that smugglers had been here. So he did. He left his burning torch.

Upstairs, Woolfe and Asada awoke immediately to the sound of their surprise alarm sounding in the basement.

They met in the hall, Asada clothed in a pair of dark, loose pants held up with a drawstring, and Woolfe wearing the closest trousers available to a fast-moving man. Neither wore shoes nor carried a candle; nor did they speak, for words weren't necessary for two men who had fought assassins of every description in some pretty low places in the world. Neither did they carry a gun, for after one shot that told the assassin where you were, you were on your own anyway.

Instead, they listened until the breaking and the screaming died down. Then they listened a little longer for that telltale sound that always came when a man was stalking you—the click of an opening door, the rustle of clothing, a board creaking.

It was only one man, they deduced after a few minutes. He was large and heavy and confident—and stupid enough to come alone and even more stupid to come up the confining staircase.

"Mine," Woolfe whispered in Asada's ear, knowing it was Quinn, relishing the prospect of the meeting. Down he went on the edge of the treads nearest the wall, silent as a cat. He could smell Quinn before he reached him, another bit of information a true assassin knew about, for a good killer came a-hunting clean and scentless.

Quinn never knew what hit him, for in a matter of seconds, he had been hit, or kicked, in the chest, his gun-carrying arm was screaming in pain, and he was on his way down the stairs. His gun came tumbling after him, end-over-end when it should have fallen and lain still.

Both Asada and George IV would have agreed on the bad luck that assaulted them that night, for the tumbling gun fired and shot Asada.

Downstairs, Quinn, whimpering and whining as great bullies do when hurt, scrambled backward and came to his feet just as smoke came floating up through the open cellar door. Woolfe listened to the sounds of Quinn's escape, hesitated at the certain knowledge that somewhere his Kingsford Hall was burning and that he loved it after all, and turned toward his friend, who was cursing fluently in several languages.

It took Asada several time-wasting minutes to assure Woolfe that he was going to live, minutes while Woolfe carried Asada into his room, locked the door against further danger, examined him thoroughly under the glare of a lighted lamp, and determined that a gunshot wound that left a bleeding groove across Asada's muscled buttocks would heal—probably faster than Asada's fierce pride. More minutes passed while Woolfe searched the Hall for other intruders and got Mrs. Maloney out of the house. Finally, he and John Spaulding attacked the fire, which turned out to be a smoking torch lying upon the dirt of the cellar floor.

Quinn sat on the edge of a small fishing boat drawn up on the shale beach, elbows on his knees, head upon upraised fists. When Oliver crunched across the coarse sand, Quinn remained in that position, a dark hulk silhouetted against the waning moon shining off the sand. He didn't stir, even when Oliver kicked his booted foot to rouse him and show his displeasure.

"I'm going to kill 'em all," the brute said, so surprising Oliver that he suspended his second kick, for Quinn never initiated the conversation.

"You'll do as I say," Oliver snarled, his temper on a shorter fuse than usual, "and you'll kill only if I give you permission." He paused to reflect on Quinn's actual words. "With whom are you displeased enough to end their lives?"

"George and his men—they're threatening to join the gang

out of Alfriston, and I'm going to kill 'em one by one. And t'other ones at the Hall."

"They're still alive? You did not kill Woolfe?" Oliver's icy words brought Quinn to his feet, scrambling for an explanation.

"Ya shoulda been there. It wuz like hellfire, with fire and smoke everywhere and an army of men attacking. They wuz waiting for us in the dark with clubs and guns."

"And the stores?"

"They wuz gone before George got there; they mustuv sold 'em to get the blunt." His eyes squinted and his voice rose. "He's gotta know we wuz behind it."

"Probably." Oliver paced back and forth with precise steps, ten paces up and ten paces back. "But proving it will be another matter." He proceeded forward for another ten steps, then stopped and listened to the thoughts in his head. "I have another plan—"

"Not in the dark!"

Oliver stared at his man, thoughtfully observing the signs of rebellion that could queer his plan. He replied in a soft, humoring voice, "We shall see . . ."

The next morning, fresh home from London, the young people from The Willows drove their smart equipage the short distance into the village proper of Kingsford and parked it alongside the green. Taryn exited first, her blue-green sprigged muslin dress flowing around her ankles as she stepped excitedly from the coach. She'd worn her favorite ensemble today, not quite admitting to herself that she was looking forward to seeing Woolfe's reaction—if, of course, he just happened to see her in it.

Taryn took one look at the village and forgot to step forward, forcing the others to maneuver around her as she stood unmoving on the grass. Unnoticed, a gust of wind lifted her hat and blew it across the green, and a boy with a hoop crushed it flat. She turned slowly while pins from her newly freed hair leapt to freedom and blew in her face. She pushed it out of her eyes without noticing its wildness.

What on earth, she thought with a finely tuned anger, has Woolfe done to Kingsford? Where was her quiet little village?

"Charming," Georgia pronounced with a sigh, looking over the shops and the prettily dressed ladies strolling along the footpath.

"It's very small," Nancy complained, staring with disdain at the stalls being constructed on the green.

Giles nudged Taryn forward and shaded his face with his hand. "What the . . . ? Where did all these people come from?"

Lionel's eyes glowed. "It must be the new race ground they're building up on the bluff." He rubbed his hands together. "I b'lieve I shall run up today and sign up for the coaching lessons, for they won't let you race unless you pay for that first."

"Races!" Nancy raised her parasol to look at the bluff. "What are we ladies to do while the men spend their days at the races?" She stormed across the street toward the shops. Taryn followed in a dreamlike trance to stand beside her.

"Subscription balls?" Taryn exclaimed, reading the ornate handbill in the shop window—Rolf's Printing Shop. "Friday evenings at the Heritage ballroom?" She turned her back to the print shop and looked around in a half circle, slowly trying to assimilate the changes. The air in the little village crackled like a thunderstorm, full of energy and impending power. And Zeus-like, Woolfe had undoubtedly generated the tempest.

New signs hung along the street where shops had once stood empty and deserted. Polson & Simpson Tea & Pastry, Kingsford's French Cloth, Lace & Fancies, Continental Furnishings and Paintings, The Heritage Ticket Sales, and The Flying Goose, with a smaller sign hanging underneath, Plays Performed Nightly.

Workmen with ladders and paintbrushes toiled in front of other shops whose status had yet to be emblazoned onto a sign. Across the green, hammering and sawing flung the scent of new wood into the air as more workmen constructed stalls. Children ran around on the grass, and housewives watched the men from their vantage point behind a table covered with jars of berry cordial and sparkling glasses waiting to be filled. Is this how Woolfe inspired such energy, Taryn wondered indignantly, as she studied the overly cheerful workmen—grog them up while they work?

What kind of whirlwind pressure had he inflicted upon these, her neighbors, to whip up this kind of animation? She was dying to talk to them, to see how they really felt about it all, vowing that if she found any evidence of cruel treatment or coercion from Woolfe, he would hear more than a few harsh words from her.

Giles moved to stand beside her. "Woolfe's made it a circus," he sneered, "and ruined the village." Taryn remained silent, for she was too overcome with her own confusion to agree with Giles. "Fix your hair," he added. She ran her hand over her head and wondered absently where her hat was.

The ladies led the way along the freshly swept footway, trailing into shops to explore every corner, examining the items for sale as devoted shoppers were wont to do in a new place. How could all this be done so quickly? Taryn wondered, for the displays in the windows were new, and the store fronts freshly painted. Some of the workmen she had never seen before.

She urged Giles and his friends into the inn, for she had caught sight of Eugene Rolf, the proprietor, near the door. "Come in," he said heartily, motioning them past a workman painting walls. "Go on back to the ladies' parlor and see what you think." While the others surged forth, Taryn hung back as Rolf confided to her, "His lordship's got my George working with those young swells from London, planning out a coaching school and telling them how to run it. Since we expect the town to fill with people, we've hired a troupe of traveling players to perform down here at the Goose.

"Come into the kitchen," he said, for everyone knew of Taryn's partiality for cooking. "We've ordered a new stove, and we're repaving the floor." They found Solly, the pig farmer, bringing his order to the kitchen door of the inn. He bowed to Taryn. "Haven't been so busy since m'wife died, I haven't, selling to the Heritage and his lordship's talking of shipping meat to Brighton." When she asked him how his health was, he grinned and said, "Never been better."

Solly made room for a farmer bringing a basket of vegetables around as well, saying, "Corn will be ripe soon, but the crop's a mite thin. Next year it should be healthy, though, for Lord Kingsford's going to hurdle sheep over the land this winter. That fellow's sure a talker since he's come back. Never used to say a word." When she asked him how Woolfe was treating everyone, he looked at her as if she were a bit simple, and before he could tell her what he thought, Giles came for her.

Giles guided her into Polson & Simpson's Tea and Pastry Shop, following Lionel and the two widows. "Ah, this is more like it," Nancy approved in a purring voice. "I declare, this is as pretty as Gunter's, only like a little doll house." She called to her sister, who had preceded them all in. "Shall we stay for tea, Georgia?" She ran caressing fingers down over her own waist. "Nothing like cream for a lady's form and complexion." She glanced back at Taryn's thin hips. "Join us, Miss Burnham, it will do you good."

Mrs. Polson, a pretty, white-haired lady whose crimped curls and fine wrinkles reminded Taryn of an iced fairy on a cake, bobbed a curtsy and moved forward slowly as they entered.

The widows made a fine show of letting Lionel seat them at the round table near the window, while Giles rushed to pull over an extra chair from the neighboring table for Taryn. She had to smile, for Giles had become jealous even of his friend, Lionel.

Taryn looked around the shop, surprisingly full of patrons for a change. The pleasant sound of chattering voices gave it a festive air. A young gentleman from a neighboring table stood and bowed at Taryn's entrance, staring in the dumbfounded manner she had begun to recognize. She smiled back at him without thinking, and Giles, his mood deteriorating by the second, glared at the blameless young man.

Nancy tossed her head at the slight to herself, resenting the sensation of Taryn's new attractiveness and the resultant defection of Giles's attention. Georgia questioned Mrs. Polson. "What are your specialties, please?" Nancy's attention turned to the complicated task of selecting just the right treats, while Taryn returned to her thoughts, her glance drifting absently to the window.

Then she blinked, waking up in an instant.

There was Woolfe outside the Flying Goose, without so much as a coat to hide his wide shoulders, standing like a ship's captain behind the wheel, legs spread firmly upon the footway. Beside him the vicar pointed to the green, while Asada leaned heavily on his sturdy umbrella. She stared at Woolfe, with his dark hair blowing against his cheek, and wondered what he'd have to say about the languishing poets of London.

"Taryn!" Giles whispered, nudging her. Taryn turned quickly away from the window, concerned he would see where her interest had wandered. Giles's eyes bored into hers, then looked outside as well. His temper, already frayed at the evidence of Woolfe's industry everywhere, rose a notch, and a flush crawled up his neck into his face.

Once more she smiled apologetically to soothe him, and he

in turn tried to be pleasant. "You're being asked what you want to eat, my dear, and keeping everybody waiting while you daydream out the window." She tried to remember what items Mrs. Polson had listed, but could think of nothing quickly enough to please Giles. "Confound it, Taryn," he hissed, "pay attention!" No matter how he tried to speak sotto voce, his words bit into the air.

She glared back at him, then turned to her hostess. "I'll have tea and pastry—whatever you have today will do." She received a pitying smile from Mrs. Polson, which, she thought with a bit of returning humor, might turn out to be the nicest thing that happened all day.

As Mrs. Polson walked slowly away, Nancy's narrowed eyes followed the fragile old lady, and her carrying voice filled the room. "My word, at the rate she moves, the cream will be curdled before we get it."

Taryn's restraint snapped. "Then, my dear Nancy, you shall certainly enjoy it, for cats love it curdled." She looked away, not caring that the shocked silence at their table was complete, and not caring that she had insulted her guest. Bad enough that she must be prevented from seeing what Woolfe had done to Kingsford, but to be trapped with these dilettantes, who had nothing better to do than make fun of a charming old lady was unbearable. She wished they would all go home and never come back. Better yet, leave them all here, and she would pack her bags and depart—anyplace away from the entire pack of them.

Then the doorbell jangled, and Nancy sat to attention, arching her impressive bosom forward and giving the newcomer a seductive smile. "Why, Lord Kingsford, come join us, won't you?"

Lord Kingsford was certainly happy to do just that, Taryn jeered silently, and he was taking a good look at the widow's seductive curves while he was at it. Taryn ignored her pounding heart while Woolfe dragged another table close, making a figure eight of the two tables and sat down in the empty space next to the provocative Nancy. The vicar sat cheerfully beside Woolfe, but Asada sourly shook his head and stayed upright, leaning on his umbrella.

Then Woolfe looked at Taryn and, bless him, stared.

The others fell silent while his gaze inspected every inch of her, from the top of her wild, windblown hair to her nearly bare shoulders covered only with tiny puffed sleeves, to the softly draped muslin hugging her body. Then he started all over again, this time on an upward slant, ending with a look that sizzled Taryn clear to her toes. She wondered how she could have ever imagined his reaction might compare to a London rake, for not one hot-eyed seductive libertine in London had come close to Woolfe's searing stare.

Before Giles could protest—or maybe because he was trying to do just that—Woolfe soon had them all cozy together, with the newcomers ordering the front counter empty of its displayed offerings. From the back came the fragrance of more baking rolls.

"Now tell me, dear ladies," Woolfe said with a wicked wink at Nancy, "what are you doing hanging around with two rackety men like this when you could be on your way to Brighton, where a couple of *nice* fellows could snatch you up?"

Sir Lionel laughed good-naturedly, but Giles leaned forward, rising from his chair as if to attack Woolfe. Taryn felt like urging him on, for her own temper was heating up to match his. This new Woolfe evidently liked to flirt and charm every woman in view. She remained silent, though, and patted Giles's hand. He gave Woolfe's mocking face a last warning glare and settled back into his chair.

The widows were busy responding to Woolfe's nonsense, juggling the conversation like the experienced ladies they were, when Mrs. Polson came back with their tray, followed by a beaming Rose Simpson. Taryn rose from her chair, hugged her, and exclaimed, "So that's why the sign says Simpson! I've been so amazed at the change in the village that I didn't pay attention. Oh Rose, what a marvelous idea, making your splendid pastries here. And your children, are they well?"

"We've moved to the shop, and the children are upstairs with my oldest and a nursemaid the vicar hired," Rose said cheerfully, "although every chance she gets, Mrs. Polson has them down to play with her."

Rose gave Woolfe a shy smile, but was so excited she had to tell Taryn the whole story. She backed toward the window, drawing Taryn with her as she whispered, "You should have seen it, Miss Taryn, Lord Kingsford had everyone loading my things into the cart, even the vicar, lifting and carrying like they were laborers—but what could they do but help when his lordship was doing the same?"

Taryn looked at Woolfe, but he had turned toward the door

as it opened once more, jingling to announce the arrival of Iris and her crowd. The party rose while all the women squealed their excitement at seeing one another, and further fuss was made over Lord Kingsford while Taryn moved to the side and Rose scuttled out of their way.

Taryn watched them all, noting how cheerfully Woolfe accepted Mrs. Johns's invitation to a party she was giving, and how he allowed Iris, while playing the innocent ingenue, to rub herself against him.

Her world was spinning like a top, round and round, and she was outside looking in, unable to stop it as everything changed with each revolution—changed from the way she had molded it in her mind into the way it really was.

She'd been making excuses for everyone all her life, telling herself lies and fooling herself with one scenario after another. Claudia would learn to love her, she would rescue Kingsford with her kindnesses and her quarterly allowance, and Woolfe had left brokenhearted and would love her forever.

The truth was that after all her endless efforts, Woolfe had come home and poured an ocean of change over the top of her little sprinkling of help, making her feel as negligible as a leaf floating around in a pond. As for his enduring love, the truth was that in a crowd of lovely, knowledgeable women, she had held Woolfe's interest only for the time it took him to note the changes in her looks. After a life of molding herself to please others, there was nothing left for her.

Taryn excused herself to no one special and left the shop. If she stayed in that room with those . . . empty-headed, inane people one more moment, her temper was going to explode. She turned into the first door she came to and stood quietly inside the shop. It was filled with old books, dusty and dingy like her life. She moved to the back of the store and inhaled.

Woolfe watched curiously as Taryn left, then excused himself and followed her out of the tea shop. He saw her wander into the bookstore, and was about to follow her inside when the vicar hurried out to stand beside him, giving him a strange look, and surprising him by saying, "Have you and Miss Burnham reached an amicable agreement?"

"What do you mean?" Woolfe said absently.

The vicar shot a nervous look at the bookstore and began walking up the street, drawing Woolfe after him. "I was wondering if she has given you her answer."

Woolfe thought warmly of his decision concerning Taryn,

and the pleasure it would be to save her from Giles. "We have a few things to settle between us, but all in all, I believe things are fine."

Woolfe thought for a moment, the picture of Taryn creeping into the bookstore bothering him. He turned quickly, leaving the vicar gaping after him, and followed her inside. He stopped to listen, then followed the noise of turning pages to the back of the store. Taryn was seated in a chair midway down the aisle, a book held loosely in her hand. She looked up, alarm in her eyes, then relaxed when she saw who it was. That alone solidified his decision.

"Taryn," he said, sitting down beside her on a short ladder, searching around in his thoughts for an inspired opening.

The sharp edge of her voice jarred him back. "You will command a high price on Kingsford, with all the improvements. Are you doing it deliberately to keep me from buying it?"

He considered her words and the far-from-friendly voice she had delivered them in. He'd been so eager to tell her of his decision, but now he hesitated. Would she hate him for withholding Kingsford from her? Not that it mattered, for the truth was the truth.

"I'm not selling, Taryn. I'm staying and claiming my own." Woolfe watched for Taryn's reaction, pleased and relieved when the first look on her face was pure joy.

Then her face clouded with worry. "What about The Willows? Am I to be hounded from my home?"

"Hounded?" Woolfe spit back the word with distaste, then remembered that starting a fight over words was not the way to begin his assault on Taryn's good graces. He'd never been good with grandiose speeches, had in fact found they offered more in humor than in sentiment. He should have paid attention, though, for he was at a loss.

He shook his head to indicate that she had it all wrong, and he said the first thing that made sense to him. "I've missed you."

"Really?" she said warily, putting her finger in the old book to hold her place. The book, he noted, was in Greek, so he didn't think it would hurt if he took it from her hand. She must have noticed the language problem, for she didn't object, but sat waiting for him to explain as he laid the tome back on the shelf.

"I tore into your people like an enraged bull when they first arrived home. Not," he explained, wanting to be truthful with her, "not that I didn't mean every word and not that they didn't deserve it . . . " He grinned as her chin lifted. "I believe I'm owed a bit of justice, even at this late date, so don't get huffy. I suspect you're just jealous that you didn't get your turn."

She smiled then, and her small laugh relieved the tension. He wished he had time to go slow now, to carefully rebuild their friendship, but she would just have to get the facts straight now because he was not a patient man. "Life's made me hard and greedy for success, but I've made a vow to myself to take care of the people of Kingsford. I can't promise you'll understand how I do things, or agree with what I do . . . but are you happy I am staying?"

She took her time to answer, but when she did, her voice was sincere. "I think it's what you should do, Woolfe, for it's time a Burnham stayed on the land. I have to admit, though that I'm worried about how you treat the people . . . making them work so hard when they've been so badly treated already."

"Work?" Her words made him angry, but he was determined to be calm. Softly, he said, "What would you have me do, Taryn? Better yet, what had you intended to do for them?"

"I've been doing what I can already with my allowance, but it never seems to be enough. I've been looking forward to inheriting my own money so I could give them what they need."

"Taryn, that way would have no end. People don't like to be given things—they like to be independent, else they have no pride. In the end they would not thank you for it, especially when you ran out of money."

"But they're so happy when I bring them—"

"Think, Taryn. Did they look unhappy here today? Wouldn't Rose rather be earning her own way, building her own future?" He could see her confusion, so he changed direction. "Think about Giles, Taryn. Wouldn't he be a better person if his mother had not spoiled him? As it is, he has no thought of anything other than his own comfort and no idea of others' feelings. He would not treat Kingsford any better than Oliver because he doesn't know how."

He could see that he had unwisely waded into troubled waters, but he had no patience for pretending, or waiting, so he went right to the heart of the problem. "You don't love Giles."

She was shocked, he could see that clearly, but he was even more encouraged by the way she hesitated. "Don't marry him,

Taryn. He doesn't love you, he only loves himself. He will never put you first—"

"Woolfe, you don't need to worry about Giles's actions, because—"

"Don't keep fooling yourself, Taryn," Woolfe interrupted, exasperated. "That's why I have tried to tell you all this—so you won't let him take all your caring and give nothing back to you." He saw the troubled look on her face, and the argument building there. He knew he couldn't wait another moment before holding her. He'd waited for too long already. And he knew what he had in mind would do more toward pleading his case against her wretched betrothal than all the words he could think of. "I'll show you that you don't love Giles."

He released her hands and cupped her chin in his hands. He pulled her against him, then bent his head to kiss her, putting all the rest of the words he didn't dare say into the warm offering of his mouth against hers. She was beginning to melt into the kiss when the doorbell rang and they heard voices out on the pathway, wondering where she had gone.

The door jingled once more, and her crowd began calling for her. Woolfe held her just a moment more, their mouths still joined. When he pulled away from her, a protesting sound escaped Taryn's throat. They both took deep, shuddering breaths as the voices grew louder.

Urgently, she whispered, "Woolfe, I must tell you—"

He murmured in her ear, "I shall see you in church tomorrow. We'll talk then."

Giles's angry voice startled her. "Taryn!" She moved from Woolfe with an anguished look, calling out toward the door, "I'm back here, browsing through the books. Come in and look for yourself, ladies, but you must be careful, for everything is covered with dust and . . ."

The voices retreated, their questions going with them, and Woolfe heard Taryn's voice calming Giles just before she closed the door behind her.

In the hours ahead, Taryn held her emotions in check as she and Giles and the others finished their tour, finding everywhere more evidence of Woolfe's influence. Everything was happening too quickly—her fledgling flight toward freedom, her new-found confidence, Woolfe's turnabout, and the renewal of their friendship.

And her worries over Woolfe's treatment of her townspeople, were they all unfounded? She'd heard no grumbling, seen no fearful glances directed toward Woolfe. Quite the opposite, she'd never seen the people so full of resolve, so excited about the future.

The last scene she'd observed that day only added fuel to the tormented confusion that burned in her mind. She'd been standing next to Giles when, across a field, she spotted Woolfe and a group of farmers working the soil, farm implements in their hands and their shirts off. She couldn't help but compare his strong, muscled body to Giles's soft, spindly form.

Woolfe's muscles gleamed hot and wet under the sun's rays. His straight hair clung to his moist neck, and his eyes were squinting even though he shadowed them with an upraised arm. She couldn't put a word to the feeling that engulfed her when she saw the dark shadow across Woolfe's chest, but for one wicked moment she wondered what touching that glistening hair would feel like.

Oh, she didn't know what she felt anymore about anything. She knew she was angry about something, but she couldn't decide what. Perhaps it was the feeling that Woolfe had beguiled her, and that she was just one of a crowd of women who couldn't resist him.

Mrs. Maloney scratched on the door to Woolfe's bedchamber the next morning. Woolfe threw one more mangled neckcloth on the floor, and stalked to the door. "Yes? I am attempting to get dressed for church—"

"Why isn't your man in here doing that for you?"

"I've told you before, he is not my servant. What's more, he doesn't know a thing about neckcloths."

His flare of temper didn't faze the housekeeper one whit. Placing her hands on her hips in a scolding way, she interrupted, "There now, m'lord, calm yourself down. I wouldn't be bothering you, but there's a man at the door says he's the Marquess of Hawksley's lawyer."

Woolfe reached for a freshly starched cloth. "Good. Call Asada in to hear this, and bring up the lawyer while I try once more to tie one of these without making it look like a four-day-old dust cloth."

He met the lawyer in the hall and liked the looks of him immediately, a light-haired, intelligent-looking man, whose neckcloth looked simple enough for him to know what the damned secret was.

"Good morning, Lord Kingsford. I am Paul Lloyds," the lawyer said, introducing himself with a handshake and an upraised eye at the starched cloth dangling from his host's fingertips. "Lord Hawksley said you were in a hurry, and I shouldn't trust your information to the mails."

"Good man," Woolfe replied, just as Asada joined them. After introductions, Woolfe inquired of the lawyer, "Have you been driving all night?"

"No, my lord. I got a late start yesterday and stopped over for the night." He cleared his throat. "Are you on your way out?"

"Yes," Woolfe said, "Can you tell me generally what you have found, say, in about ten minutes?" He led the way back into his chamber and sat before the mirror. "Go ahead while I strangle myself with this blasted thing."

"Certainly," Lloyds said, watching Woolfe's inept movements. "The gist of the matter is that Mr. Chastain has falsified many documents, pocketed most or all of the money, and kept your cousin and his uncle before him on a pretty tight budget."

"For Kingsford only, or for Miss Burnham's estate as well?" Woolfe queried, exchanging a meaningful glance with Asada.

"Briefly, he had Richard's signature forged on the land sale for both his home and the inn up on the bluff."

Woolfe whistled and turned to face him, the neckcloth half tied. "The *sale* of his home? Geoffrey said that he had *leased* the land for The Willows. And he cheated Señor Esteban?"

Lloyds nodded, adding, "Or they were in collusion. In regard to Miss Burnham's estate, he has been reporting extremely high expenses for Miss Burnham."

"Did you find any evidence that my cousin had made inquiries on behalf of Taryn?"

"We did, indeed, but it looks like Mr. Fletcher was ignoring Geoffrey's inquiries."

Woolfe sat still for a moment, calculating from all angles what Lloyds's findings could mean. "Did you bring Geoffrey's notes and records with you?"

"In light of the seriousness of what we have found, I have had fair copies made of our findings for you, and all original documents are in my safe in London. I have also sent Lord Hawksley copies of these findings in a sealed envelope to be opened in case of your . . ." The lawyer turned red, but didn't back down. "I must do what I think is most appropriate, my lord."

"Don't apologize, Lloyds, not at all. You're worth your weight in gold, just as Hawksley said."

The lawyer's fair skin flushed again. "Shall I bring charges against Mr. Chastain this week?"

"Go ahead, Lloyds, although it puts me in a bind. Miss Burnham has been expected to marry Chastain's son, and that makes it a ticklish situation. I am launching a campaign to talk her out of it—in fact, I'm going to be late for church."

"In that case," Lloyds said hesitantly, "would you like some help with your neckcloth?"

More than a few moments later, Woolfe pulled the curricle around to the parking area in back of the church, muttering to Asada. "I had no idea we had such a devout crowd in Kingsford." Coaches filled the smoothed area, parked every which way. Coachmen stood together, discussing their betters in the cool morning air. Woolfe managed to squeeze the curricle into a space closest to the front door.

They slipped quietly into the church, but at the *swoosh* of the door, every head turned. The vicar looked surprised, then delighted, to have the Earl of Kingsford honoring his service. Then, as if reconsidering, he stepped back with a flush of alarm upon his face.

Indeed, it appeared the entire congregation found his presence quite remarkable—and with good reason, for he hadn't entered the doors of this church since his father had disappeared.

Wondering if his own face was red from being strangled by his neckcloth, Woolfe lifted his hand to pull it away from his throat. Everyone continued to stare, and finally Woolfe realized they were waiting for him and Asada to take their places in the family pew reserved for the Earl of Kingsford on the left side of the church.

He took a step forward to do just that, and realized that the Kingsford pew was already occupied—by Oliver, Claudia, Giles, and Taryn. He swore under his breath, filled with rage at seeing the thief who had made his and Taryn's lives a living hell sitting in *his family pew*.

He'd be damned if he would join them, thus tacitly accepting Oliver's usurpation—nor would he back down and sit tamely elsewhere. He hesitated, his attention caught by the enchanting vision of Taryn, gowned in some frothy pink confection with silk roses on her gown and a chiffon bonnet. Taryn had every right to be there, he thought, but he would throw the rest of them out, manners be damned. He stared at Oliver, his intent clearly on his face.

Oliver stood, almost as if drawn up against his will, a deep hatred upon his features. He motioned to the rest to follow him across the aisle as Woolfe drew near the pew. Claudia and Giles were clearly resistant, but heeded Oliver after he murmured a few harsh words in their direction. A wave of whispers flew across the church.

As Taryn followed, Woolfe bowed and waved her back to the pew. She threw him an imploring look and followed her relatives, sitting on the aisle directly across from him. Not a sound issued forth during the drama, but Woolfe was too seized by his emotions to care. Later, he promised himself, he would take that choice away from Taryn and set her free from their grasp.

He ushered Asada in before him, then seated himself. Looking deliberately around, he examined the congregation, noting with a warm pride that he could identify most of them, farmers and merchants alike. Also sprinkled in the pews were a goodly number of stylish visitors who had come to gawk at the new earl, and his outrageous new businesses.

Woolfe smiled and settled back in the pew while the vicar cleared his throat. Reverend Sefton shuffled papers on the podium and finally settled on the next piece of business.

"Mr. Chastain, an honored member of our congregation, has asked to have the banns called for his niece, Taryn Burnham." The vicar stalled, his eyes nervously looking at Woolfe.

The banns for Taryn?

Woolfe turned to look at Taryn as voices broke out. Her eyes were wide with some unnamed emotion—shock?—and Giles was whispering in her ear. Woolfe wondered if being kicked in the stomach by a horse felt like this—sick, breathless . . . and mad as hell.

He stood, ignoring the gasps that hushed the room, feeling the greatest urge to leave Kingsford without waiting another minute, and let the whole lot of them take whatever they got from the first person he could sell the mess to.

Then he looked at Taryn, and she looked up at him, her face flushed and wondering what he was going to do. He remembered the way her lips clung to his yesterday in the bookstore, and how she couldn't say she loved Giles. He remembered how she'd clung to him six years ago and told him what? . . . that *it had been arranged for years* . . . not that she'd loved Giles then either.

What a fool he'd been—then and now.

Taryn was his. She had always been his, from the very moment he had taken the first whip lash for her, and she'd sacrificed her own free will to save him.

He had one brief moment now to make his move. He stood, never taking his eyes from hers.

You're mine, Taryn Burnham.

Taryn watched Woolfe step toward her, the desire in his eyes so intense it took her breath away. She thought once again of their kiss the day before, how she had lost her entire being in that meeting of mouths, how the world around her had disappeared, like finding the answer to life, like welcoming Woolfe home with a heart that was whole at last.

Woolfe tore his gaze from hers to look back at the vicar. She heard whispers all around her and Giles's growl at her side. She pushed the noises away, like the buzzing insects they were, and riveted her attention on Woolfe and the vicar.

The vicar gulped, and his glasses slid down his nose. He rescued them and looked at the paper in his hand. His glance moved back and forth across the church, to Oliver and then back to Woolfe.

He looked again at the paper and said, "So let the banns be called for Miss Taryn Burnham and—" His voice broke off in a sharp squeak as Woolfe stepped out into the aisle. Once again, the poor man's spectacles fell down his nose, clinking on the pulpit, on their way to the floor.

The vicar stepped back, looking downward to locate his wandering eyeglasses. A loud *crunch* echoed through the silent room. He bent down behind the pulpit, out of the congregation's view, and a sound of mourning erupted from his invisible form. Finally, he came back into view, his bent glasses sitting on the bridge of his nose, while he struggled to slide the stems atop each bright, red ear. Eventually, he had them in place.

A titter broke out, quickly smothered. The vicar glared at the sound, for he clearly had reached the end of his patience. He smoothed out the crumpled note and began again. "Let it be read that the banns are now declared for Taryn Burnham—"

He paused again, just now realizing that his left lens was shattered.

He blinked and stubbornly intoned, "For Taryn Burnham and—" He stopped in horror as he saw clearly—through his right *unbroken* lens—that Woolfe was stalking forward with murder in his face—toward him.

In a weak voice the vicar quickly concluded, "And for Woolfe Burnham, Earl of Kingsford."

Chapter Fifteen

To Taryn, the ensuing moments proceeded in a slow, lingering, *underwater* manner, enabling her to register them each clearly, even though they happened in a matter of seconds.

Still sickened at Oliver's diabolic conniving to force her hand in this manner, she found herself almost unable to comprehend what had transpired seconds later.

The vicar had called the banns for her and Woolfe?

She could not take her gaze from Woolfe as he turned away from the vicar to face the congregation, his anger manifest in his rigid stance, furious expression, and the silent, icy air about him. It frightened her, not for herself, but for him. Suddenly, they were children again, and he had angered Oliver and she knew Woolfe was going to suffer. She rose from the pew to stop him, but Giles held her fast.

She turned toward Giles to protest, then glanced past him at Oliver. Woolfe's voice began, echoing like a drum in the quiet church, "Please forgive me for being late, but my lawyer arrived a few moments ago with some important news, and I was briefly detained."

Taryn saw the resultant alarm ripple over Oliver's features and the angry way he silenced Claudia. Taryn looked at Giles beside her and saw the impotent fury on his face as he looked at Oliver and realized that Oliver wanted him to remain silent as well.

She turned back to hear the rest of Woolfe's words, shaking off Giles's possessive grasp. Woolfe held out his hand toward her. She wanted to tell him he must not, that the vicar had made a mistake, but she could not shame Woolfe in front of all these people, not when he had suffered years of humiliation before them, and now had gained their respect.

She moved toward him and could feel the anger flow from him as she took his hand. He pulled her beside him, placing his arm around her waist, and continued his comments. "I know you all—and Taryn's family especially—will wish us happiness . . ."

Taryn looked at her relatives, suddenly acknowledging for the first time that they *should* wish her happiness. But did they? Oliver looked through her, just as he always had—as if she was a commodity to be used. Claudia was looking at her with loathing—not just annoyed with her, or greedy for her money, but hating her in a truly personal way.

Giles? Even now her heart went out to him, for he wouldn't look at her or anyone else. He was embarrassed in front of his friends, she knew, and angry with Woolfe, as always. But did he care about her? Did he want her happiness? If this capricious mistake the vicar had made had been true, would he wish her well, ever put her before himself?

Woolfe's words echoed in her mind, *I know you all—and Taryn's family especially—will wish us happiness. . . .* She didn't know the complete answer about Giles, her childhood friend, but at last she understood the question.

Woolfe relaxed and spoke above the whispers that were beginning to spread throughout the congregation. "Now, as you know, one reading of the banns does not a marriage make, so with your permission, I shall borrow Taryn for a short while to step up my courting technique."

As he drew her down the aisle with him, a cacophony of voices broke out. The social set gasped with delight and promised themselves to write to their friends. The gambling youngsters took bets on the outcome of next week's banns, for Giles had bragged about his little homebody heiress, and here he was looking as though he wanted to murder Woolfe. The country folk pelted Woolfe with homey solutions for securing his bride. Taryn blushed at the more earthy suggestions given to Woolfe on the capturing of an indecisive female—ranging from barely veiled advice on getting her with child, then sending for the clergy, to offers of proven aphrodisiacs prepared from old recipes.

Asada bowed to Taryn and wished her many sons. To Woolfe he announced his intention of spending the day with Señor Esteban. John Spaulding offered to take Mrs. Maloney for a long walk should Woolfe wish to show Taryn the progress on the Hall. Alyce jumped up and hugged Taryn, telling her to catch him quick, and Cook pulled on Woolfe's coat, while he in turn grabbed her in a bear hug right in front of everyone.

"You will all excuse us, won't you?" Woolfe said charmingly. "I've got to begin my wooing before I forget all your advice." He smiled as he navigated their escape from the church.

"Oh, Woolfe, I had no idea that Oliver planned to call the banns for Giles and me this morning," Taryn said as soon as he had them settled in the curricle.

"I didn't think so, after seeing the shocked look on your face."

"But, Woolfe, then you frightened the vicar, and he panicked and named you instead of Giles." She glanced at Woolfe's stony expression and wished she knew what he was thinking. "You didn't have to pretend it was all right, you know. You could have just said that the vicar made a mistake."

"Do you think so?" he asked absently, just as if they were commenting on the trees they were passing.

"Why didn't you correct him? Everyone would have understood."

He looked at her then, a bitter sadness falling over his features. "But would you?"

"What do you mean?"

"Would *you* have understood if I tamely handed you over to Giles once more?"

That silenced her; indeed it took her breath away. She was afraid to ask him to elaborate, for that remark could mean a lot of things. Pride kept her from asking if he truly wanted her for herself, and cowardice kept her from asking if he'd let the banns be called for him just to hurt Giles and his parents.

"Would you like to see what we've done to the Hall?" he asked in a conversational tone that confused her even more.

"Yes," she answered, willing to go anywhere just to see if this stolen time might give her answers.

He drove slowly up the knoll toward the Hall, proudly letting her see the improvements on the grounds. The encroaching weeds were being cut back. Clinging ivy had been stripped from the front of the hall, and below the library window a cluster of young rose plants grew with their leaves shiny and dark green against the stone. The heavy front door wore a new finish, and its knocker glared brassy gold like a haughty gypsy's bangle.

Woolfe hopped out of the curricle, brusquely drawing her

with him. Unlike her own Willows, which boasted a tall set of steps into the front foyer, the Hall's entrance was a simple step over the threshold into the tower entrance; she wondered how long it had been since she had entered this mansion, then realized that she had never come back after they moved away. No, to remember Woolfe when she had grown lonesome, she had gone to the cottage and thought of him there.

"I should have brought Mrs. Maloney along as a chaperone to give us respectability," he said. "I have engaged her to replace Parsons, as you know."

Taryn remembered very clearly that she now had to contend with the sour old crab in her own kitchen, one more episode of Woolfe's running roughshod over anyone in his way. This entire drama was looking more and more like revenge.

He pulled her with him toward the old library, eager to show off his hard work. His large hand engulfed hers as he opened the door, grinning as though he'd created a masterpiece. He had indeed, she thought—a masterpiece of chaos—but his look was so eager for approval, she hadn't the heart to tell him what she thought. The room was stripped to bare floors, and the mildewed carpet lay folded, ready to be carried out, along with a pile of moldy books. The bookshelves were sanded smooth and stained halfway around the room, and the paneled walls glowed with a rich burnish of oil. On second viewing, she realized, it was a masterpiece—in progress.

When she told him as much, he grinned and promptly drew her up the stairs, discussing plans for the dusty, echoing ballroom, peeking into the empty music room, sadly empty without Woolfe's mother's pianoforte. She wondered if he'd noticed that it now resided in Claudia's house.

Without looking at the other public rooms, he led the way up the next flight of stairs and stopped at the open door of the master suite. She stepped forward, fascinated by what he had done to the room. The old dark-paneled walls had been cleaned and refinished, and they now glowed with a rich oak brown patina. She strolled in, stroking the new green velvet drapes, velvet so rich that she wanted to wrap herself in the soft, fleecy cloth. He came in behind her, noting her fascination. "A little gift from the local smugglers."

Her mind worked quickly. She turned to where he stood leaning against the bedpost. "And the new fabric and furnishings in the shops in the village, are they—?"

"Compliments of Oliver's smuggling ring. As you recall, I

offered to give them back if he had receipts, but he declined and decided instead to send his smugglers to storm the Hall. Luckily, we sent them packing."

Taryn cried out. "Oh, Woolfe, how horrible." Woolfe shrugged the way he always had when he'd triumphed. Taryn whispered, "You *do* want revenge."

"I want him stopped."

"Can you call a magistrate? Do you have proof?"

He sat upon the green velvet counterpane, his face giving nothing away. "I told the truth this morning when I said my lawyer had arrived with interesting information. As to your inquiry, Geoffrey asked Mr. Fletcher to give him information about your estate, but had never received an answer. My lawyer said this morning that he has proof that Oliver has been systematically stealing from our inheritances, and even falsified the purchase of The Willows, as well as the Heritage."

Taryn gasped, unable to speak for a moment, trying to comprehend the ramifications of these findings. "He's here now with the proof? May I speak with him?"

"He's gone back to London to start legal proceedings against Oliver."

"Oh," she said slowly, "did you . . ." She waved her hand aimlessly, as if at Woolfe's anger. "The banns—did you do that on purpose then to pay Oliver and Claudia back?"

He watched her closely and took his time answering. "I deliberately stopped the vicar from declaring the banns for Giles," he said, enunciating every word clearly, "to stop you from making an unacceptable mistake. I—"

Her heart felt like he had dipped it in ice. "Unacceptable? You arrogantly interfered because *you* decided . . ." All at once, the rebellion that had been simmering inside her for weeks boiled over.

She lifted her chin. "Do you have any idea how sick I am of everyone making my decisions for me?"

Woolfe tried to answer, but she wouldn't let him. "Claudia decided I was to live with her, that I was to marry Giles. Oliver decided to make free with my money." Her tone intensified. "You decided to interfere with my whipping, and put yourself into jeopardy for years to come. Then, without a single clue, you suddenly kissed me and, giving me one second to realize how I felt, you trotted off and left me alone with them—after letting me think that you loved me—hah! You certainly argued with me, didn't you? You certainly worried about me and came back to see how *my life* was, didn't you? Oh no, you couldn't get out of here fast enough, with your cursed Burnham *wandering* blood. You left me weeping, thinking of your broken heart and how noble I had been to send you away to save your miserable life and your miserable money-making dream!"

An incredulous expression flooded Woolfe's face, and he opened his mouth to speak, but she rushed on, her eyes spitting fire. "Then after you left, I decided that I could do very well without you all—my relatives, Giles, and most particularly, you. I begged Geoffrey to help me overturn my father's will, and he informed me that my father had not commanded that I marry Giles, but merely gave his permission to do so if I wished."

She ignored his amazement. "Geoffrey said he believed that my father set up a trust to ensure my independence when I reached my majority, but Geoffrey was worried that Oliver had managed to get his own man appointed trustee."

"Why did you not inform me of this?" he asked, his brows lowered and his voice indignant.

"Think, Woolfe. You were so full of anger and revenge. I couldn't trust you not to blurt it out to Oliver, never caring how it might hurt me. And I see that I am right, for look what you deliberately did this morning. She marched over to him and grabbed his perfectly tied neckcloth. "Do you think I am an idiot?"

She gave the neckcloth a furious jerk. "*You* are the idiot to think that you can push me around like a pawn—just to thwart them, to get revenge on Oliver. You are an *imbecile* to think that I will let you have the second bann called, much less the third, just so you can punish them for hurting you, and then leave me once again, but this time standing at the altar.

"Oh, no, you are going to continue Geoffrey's work in freeing me from Oliver, then you are going to accept my offer of buying Kingsford, for I have no intention of letting you change your mind next month, taking off on another jaunt around the world, and breaking the hearts of my people."

The laughter disappeared from his face. "You do not trust me to look out for you?"

"Haven't you been listening to me, Woolfe? I have just declared my independence from *everyone*. I shall live alone with Cook and Alyce, but I shall never marry anyone. Never again shall I let anyone control my inheritance or my life."

She turned to leave, throwing one last dart over her shoulder. "Maybe after I have become a rich, independent woman, I shall take a lover—perhaps Giles. What do you think?"

She gasped as he snaked his arm around her waist and fell back on the bed, pulling her down with him. She wiggled and tried to get away, but he held her fast. Oh, she thought, don't let him hold me, don't let him touch me, or I shall never be able to think.

Desperate now, she taunted him, trying to frighten him away. "Or perhaps, after all, I shall let the poor vicar have the last laugh with his mistake, and shame you into marriage, and I shall become a shrew just like Claudia and dedicate my life to tormenting you. All I have to do is let the banns run with a life of their own—and after your public announcement, how will you get out of that?"

She was sorry the minute the words left her mouth, for the most contemplative, *predatory* look came over his face. She argued with herself that it was better than laughing at her, as he usually did, but it didn't stop her from recalling that here she lay in a bedroom, challenging a man who had given her three kisses she would never forget.

No, she thought, squirming out of his arm to back up against the headboard, she wasn't going to let him know he had that powerful effect on her, not when he looked at her with that expression.

One part of Woolfe's brain tried to think of a crafty reply that would bring another delightful flush of anger to her cheeks. The other grinned, eyeing the curve of her enticing breasts under the soft summer dress and the way her stocking'd legs twisted to push her back against the headboard.

His Taryn, who was waiting for his answer about how he was going to keep the banns from going on with a life of their own.

The truth was that he *wasn't*. He was going to cheer the banns on, give them Godspeed. Bless the vicar for choosing to call the banns for Woolfe in order to save his own hide. Bless Taryn for lying to the vicar in the first place, and for setting it all up. Bless the way she melted at his touch. Hell, he thought, bless them all.

But most of all, bless his own devious mind, his bullying ways and his stubbornness. He would think of a way to make her see that she wanted him more than the people of Kingsford, and even more than the independence she thought she craved. And no matter how she argued, she was going to love him back. She was going to be so happy when he got through with her.

But first, he was going to start his courting. Now.

Woolfe gathered Taryn into his arms and held her close. It felt so good, so right, so *necessary*. She shivered as he slid his fingers up her bare arms, and he marveled how his hands ached to feel every part of her. Her fragrance, roses and woman, drew him.

"Woolfe," she protested, but he buried his face in her hair, nuzzling and breathing deeply, reeling with the overpowering wildness that poured through him, that need to be closer. His lips found her neck, soft and warm with a pulse beat that matched his own. His lips opened to taste her—her neck, her soft chin, her hot mouth.

He couldn't stop, not when all those years without her cried for fulfillment. His mouth devoured hers, not gentle now, not nurturing, but taking what he needed, binding his soul with hers. Her arms came round him, her soft breasts pressed into the contour of his chest. Yes, Taryn, he thought, want me back, welcome me home at last.

He deepened the kiss, tasting her lips, delving into her mouth—

She gasped and pulled away, shaking her head frantically. He ached to pull her back, but this was Taryn, his Taryn, and he was no ravening beast to frighten her so. He waited for her to catch her breath, teasing to calm them both down. "Weren't you through berating me, darling? Shall I get the broom for you to beat me with?" She scowled at him, but her eyes were laughing. "Are you still angry?" he asked.

Warily, she scooted sideways toward the edge of the bed. "Oh, Woolfe, you make me crazy, you know."

"I know, and I am sorry. I've been waiting these long days to speak with you, and then in the bookstore we were interrupted." She nodded, waiting for him to go on. "Let me take back all the mean things I said to you, Taryn, for we've known each other since we were children, and we went through more together than anyone will ever know."

His hand rested on hers, halting her flight. "We were probably meant to be together, but life tore us apart and we went our own ways. That doesn't take away from us our beginning, our caring, or our belief in each other. No matter what it seems, I know you don't wish me harm . . . and I hope you'll know I don't mean you harm either."

His throat was choking up, so he quit talking and brought her hands briefly up to his lips before he cleared his throat and started again. "When I heard the vicar call the banns this morning, I knew why I had come home, why I was so adamant about stopping Giles from having you." He caressed her hair, letting the pins fall out, one by one. "I love you, Taryn."

Her mouth fell open, and she stared at him, a flush of dusky rose flooding her ivory skin. "Taryn, dearest, I have loved you for so long I don't know how to do anything else. I banished you from my thoughts when I left and believed I'd exorcised you from my heart as well . . . but when I saw you again, it was like a mighty blow. I knew you still had the power to hurt me, so I fought it with all I had, and hurt us both in the process."

He threaded his fingers through her thick tresses, bringing the fragrant tendrils to his face to inhale their sweet scent. "I know I should be unselfish and let you see if you can love someone else, for you haven't had a thimbleful of experience. If I were a gentleman, I would let some other fellows court you. I'm not a gentleman, Taryn, but I have traveled halfway around the world and have never met anyone deserving of you, or who would love you as I do. I shan't let you throw yourself away on anyone else when I am here, willing to lay my entire life and fortune at your feet, willing to do anything . . . except let you go."

She smiled, an enchanting, guileless smile, and leaned forward to sip a little kiss from his lips. The soft touch shocked him to the core, and he had to fight the urge to devour her on the spot, telling himself to go slowly, to protect her virtue from his own surging desire. She leaned forward again, pressing her hands against his chest, intent on kissing him once more.

The moment her mouth touched his, he suspected he was in trouble. Her mouth softened and opened, an elemental, earthy reaction that surprised him, yet was so much a part of this compassionate woman he loved with all his being. How could he go slowly when she gave herself at first touch? He pulled away, but she moaned in protest and wound her arms around his neck, molding her mouth to his, wildly trying to get closer—like Rose's infant searching for sustenance.

He fell back on the bed, and somehow his hands once again swept her down with him, still caressing, but lower now, on the curve of her hips. One of her long legs fell over his body, innocently winding itself between his. His heart was pounding so hard he couldn't breathe, but the rest of his body had more lusty things in mind.

Without asking, his arms rolled her onto her back, and his mouth deepened the kiss, seeking and tasting, while his hand moved to the small of her back, his fingers stretching downward to caress the warm, erotic spot that intensified the heat.

He gulped and took a deep breath as Taryn arched tighter into his arms like a purring feline, eyes closed, lips slightly open. It was time to stop, he told himself, but the moment her innocent tongue answered his, he was lost.

She whimpered deep in her throat, and he knew the moment she, too, realized the danger they were courting. She stopped then and rolled up into a ball facing him, leaving him in the most painful agony he could ever remember.

"Oh, Woolfe," she said, gasping for breath, "you've got me so confused. If we don't stop now, we'll be making babies, and then we'll never get the banns stopped."

Chapter Sixteen

Woolfe said in wonder, "Is that what you think, Taryn, that I want to stop the banns?" When she didn't answer, he searched her face, adorably flushed with the abandon of the past moments. "Be sure of one thing, Taryn—I have no intention of stopping them. At the moment my only thought is taking you to our marriage bed and keeping you there—for about a year, or until we die, whichever comes first. Actually," he mumbled, thinking of the shape she'd just left him in, "that could come at any time."

"Woolfe . . . you must realize that until a very short time ago, I was on a course going in one direction, and now you've set me on another. Think about what little time we have had together since you returned. We need to get to know each other once more, and I need to feel more secure that you do love me . . ."

He rose to a sitting position, pulling her up after him. She rested her head against his shoulder. "Please don't be hurt by what I say, Woolfe, just be my friend and understand me as you used to do. I do not want you or anyone else to make decisions for me. I am not one of your villagers, someone with whom you can bluster in, ask questions, then decide what you want to do with them. If you love me, you must stop and really see me, and listen to what I say . . ."

Woolfe lifted her chin and looked into her eyes. "I'm listening now, Taryn, and, just once, I would like to hear you say you love me."

She grinned, her eyes alight, sharing her secret. "I think I have loved you since the first time we met, Woolfe. I've felt so . . . empty since you left." He leaned toward her, but she nudged him away in a busy, practical manner. "No more of that. I must fix my hair before everyone thinks the worst of us." She crossed to his dressing table and appropriated his brush. He sank back down on the bed and watched her, seeing their life together.

Finished with her tidying, she walked to the door. "I must talk to Giles and tell him I cannot marry him. I hate the thought of hurting him, but—"

"Taryn, you are not going to go back to that house."

"Of course I am, Woolfe." She turned back to reason with him. "I cannot move in here with you, nor can I leave without speaking to Cook and—"

"You ask me not to tell you what to do, Taryn, but if you want that to work, you will have to really *think* about things yourself. Think how they controlled you when you first came to live with them, and think how they never let you get too far out of range. Think seriously about how they would react if they thought you and your money were lost to them."

He wasn't smiling. But then, neither was she.

That's how Oliver found them. Oliver—whom everyone knew never carried a weapon, always letting his brute do his dirty work—suddenly had a pistol against her head and Quinn beside him, his whip on his shoulder. "Planning the nursery, girl?" Oliver said, winding his arm around her throat. "Or have you two been planning what you'll do together with my money?"

"She's not going anywhere, Oliver." Woolfe started forward.

In a cold voice Oliver said, "I shall kill her, you know, before I'll let you take her." She knew Oliver meant it, and so did Woolfe.

Woolfe stopped, and Taryn could have cried at the look in his eyes. She tried frantically to think of some way to salvage the situation. She struggled to break loose, but Oliver's arm was an iron vise around her neck. She cried out as Woolfe let Quinn bind him with a rope he pulled from his greatcoat pocket.

"Let him go," she begged. "If you harm him, I shall never marry Giles. I shall tell everyone what a monster you are. If you kill him, I shall kill myself—or you, if I get the chance."

Woolfe said hoarsely, "I told the truth in church, Chastain. Lord Hawksley's lawyer came by this morning. He has proof of your dealings locked in his safe and orders to begin proceedings against you. If I die or disappear—or if Taryn is forced to marry Giles—you will lose everything, including your neck. Let her go."

Oliver paused for a second. "Very well, we shall compromise. I shall hold Woolfe hostage against Taryn's willing marriage to Giles, then I shall free Woolfe."

"Do not believe him, Taryn—" At Oliver's nod, Quinn viciously swung the butt of his gun against Woolfe's head and knocked him unconscious.

Oliver gave his directions to Quinn. "After you have deposited Woolfe safely away, find the foreign devil and kill him."

Asada, favoring his wounded hip, strolled quietly through the woods toward the Hall. A noise, one of rustling leaves, sent his gaze searching the perimeter of the horizon ahead. His search paused for the blink of an eye, but he strolled along without missing a beat. As he neared the danger spot, he moved suddenly, and before his prey could discern his intentions, he had him by the throat.

He pulled him onto the moonlit path as his captive gasped, "Leave off, Mr. Asada, I was waiting for you."

"Spaulding?" He released him and asked urgently, "What is wrong?"

"His lordship is gone. He and Miss Taryn left together after church and must have come to the Hall, but they're not here now. His curricle is in the drive, and the horses have been standing too long." He rubbed his throat. "First I went over to The Willows to see if Miss Taryn was there, but Mr. Chastain has the place surrounded by his hoodlum smugglers. When I came back, I saw some of Oliver's toughs slinking around the Hall, so I came out here on the chance that they were waiting for you."

"Good man. Where is Mrs. Maloney?"

"At the Hall, ready to do in Oliver herself."

"He is a dead man."

"His lordship?" Spaulding exclaimed, stepping back in alarm.

"No," Asada said in a lethal voice, "Oliver Chastain." He stood unmoving for a moment. "Go back and behave as if nothing is unusual. If Mrs. Maloney becomes frightened, take her somewhere safe where Oliver's men cannot find her. Depart from town if necessary, but do it quietly. I depend on you to be wise in this."

Spaulding stood to attention. "Godspeed, Asada," he said, then hurried quietly toward the Hall.

Several hours later Asada slipped into the private rooms of Señor Esteban and stood still in the darkness to listen for sounds. His keen ear led him to the bedside of his target, where he stood for a moment, praying for wisdom and discernment. He pressed a knife to Esteban's neck and slowly applied pressure. "Señor Esteban, I have come to speak with you."

Esteban barely moved. "My time is yours, Asada."

"Oliver Chastain, in one of his last moves on earth, has captured my friend, Woolfesan. I wish to know if you are my enemy in this, or my friend."

Esteban jerked, trying to get up. Asada leaned forward, and his knife bit deeper. Esteban eased back onto the pillow. "Oliver has Woolfe? Is he still alive?"

"This I do not know. Oliver took Woolfe from the Hall today. I have gone to The Willows, but the place is guarded like a fortress. I am unable to find Quinn, so he may be with Woolfe. He, also, is a dead man." He paused, watching Esteban's face, then sat back on the edge of the bed, his weapon unmoving.

"I am with you, Asada. Let me up."

Asada looked at him for a long moment. "Your oath, sir."

Señor Esteban glared daggers back at him, then sighed heavily. "I swear on the life of my son, Woolfe Burnham."

The air was electric between them. Finally, Asada withdrew his knife. "You are the unworthy pirate Woolfesan has been searching for? Be glad he does not know who you are, else you might find his knife at your throat."

"He hates me?"

"Ask to see the scars on your son's back—from the whip of Oliver's henchman, Quinn. He was at their mercy for many years."

Esteban's eyes grew glacial. "Thank you for telling me, Asada." He sat up and slowly pulled the covers off to the side, uncovering a gun nestled beside him. Grinning, he boasted. "I could have killed you at any time, you know. It was pointed at your heart."

Asada's stern visage relaxed. "I doubt that, Señor Esteban."

"Had I missed, the shot would have brought my men running. They would have torn you to pieces."

Asada smiled. "They would have to be more skilled than the two unconscious men I left in the hall outside." He stood impatiently. "Enough. Let us plan."

Esteban stood and dressed quickly. "This is going to be

tricky, Asada. We must operate on the assumption that my son is alive. And no matter that I want to attack The Willows in force and kill that maggot, Oliver, the truth is that we cannot. Lest we trigger Woolfe's death, Oliver must not suspect that I am his enemy, nor can we let him find you." At Asada's thoughtful nod, he continued, "We'll set my men searching and questioning, but our need for caution will necessarily slow us down. In the meantime, Oliver's every movement will be under our scrutiny; we can only hope that he will lead us to Woolfe."

Taryn's bedroom door flew open, and Claudia stalked in. Taryn, sitting at her bedroom window, turned and stared at her aunt, sick with anxiety at her wrathful entrance.

"Now you've done it, Taryn Burnham. You've encouraged that mongrel, Woolfe, to come chasing after you once more, and caused our family a humiliating scene in church. *Church,* mind you, when this should have been a triumphant, festive day for us. You've made a laughingstock of your cousin. Poor Giles is beside himself."

"I am sorry, Aunt Claudia. I did not encourage Woolfe at all. You may ask anyone who has ever seen us together, and they will tell you that we are always fighting."

Claudia came closer and snarled in Taryn's face. "You left church with him willingly, you hussy—everyone saw you. And, you were gone for hours, doing who knows what."

"I went to speak with him in private, to talk some sense into him. He showed me the Hall, and then Oliver came to get me." She had no idea how much Claudia knew about Oliver's vile threats, but had to try to win her assistance. "Uncle Oliver has taken Woolfe and is holding him captive to force me to marry Giles, Aunt Claudia. Did you know that?"

Claudia looked surprised, but not overly alarmed. "Perhaps he feels Woolfe is a dangerous man and wishes to subdue him to keep you and Giles safe. It will not hurt Woolfe to be restrained for a few days, for Oliver has obtained a special license, and this Sunday you will marry Giles—willingly—in front of witnesses. That way, no one will be able to overset the marriage."

Taryn felt as if she'd been stabbed, the pain within her was so intense, for Woolfe's peril was even more critical. Urgently, she said to Claudia, "Oliver is a dangerous man, Claudia. He says that he will release Woolfe after Giles and I marry, but I know that he will kill him then."

Claudia was furious. She slapped Taryn across the cheek, making her eyes water and her head ache. "You are the vicious one, missy, making up stories like that. No wonder Oliver has you locked up. Just like your mother, always making trouble and swishing her tail after the men."

Taryn grew quiet. "My mother?"

Claudia paced away from Taryn, then back again, her wild eyes seeing something from the past. "Your father was courting me first, did you know that? Oh yes, your father adored me. Then that bitch came round and seduced him and forced him to marry her. I laughed when they died."

Taryn held her expression tightly in place, not allowing a single muscle to change or in any way show her horror. "I am surprised you took me home with you, then."

"Well, I have had my revenge, though, haven't I?" She laughed. "And now my Giles will get it all."

"I haven't seen Giles. I wanted to apologize to him."

"The only time you will see him is on Sunday. You'll not have a chance to work your wiles on him until your wedding day, and then it will be too late—"

A harsh voice cut through Claudia's monologue. "Claudia, I told you the girl was to have no visitors."

"I just had a few words to say to her, Oliver. I am going now."

Taryn knew she had to see Woolfe, yet Oliver must not know that Claudia had revealed the secret of the special license. Frantically, she tried to form the words that would convince him. "Uncle Oliver, I wish to see Woolfe in person this Saturday, and the following Saturdays as well. If I do not, I shall not cooperate with you. I mean that, for if you have killed him, I will make it as difficult as I know how."

Oliver stared at her for a long, tortuous moment, his eyes unblinking like a snake. "Very well, Saturday evening before dinner."

Woolfe awakened in the floor of a cave, sprawled on a mountain of rope. He began to rise, then thought better of it, for his hair was not only stuck to the rope, but the effort of moving at all made his entire body hurt clear to his toes. Damn, he was hot, for there was no air in the dark, fetid hole.

He moved again, cautiously, almost crying out as pain shot

through him once more. The next few moments as he tore his hair loose, were not the ones he would ever want to dwell on, should he have a future. Succumbing finally to nausea and a suffocating heat, he sank into the welcome relief of unconsciousness.

His first thought upon awakening once more was to seek some measure of coolness. He still wore his coat and shirt from his sojourn to the church, and if he could just remove them . . . he tried to move his hands and feet to see if he could escape Quinn's bonds. He wiggled his hands once more, determined to free himself.

Only a few seconds passed before he heard Quinn's scuffling footsteps. Giving Woolfe a slow, satisfied look, Quinn untied the ropes on his feet, retied his hands in front of him, then added a chain tether to his hands. "This is to let you take care of your own stuff, cuz I'm not no nursemaid," he said, dragging Woolfe across the cave and fastening the chain to a ring secured in the rock wall.

"Here's water," he said, pointing to a dark streak on the cave wall. Woolfe's gaze followed the trail and saw that it dripped slowly into a concave hollow on the dark side of the rock, then trickled over the lower edge of the pool to disappear into the side of the cave.

Quinn dragged over a bucket and clanged it against the wall near his hip. The miasma of smoked fish rose from its shallow depths, and Woolfe could see intermingled with that several loaves of dark bread. He should be thankful, he supposed, that they expected him to be eating for a few more days at least.

"Chastain's keeping us here together, cozylike, but if you try something, remember my friend and I have guns. One try for freedom, and you're dead." Woolfe looked toward a distant lantern's glow, dismayed to see a second guard.

And so the days went, Quinn and his comrade playing cards, drinking and arguing while Woolfe plotted his escape. Each day he walked back and forth as far as the long chain would allow, his headache diminishing and his strength growing, although much too slowly. He constantly pulled at the metal ring, reducing his wrists to raw sores, but knew it would take a month to loosen—time he did not have.

His thoughts were anguished, demented with worry about Taryn. When early one evening he heard her voice, he thought he had slipped into the realm of insanity.

She was angry. "Get your filthy hands off me, you depraved fiend!"

What on earth? His heartbeat raced up into his throat, choking him. He tried to rise to his feet, but before he could do more than kneel, she stood in the light before him.

Oliver called Quinn, and the brute appeared before Woolfe with his gun at his head. Taryn ceased struggling and stood stiffly staring into space, her hand clenching on the handle of her lantern. Enraged, Woolfe could only watch impotently while Oliver slowly ran his hands insultingly over her body. "Just looking for weapons, my dear."

When he had finished, she addressed him coldly. "I'm waiting for you to leave. That was our agreement."

"You have five minutes, girl," Oliver snarled and left with Quinn.

Taryn looked at Woolfe then, and her face crumpled. "Oh Woolfe," she murmured, setting the lantern down, "you look terrible." She slumped to her knees beside him, caressing his bearded face and kissing his lips. She sat down on the musty dirt of the cave, and he maneuvered his legs to sit beside her. Staring at his injured wrists, she reached into her pocket and brought forth a small bottle of brandy. "I insisted on bringing this in case you had injuries. Shall I pour it on your wrists? Woolfe shook his head, one of his plans taking a more hopeful shape as she set the bottle on the ground.

She raised her hands to her head. She raised her voice and spoke in a false, affected tone. "This whole thing has given me the headache. It feels like my hair is strangling me." She proceeded to take the pins out of her hair and pull it free. She shoved the pins under his knee and murmured, "How are you, really?"

"As you see me, Taryn. How the devil are you?"

"Locked in my room, but otherwise all right. Do you think they can hear us?"

"Probably not. Why?"

"I braided my sewing scissors in my hair, and they're now under your knee with my hair pins, good strong ones. It's all I could find in my room."

He didn't know whether to laugh at her inventiveness, or howl at the moon that it was not enough. "Thank you, Taryn. Have you heard anything about Asada?"

"No." She paused, then said slowly, "Oliver told Quinn to kill him. I don't know if he did." Her voice wavered. "Oh,

Woolfe, listen to me. Tomorrow Oliver is going to produce a special license and see to it that Giles and I are married at once. You must free yourself tonight, for I know he will never let you go."

"Damn him to hell," Woolfe whispered. "You listen to me, Taryn. Don't let him marry you to Giles. Once he has his hands on your money, your life won't be worth any more than mine. He will arrange a little accident for you to keep the truth from being known."

"That very thought has occurred to me as well. You're right, of course. I shall do whatever it takes to ruin his plans."

"Good girl." He looked at her tenderly. "Now tell me that you love me."

She swallowed. Her voice was just a thread of sound. "I *do* love you, Woolfe. I just wish I had gone away with you six years ago."

"At the Hall," he murmured softly, "you said you sent me away to save my miserable life—is that true? You loved me then?"

She reached out and touched his face. "I didn't know until you were going away. We would have never made it with Oliver after me, and if you had stayed, Quinn would have seen you dead one way or another."

"So you lied."

"I told you what was the truth up to that minute. It broke my heart to send you away." He was silent so long that she went on to explain. "You never indicated in the least that you loved me, Woolfe. You always remained so blasted aloof."

"Pride. I wasn't going to beg, Taryn."

"You should have tried at least mentioning it." She kissed his cheek. "Next time you propose, try giving me more than ten seconds to make up my mind."

"Next time I propose," he said, turning his face to capture her soft lips, "I'll just heave you over my shoulder and run like hell." They held the kiss, a kiss so light that it amazed them when the magic instantly simmered. His chains jingled as he rubbed his thumb over her mouth. "I love this tooth," he murmured. Her lips moved to nip at his thumb, then stayed to kiss it.

He pulled away, his voice low and urgent. "Taryn, if you can get away, do it. Don't worry about me. Whatever they have in mind, they are going to do it anyway. Save yourself, and I'll get free—thanks to you," he lied. "This way they have us both."

She was silent for a moment. Then she began to cry.

"Taryn . . ." Just a whisper of sound emerged. He pressed his forehead to hers and closed his eyes.

Quinn's shuffle grated across the rocks near the entrance to the cave, and Oliver's voice drowned it out. "Quinn, take the girl outside."

Taryn hugged Woolfe fiercely, then stood. Hurrying to get past Quinn, she rushed ahead of him out of the cave. Oliver stood looking down at Woolfe. "Just think, Woolfe, this is the closest you'll ever get to having the girl in your bed."

"You're very brave, Oliver, with trussed up men and helpless females."

"I very much prefer girls—young girls," Oliver said smugly.

A horrible thought occurred to Woolfe. He offered the bait. "Like Martha?"

"Precisely," Oliver boasted with relish. "I like them when they're young and too frightened to fight." He shrugged, dismissing his guilt. "The wench resisted and went out the window for her mistake."

"One day, Oliver, you'll pay for all your sins. When the evidence comes out—"

"By the time your officious solicitors come around, you will be dead and I'll have so much money at my disposal that I'll be able to buy all the lawyers I need and bribe the judges. Or leave the country—my choice. As for any discrepancies, Fletcher will take the blame for that."

Oliver stared at Woolfe for a moment and with a sly smile, added, "And you won't be any more bother to me than your father was."

Woolfe's head came up, and Oliver laughed. "Did you know your father was a provincial just like you, mucking about like a farmer when his nose wasn't in the estate books? Getting rid of him was nothing personal, but I wanted his job and he was in the way. I had him shanghaied by my men and sold him to slavers." Turning, Oliver gave final instructions to Quinn. "When you hear the wedding bells, kill him."

Oliver delivered Taryn to her room just as Parsons was leaving. Taryn sat at her dressing table, looking with distaste at the dinner Parsons had left, for she had no appetite whatsoever after seeing Woolfe's condition and the danger of their situation. She lifted the glass of fruit cordial to take a sip when she heard Oliver's voice just as the door was closing behind them.

"Leave her door unlocked tonight."

Taryn choked, swallowing a huge gulp of the drink, then coughed and choked as the liquid tried to rush down the wrong way in her throat. "Ugh," she moaned, for the cordial had tasted horrible. She reached for a piece of bread and brought it to her mouth to kill the taste—then she thought about it.

The taste was *laudanum* . . . and Oliver's command was *ominous*.

She waited in a daze for her thoughts to calm down. Why had Oliver said that? Did he intend to take his fury out on her late in the night? And the drug, why would Oliver want to put her to sleep tonight?

She scrambled off the chair and looked down at the glass, sick when she saw that it was half gone. She had drunk too much of the stuff and would be asleep before she knew it. No, she told herself, she had no intention of lying helpless for whatever evil plans Oliver had for her. She must expel the drug, but how? How indeed, did anyone produce a purge of this sort?

Salt . . . or oil . . . or anything that would make it all come up again. She ran across the room, grabbed the large pitcher of water, and hurried back to the food tray. She picked up the glass of cordial and went to pour it out her window. Ugh, her mouth tasted terrible.

She poured water into the glass, reached for the small salt cellar on her tray, and, taking off the cover, poured the contents into the glass. She stirred it with a spoon, frantic when the water turned cloudy and the salt didn't seem to dissolve at all. Without giving herself a moment to think, she downed it all in a few gulps. Oh mercy, it tasted awful, and made her tongue feel like she'd swallowed gravel. Half the salt rimmed the inside of her mouth, and the other remained on the bottom of the glass. She filled it with more water and swallowed that on top of it. Her throat spasmed, and she waited for it to erupt. Nothing, nothing at all happened.

She ran to grab the bowl across the room and brought it back to her dressing table, now littered with debris. She looked in the mirror—her hair was all over and her eyes were red. Salt clung to her lips, and she looked like a bedlamite. She took a deep breath and stuck her finger down her throat, but nothing happened. She tried the spoon, pushing it farther down. She gagged, but still no progress.

She looked around, wiping her mouth on her sleeve. She needed to escape, but how? Her room was up three stories, and no handy tree waited beside her window. She made herself choke again, frantic to evade the drugged sleepiness that would soon overcome her, determined not to become a victim this night.

Whatever—or whoever—was coming tonight was not going to find her helpless, she vowed. Eventually the salt would work—it must—and in the meantime she'd find a weapon.

She found it upon her mantel, a brass statue so heavy it hurt her wrist to lift it. She placed it upon the far bedside table, intending to settle herself on that side of the bed. Then she went hunting again, for she had no intention of submitting to anything without a fight.

She was in bed fully dressed, weapons at the ready, trying to keep her drooping eyes open, when her door handle rattled and someone slipped in her room. She heard the sickening sound of clothing being removed and bare footsteps scuffing across the carpet, coming in her direction.

She reached for her heavy statue, and wondered as the night visitor lifted the covers on her bed if she could go through with it. She raised the statue and waited until he leaned over her. As the smell of liquor from the stranger's foul mouth came close, she swung her wicked weapon, over and over again, hitting his shoulder, his arm—but when it connected with his head, the statue slipped from her fingers onto the floor.

They both groaned in pain, but Taryn had enough fear-inspired energy flowing through her to reach for her second weapon. She jabbed her long hat pin in the man's shoulder, once, twice, and a third time.

He flipped off her and fell heavily back on the pillow beside her. Giles's drunken voice whined, "For God's sake, Taryn, leave off before you kill me."

"Giles," she gasped, scrambling out of the bed, "what are you doing here?" Her head swam with the effects of the drug.

"M'father told me to."

She lit the candle and looked at him. Blood dripped from

the side of his head onto her pillow. He was reaching across to his arm, where the hat pin still skewered his flesh.

"He told you to rape me?"

"I've got to, Taryn," he said, pulling the pin into the air. "I've got the French pox, and the only way to cure it is to make love to a virgin." She couldn't believe what he was saying—surely he must be making up the story? She knew that stubborn tone in his voice, though, and suddenly realized he meant to do it no matter how it might hurt her.

"Hell, if you just let me do it once, Taryn, I'll never bother you again, not even after we are married."

"What?" Heavens, had the clubbing addled his brains? She closed her eyes to think, then when it seemed impossible to open them again, she rubbed them hard and pinched her cheeks to wake up.

"It makes sense," he slurred, "for after I'm cured, I won't want to get it back from you."

Her throat spasmed, and not from the salt. Giles was telling the truth, then. He was breaking her heart, even as he validated Woolfe's prediction. Her Giles, whom she had cared for all these years, would cheerfully resign her to such a fate without a thought. She finally got herself under control and scurried around the bed to pick up her weapon from the floor. Giles turned white when he saw the statue in her hand; even in the candlelight she could see his terrified look and decided to take instant advantage.

She raised it in the air. "You are *not* going to rape me, Giles Chastain. As a matter of fact, you aren't even going to *touch* me . . ." She paused to see the effect of her words, and gulped again when she saw that he wasn't going to give up. Thinking quickly, she continued, ". . . that is, until we are married. I'm not a girl to be taken before marriage, and I don't care if you have the French pox, whatever *that* is."

She knew perfectly well what that frightening disease was, for servants talked about everything, but it wouldn't do for Giles to realize that. She went on. "You can wait until we're married to cure your problem, for Oliver . . . is having the banns called tomorrow at church." She had almost mentioned the special license, but then Oliver would know that Claudia had revealed his secret.

"Church? Oh, no, tomorrow can't be Sunday," Giles moaned, his hand drifting to his head. "I'll never make it to church, Taryn. Not only have you brutally attacked me, but when m'father finds out you've beaten me, he will thrash me again."

"What makes you think I shall want to marry you if you rape me, Giles?"

"Once the servants find your blood on the sheets, the story will get out and you won't have a choice. Nor will Woolfe bother with you again." He sighed. "I don't think I'm up to raping you tonight, Taryn, even if I try. Every bone in my body hurts."

Her throat swelled with horror as he talked, for with every word Giles revealed how self-absorbed he had become. He was thoughtlessly willing to destroy her reputation—and her. How could she have not seen how very like his parents he was? Whatever kindness he had shown her as a child, he was now truly Oliver and Claudia's son.

And, she thought, wiping the tears from her cheeks, how horrified Cook and Alyce would be to hear of this. How, too, would the story of her downfall spread like wildfire, branding her as wanton and Giles as a man who naturally took what was offered.

Giles's voice sniveled, pathetically lamenting his woes. "M'father will be back to check to see if I did it, though, so I don't have any choice." He touched the blood on the side of his head. "Promise you won't tell my father you did this, Taryn."

Taryn's thoughts flew. There was a way to stave off his attack, at least for tonight. She plucked the bloody hat pin from his unresisting hand and hid it in the drawer of her table. "Stay there while I get into my nightgown." She hurried behind her dressing screen and, tearing off her clothes, dropped her nightgown over her head, then rushed back to the bedside. Jerking the covers back, she flung an order at Giles. "Move over."

He sat, reaching frantically for the sheet to cover himself. "Where's your modesty, Taryn? I'm undressed here!" She glanced away, curious, but too busy to ponder the strangeness of the human male.

"Move over on the other side so he won't see your poor head," Taryn ordered, watching impatiently while he moved laboriously across the bed, clutching the sheet as if he were the frightened virgin. She rubbed the spoiled side of the pillow on the bottom sheet to give the impression that Giles had obeyed his father. Turning the pillow over clean side up, she climbed in beside him and pulled the covers up.

"How would I look?" she said, breathless with anxiety.

"What d'you mean, how would you look?"

"If you'd done that to me, how would I look?"

"Happy," Giles said mutinously, "ecstatically happy."

Taryn was on her side, holding her eyes open with her fingers and watching Giles snore when Oliver sneaked in to check on his son's success. At the sound of the door opening, Taryn pasted on a serene little smile and tried to breathe evenly with her eyes closed. Her skin crawled when Oliver lifted the covers for a brief moment, then stopped to run his fingers slowly through her hair. When Taryn thought she could bear it no more, he finally left.

Then she threw up.

Chapter Seventeen

Woolfe spent the next part of the evening trying to pick the lock that held his chain to the wall. He bent pins, dropped them in the darkness, cursed them, and tried again. In desperation he tried the little sewing scissors on the lock, promptly broke the tips off, then spent the next measure of time fruitlessly attempting to saw through his ropes with what was left of the scissors.

Time was running out, and he had to try a more desperate move. He racked his brains for a solution, then realized that perhaps Taryn had provided him with one after all. Reaching for the flask of brandy she had brought him, he swished the fiery liquid through his mouth, poured the rest on his shirt, and sprawled against the wall of the cave.

"H'lo Quinn, you coward," Woolfe roared in what he hoped sounded like a drunken bravado.

"What?" Quinn bellowed, while his companion chuckled behind him. Quinn swaggered into the cave's depths, his gun drawn.

"He's afraid of me," Woolfe confided to Quinn's companion, who had followed Quinn. "Big gun, little man—you know what I mean. I beat him in a fight six years ago, and he's too afraid to come near me without his gun."

Quinn struck him with his doubled fist. It hurt like the devil, but Woolfe knew better than to let Quinn know that. "See what I mean?" he said and laughed, "a fair fight scares him spitless." He turned to Quinn and taunted, "Give your gun to your friend and face me like a man, you fraud."

Quinn pulled his fist back to strike again, but stopped when his companion laughed even louder. Breathing hard, Quinn turned to his friend and smacked his gun into the other fellow's hand. He turned back to Woolfe, fists upraised. Woolfe rattled his chain. "I'm not fighting with these on, Quinn. I don't fight scared babies." He slumped down and closed his eyes, a picture of drunken boredom.

"Unlock him," the companion said in disgust. "I've got him covered."

Quinn produced the key and released the chain. Not bothering to untie the ropes, he whipped a gleaming dagger through them, severing them like butter. Woolfe staggered upward, fiercely exultant. Quinn sheathed his knife into his boot and moved cautiously backward, ready to attack. Woolfe peered around as if unable to focus.

Staggering sideways as if searching for Quinn, he moved closer to the companion who held the weapons. He bowed to him, a silly grin on his face. "Gentleman, thas wot you are; I'll do the same for you someday." Woolfe turned casually away, then suddenly twisted in the air and kicked the gun-holder in the head, putting to an end the danger of his weapons as the man sank silently to the ground.

Quinn roared and charged. Woolfe stepped aside and struck Quinn as he rushed by. Quinn shook his head and turned to charge again, leaping forward like a maddened bull. His massive fingers closed around Woolfe's throat, pushing Woolfe to the ground. Woolfe panicked as he realized how his confinement had weakened him. Then, as Asada's endless lectures flowed from his memory into his trained limbs, Woolfe's hand swung to the base of Quinn's thick neck. Quinn roared in pain, rolling off Woolfe and staggering to his feet. Woolfe leapt up, swallowing hard and trying to breathe. He moved in front of the rock wall.

Quinn rushed Woolfe once more, but found only air before him—and the rough rock of the cave's wall. After that it was only a matter of seconds before Woolfe efficiently dispatched his old enemy into a peaceful sleep.

A loud noise suddenly echoed through the cave, a clamor filled with the sounds of men yelling and shots firing. Woolfe swore as a flickering torch came to life at the opening of the cave. Footsteps ran quietly toward him, the touch of light feet against sand and rock. Woolfe crouched against the cold, dark wall to wait. When the breath of moving air hit his face, he leapt into action, and promptly found himself flat on his back.

"Woolfesan, it is Asada, and you are too slow as usual."

Woolfe's grin spread jubilantly across his face at the wonderful sound of Asada's voice. "I thought they might have killed you."

"No, Woolfesan, it is your enemies whose days are numbered." Asada reached for Woolfe's hand and brought him upright, whispering urgently. "Are there more guards in here?"

"Quinn and another, both asleep for the evening."

"I shall tie them up and retrieve them later."

Woolfe looked toward the cave's entrance. "And the other guards?"

"Eliminated. Go to the entrance and let Esteban know you're safe."

"Esteban is with you? You trust him?"

"Oh, yes." He nudged Woolfe ahead of him. "He's waiting outside. We'll go to the Heritage."

"Forget that. We need to get Taryn."

"The Willows is a fortress, Woolfesan. We have a plan, but must wait until our enemies come out of their lair. It is an omen that your heiress is to travel to a holy place tomorrow just as her warriors are ready to bring her to safety, a fitting part of the plan."

Woolfe hesitated, fighting the overpowering compulsion to roar ahead, no matter what the odds. Then, contemplating what plans Asada and Esteban must have made between them, he smiled, grateful to hear one more of Asada's lectures. He hurried to the exit of the cave. Woolfe breathed deeply of the damp sea air. Nothing had ever smelled better.

Esteban materialized out of the darkness. "Woolfe." He slapped him on the back and added gruffly, "Grateful to see you in one piece."

Woolfe nodded, grinning. "Thank you for your help, sir." Asada joined them, and the men hurried silently up to the Heritage. Woolfe followed Asada to Esteban's private entrance, and Esteban went by way of the kitchen to order a hot bath and a large meal brought to his rooms.

"Food and water will be here soon, Woolfe," Esteban said when they met in his private parlor.

"I should be mucked out in the stables," Woolfe replied, rubbing his bearded face, exhilarated to have been sped to safety this soon. He looked at Esteban, and confessed ruefully, "I often wondered if you were in this with Oliver, you know."

Esteban scowled. "The devil you say! When have I ever shown such poor taste?"

"My first suspicion came when I spied a Burnham family Rembrandt upon your wall."

Esteban's countenance cleared. "Ah, well. I have always admired it and bought it from Oliver, who has no taste whatsoever. It was upon his wall at The Willows, you know, as are several other treasures from the Hall."

"I shall retrieve it from you, as well as the others, and return them to their rightful place," Woolfe said grimly.

Esteban's voice rose, clearly willing to debate the point. "Well, as to the Rembrandt, young Woolfe—"

"Gentlemen," Asada's amused words interrupted, "perhaps we should suspend these negotiations while I offer the introduction Esteban seems reluctant to render himself. Esteban?" he inquired.

Esteban's face flushed. "Thank you."

"Well then," Asada said with relish, "Woolfesan, please meet your father, who has placed his unworthy person upon this hill, waiting for you to come home."

Woolfe's mind went blank as emotions swirled around him and set his heart beating—his father? He stared at Esteban for a second, then turned to the window to gaze into the dark. His father, who had left him . . . this man whom he now admired—and yes, had respected—was his father? Woolfe looked back at Esteban, comparing the image he carried of the man he barely remembered with these scarred features before him. The only reality he could find in this unbelievable moment was that Asada never lied.

Woolfe said the first thing that came to mind. "Oliver had you shanghaied, you know."

"The devil, you say—"

"That was over fifteen years ago, Esteban." His icy condemnation roused Asada to protest.

"Do not judge in ignorance, Woolfesan."

Esteban spoke finally, his voice hoarse with emotion. "I regret . . . more than you can ever know . . . that I was not here to prevent what Asada tells me was . . ." At this, Esteban stopped for a moment. "I know you cannot love me the way you would have had Oliver not robbed those years from both of us. I ask only for a chance to become acquainted with you, and perhaps to build something worthwhile."

Woolfe replied carefully, trying to find words that explained his hostile feelings, yet offered the hope his father wanted. "I'll admit I've hated you for deserting me. I suppose I'll need some time to get my mind turned around to the real facts, whatever they may be. If it will help, I was mightily disappointed when I thought you were a friend of Oliver's, for I believed you and I had the beginnings of a friendship."

"More than generous," Esteban replied fervently. He paused, then asked, "Why the devil did Oliver have me kidnapped? It makes no sense. I barely knew the man."

"To get your job, he said, part of his nefarious plan to gain control of Kingsford."

Esteban stood silently, his thoughts inwardly focused. "I would like to ask one favor from you both, one that is very dear to my heart."

"Yes?" Woolfe inquired, amused that even in the midst of a momentous occasion, Esteban—his father—thought to bargain.

"Oliver is mine."

Woolfe hesitated briefly, then grinned. "Shall we trade for the Rembrandt?"

Sunday morning dawned, and Taryn's fighting blood rose to meet it. She had ousted Giles before he had time to recover from his stupor, and had gleefully burned Oliver's precious evidence, the spoiled linen. She was furiously determined to make certain that Oliver's evil plans would not come to fruition, and if possible, neither would Woolfe's life be forfeit. Endless prayers had been sent heavenward from her pleading lips for his safety. Now it was up to her—and to him if he had escaped.

Taryn let Parsons dress her for church, playing the part of a drugged victim to lull Oliver's caution, as well as enacting a little revenge on Parsons for delivering the hated opiate to her the night before. Enjoying herself enormously as she pretended to be almost incapacitated, she fell asleep against the wall and slid down as Parsons washed her face. When the crone lifted her dress over her head, she flung her arms around Parsons's neck and bore her to the floor in a painful thump—with Parsons on the bottom. While Parsons braided her hair, Taryn slid off her stool three times, feigning sleep in a heap on the floor. Parsons finally let her hair hang straight with a ribbon at her neck.

When Oliver came, she gave him some of the same treatment, letting her hand slide over his coat as she descended to the floor. She let them gather her up again, shaken and dismayed that her furtive inspection of his coat had betrayed the presence of his gun. "How much did you give her, you idiot?" Oliver hissed.

Parsons glared at him and said not a word. Taryn let her legs go limp down the stairs so they had to carry her between them, and when Giles met her at the bottom of the stairs in the foyer, she threw her arms around his neck and wounded head and screamed, "Giles, darling," smiling when he winced.

The hardest moment was Giles's shamefaced words spoken quietly to her ear. "God, I'm sorry, Taryn. I can't believe that I—"

Back in the hall the kitchen door opened, and Cook came hurrying forward. "Bless me, what's the matter with our Taryn?"

"Get back in the kitchen," Oliver snarled. Cook looked shocked at his fury, but backed very slowly away. Taryn lifted her head off Giles's shoulder and stared at Cook, her eyes clear and alert. Cook threw her apron over her face, turned, and ran back to the kitchen.

Outside, Taryn stopped, knowing she must not overdo the drugged act, for she did not want them to forbid her entry to the church. She took a deep breath of air and said, "Umm, nice," and leaned only very lightly against Giles. Claudia joined them in the carriage, completely ignoring Taryn.

When Taryn's party entered the church, the congregation grew hushed. Oliver and Claudia, pulling Giles and Taryn behind them, marched into the Kingsford pew as if they held the mortgage on the place, and seated themselves with a regal flare. Parishioners and visitors, packed tightly together in the pews, watched the drama, then quickly began whispering among themselves.

Taryn sat very still, keeping up the pretense of submission, while feverishly searching through the congregation for Asada. When she didn't find him, she knew that she couldn't keep looking for rescuers. When Oliver made his move, she would scream her accusations to the ceiling and take the chance of Oliver using his pistol on her.

Reverend Sefton locked his shaky knees in place, and like a man going into battle, reconnoitered his congregation to target the expected danger spot. His gaze sped toward the family Chastain, who had reclaimed the Kingsford pew. Behind them were their servants, Alyce, Cook, and . . . *what the devil?* . . . the ugliest, dark-skinned, squinty-eyed housewife he had ever seen, in a purple, wide-brimmed bonnet.

Oh well, he thought resignedly, the place was full of strangers and most of them irreverent tourists who'd come a-gawking after another story from Kingsford and its peculiar inhabitants. From his bird's-eye view, he could identify them all.

The social set had imported their friends, for the entertainment to be found in Kingsford was better than a waning season in London. Young Iris Islington and her set were here as well, mad as wet cats so the vicar had heard, to have missed last week's excitement. The young gamblers, increased twofold, perched upon chairs they had rented from the Heritage so they could sit on the outside aisles, whispering among themselves and surreptitiously passing betting slips between them.

If this was not enough to aggravate a new vicar who had chosen the clergy in search of a pleasant, *comfortable* life, now he must find the courage to stir up the mob once more.

Firmly taking his gaze from the sight of Oliver watching him with a dangerous look on his face, the vicar reached up to adjust the new glasses that he'd spent the entire week obtaining in London, glasses that *curved* around his ears and had yet to become dislodged. He cleared his throat twice before he got his vocal cords going, praying that he was not venturing into this nightmare alone—and that he had indeed chosen to side with the man of power in Kingsford.

"I have been instructed to call the second banns for Taryn Burnham and . . ."—he spied his hero, the earl, walking round toward the parishioners' pews, his lordly nod telling him to go right ahead and finish—"and for Woolfe Burnham, Earl of Kingsford."

Miss Taryn Burnham wore a look of incredulous wonder, and the vicar's own throat tightened to see joyful tears sliding down her face.

Oliver stood, yelling, "No!" at the top of his voice, his face red as he struggled to free his arms—arms bent painfully behind his back by the ugly housewife wearing the purple bonnet who stood in the pew behind him.

Claudia Chastain was the vicar's next concern, for she alarmed the vicar almost as much as did her husband. She had a vicious hold on her niece's ear, pinching it and yelling into it at the same time. Young Giles sat on the other side of his mother, holding his head in his hands, and seemed to be talking to the floor.

The gasp of delighted surprise and the hurrahs from the villagers—and from half the young gamblers—told him the sentiments of his congregation. The vicar had learned a few things since that rather frightening Earl of Kingsford had come home to turn the valley upside down, and seeing His Lordship cheered on by folk who had been part of that whirlwind of action—and hearing his own name mentioned in part of that approval—broke a chink in the pride and ignorance that the vicar had brought to Kingsford. He blinked a few times and took another good look at what was happening in his congregation.

The vicar memorized each exciting, nerve-wracking event that he observed from his high vantage point that day. By now, no one sat; indeed, they buzzed and moved busily throughout the room, much like a hive of industrious bees.

While the lovers, Woolfe and Taryn, were the focal point of their buzzing conversations, no one save the observing vicar took notice of the trouble they were having trying to reach each other through the tangled, moving hive of people.

Taryn, her face blazing with emotion, looked longingly across the room toward her earl. The Earl of Kingsford, for his part, was plucking the parishioners up one by one and depositing them out of his path. Taryn, fighting off her haranguing aunt on one side and trying to climb around Giles on the other, finally turned to Claudia, made a fist, and punched her aunt twice in the face. The vicar paused to savor the moment, determined to remember the picture of the intimidating Claudia, dazed and *silent* while her eye swelled up and her nose bled down the front of her dress.

His Lordship, the Earl of Kingsford, had clearly reached the end of his patience, for as soon as he dislodged one obstacle from his path, another would move in and fill the empty space. He finally tipped his head back and bellowed for silence, which brought an immediate end to the noise and confusion.

Holding up one hand, he began to speak. "I don't plan to make a practice of giving a speech every Sunday, and I apologize to Reverend Sefton for doing so today, but we have a problem here that my own people have a right to know about. Before I tell you what that is, I believe I'd like my betrothed to let me hold her for a moment." By now he had made his way to her pew, and she had scrambled rather hysterically to his side. A sigh of feminine approval met the touching reunion.

"Oliver Chastain," the Earl of Kingsford began, with his arm tight about his fiancée, who was clinging to him with both arms, "has ruled this valley under the guise of serving the Burnham family. He has done so by stealing funds, by forging documents, and by exacting an uncivilized cruelty upon my people. In addition, he tried to kill me by hiring highwaymen to stop my coach, and held me captive this last week with the intention of disposing of me today. Each of you could probably add something to that list yourselves, but the most savage thing he did in this valley was to cause the death of Martha Dresden, the daughter of our beloved Cook."

Then, as the vicar was to whisper to himself later when he recalled the scene, "the hounds of hell broke loose." Cook swung her reticule and hit Oliver in the head, then, in swinging it back to get another good shot, she accidentally hit the arm of the ugly housewife, who then lost hold of Oliver. Oliver snarled, reached inside his coat, and brought forth a pistol.

His wife, Claudia, jumped up and attacked Oliver, screaming, "You were practicing your perverted habits on a member of our household? Put that gun down, you fool, our neighbors are looking." She went on in that convoluted vein, grabbing at his arm until it seemed Oliver lost complete control of his senses, for he said, "You worthless bitch, you've made my life a living hell, and to think I put up with it—and still don't have the girl's money!"

Then he aimed the gun at Claudia and would have shot her had not the ugly housewife behind him knocked the gun out of his hand. Oliver glanced behind him, took one horrified look, and ran out the church door.

All in all, it had been a most unforgettable and enlightening day for a vicar who had just discovered that he quite liked his job after all.

Outside, Oliver stopped short at the sight of Señor Esteban sitting calmly holding the reins of his carriage. Esteban drawled, "Well, Oliver Chastain, you look like a man who could use an ocean voyage."

"Thank God you are here," Oliver said and scrambled up beside him.

Esteban said rather seriously as he started the horses, "Amen to that. I know *my* prayers have been answered."

Chapter Eighteen

Taryn, not wanting to dull the bright edges of her newfound happiness, put off the dreaded interview with her aunt and cousin. Her sympathy and her anger warred back and forth, the pendulum of her emotions causing her more grief than if she had overcome her cowardice and got it over with. Finally, Woolfe bundled her into the curricle and drove her to The Willows.

"Unlike you, Taryn, I am looking forward to this," he said.

She stopped halfway up the steps. "Looking forward? . . . I cannot even imagine what I am to say to them. On one hand I am furious with them both, and on the other, I feel so sorry for Claudia and Giles being shamed by Oliver, losing the respect of their friends—"

Woolfe groaned. "This is not the time to let your merciful nature rob all the justice from this situation, Taryn. Let me do it for you."

She straightened her shoulders and walked up the stairs. "Promise me you will let me speak for myself, no matter what."

He kissed her cheek. "We'll see."

The door opened and Claudia stood at the top of the stairs. Despite her purple-yellow eye and swollen nose, Claudia's blazing expression looked quite ferocious. "Oh my," Taryn said, looking at her own handiwork upon her aunt's face. She stepped backward into the rock-solid chest of her betrothed.

Claudia grabbed Taryn's sleeve to pull her into the house, but Woolfe's hand shot out and pried Claudia's fingers loose. Her eyes widened as if seeing him for the first time, then she tossed her head and marched back into the house. "Well, missy," she began as Taryn followed her in, "it's about time you got yourself home." Woolfe stepped into the hall and closed the door behind him.

Claudia's eyes glittered. "How dare you disappear with

this . . . this *savage*. Why, not one person has come by to see us or issued an invitation, and I know from Parsons that the valley is full of our friends. Our own guests left so fast I hadn't time to tell them how wrong Woolfe was. How can I hold my head up after you have gone whoring at the Hall with Woolfe Burnham?"

Woolfe growled deep in his throat, nearly choking in his bid for control. Taryn stepped toward her aunt. *"Whoring?* I beg your pardon, Aunt Claudia, but Woolfe has sent a note to his lawyer to hire a proper matron to live with me, and he and Mr. Asada have moved to the Heritage. In the interim, I have the chaperonage of Cook and Alyce and Mrs. Maloney to—"

"That's another thing, you miserable girl. How dare you entice Cook and her daughter away from The Willows where they belong? I insist that you return them immediately."

Woolfe could contain himself no longer. "This is the most ludicrous . . . Taryn, this woman has no sense of reality. Why do you even—"

"Claudia," Taryn said patiently, ignoring Woolfe's outburst, "how can you expect them to return to Oliver's home when he was responsible for Martha's death? Surely you must realize—"

"Do you have any idea what kind of meals we are forced to subsist on? Or what humiliations we have suffered when the shops refused to honor Parson's order this morning? Without Oliver here to pay the bills, everyone thinks we are paupers. You just march down to the shops and set things straight!"

Taryn spoke to her aunt in a tone one used for fractious children. "Aunt Claudia, I am not your servant—"

Claudia's face contorted in an ugly sneer, and her words deepened into an eerie, venomous cadence. "Well, I should have known you would turn out this way, Taryn Burnham. You're certainly a true daughter of your mother, selfish to the bone, ready to take whatever you want away from me. I'd hate to tell you how miserable she made your father, and how he must have regretted the day she seduced him—"

Taryn grabbed a fistful of Claudia's dress and shook her out of her trance. "If you do not want another purpled eye to match the one I gave you, you'll not say another thing about my blessed mother. My father escaped a horrible fate the day he chose my mother over you, Claudia Chastain. You are the most miserable, *cruel* woman in this world, and you have made my life a living torment from the moment I came here."

Woolfe chuckled as Taryn took a deep breath and resumed

her attack. "And even worse than the misery you put me through, just think of the beatings you inflicted upon Woolfe —Woolfe, who never did anything to deserve it, but only tried to keep your monster husband from hurting me, an eight-year-old child who had just lost her parents."

"Taryn?" Giles's voice came from the top of the stairs. Taryn looked up and, breathing hard, let go of Claudia's dress. Claudia backed away toward Giles, her eyes wild but wary.

"Giles." Taryn acknowledged her cousin without inflection, surprising Woolfe with her coldness.

"Taryn, where in the hell have you been? Parsons said you'd be with *him*," Giles said, his gaze darting toward Woolfe. "Don't tell me you believe the lies he told about m'father?"

"You think they are lies, Giles?"

Giles started down the stairs, rolling his eyes to show his impatience with her logic. Woolfe watched the two of them carefully, aware that Taryn was speaking to Giles as if he were a stranger.

Aggressive now, Taryn challenged her cousin. "What part of the story do you think is false? The part about killing Martha?"

Giles looked to his mother for help, but he could see that Claudia knew that part was true. He turned back to Taryn as she continued, "The part about cheating Woolfe and me? The solicitor has the proof—forged documents of sale for The Willows and the Heritage."

"We don't own The Willows?" Giles asked, sitting down heavily on the step behind him.

"Or do you doubt the part about Oliver's intentions to kill Woolfe?" Taryn asked, her eyebrows raised. "I, myself, heard him order the murder of Asada, and know for a fact that not only would he have killed Woolfe, but, eventually, he also would have killed me as well."

Giles waved his hand as if to ward off further lies. "Don't let your dramatic imagination run rampant, Taryn—"

"Think about it, Giles," Taryn insisted, her voice now brimming with emotion. "Any man who would order his own son to rape his cousin and deliberately give her a deadly disease, just to ensure that he could get his hands on her money would—"

Woolfe leapt forward. He moved so fast that he had Giles around the throat before he knew he had done it himself. Claudia was screaming, and Giles's eyes were beginning to bulge by the time Taryn tugged at Woolfe and said, "No, Woolfe, don't—he didn't succeed!" Woolfe looked at her, and his expression softened. He dropped Giles on the stairs and pulled her into his arms, running his hands over her shaking shoulders. Looking at Giles over her nestled head, he said coldly, "Lucky for you that you didn't succeed, or you'd be a dead man now. As it is, I'll have the satisfaction of seeing you die a horrible, lingering death."

"I don't believe you," Giles blustered, trying to extricate himself from his mother's clutching arms.

"You harlot," Claudia screamed, "You dare to tell such lies when you probably tried to seduce him yourself."

Taryn took a deep breath and bit her lower lip. "I have come here to discuss what to do with both of you. I had a certain amount of sympathy when I came here, but just being near you both has changed my mind. You are making it much easier to do what I must."

Her voice shook. "You are to leave this house. You have three days to pack your personal belongings. You will be provided transportation, and Woolfe will check every item you plan to remove from the house. You will not take anything that belonged to his family, or I will toss you out in the lane with nothing more than the clothes on your backs."

They both made protesting noises, but Taryn was firm. "Take Parsons with you, for she is no longer welcome here in Kingsford. You, Claudia, have a pension from my grandfather, which should be more than sufficient to maintain you comfortably. If you practice reasonable economies, or if Giles is lucky at gambling, you should be able to stay out of debtor's prison. Or, you could go to work, Giles."

At Giles's unbelieving shudder, she finished. "You are fortunate that I am in a generous mood, for if Woolfe had his way, both of you would be brought up on charges."

Taryn's courage lasted almost the entire way back to the Hall, then it wilted into a bundle of shaky regret. "Oh, Woolfe, why do I feel so guilty? I know I am not responsible for them, but already I'm worrying about what they will do."

"Taryn, it is not so strange that you feel they need you, for you have been providing for them since you were a child. You have been the source of their livelihood, were even expected to give yourself in marriage to perpetuate that fact. And, instead of thanking you for it, they have been pounding into your head that you owe it to them, that you were an ingrate for giving them anything less than absolute servitude."

"I know, Woolfe," she said, taking a deep breath. "I shall just have to be strong and stand on my own two feet."

Woolfe reined in the horses in front of the Hall. "Nothing will completely erase the pain of your childhood, Taryn, but when we are married, you may borrow my two feet as well, for I'll not let your relatives ever bother you again."

He pulled her close and gently kissed her hair. She smiled and nuzzled his neck, then turned her face to seek his lips. For both of them, it was meant to be a comforting caress, but the moment their mouths touched, the fire between them ignited.

His blood pounded heavily through his veins, rushing even more wildly as Taryn's hands slid round his back. His mind, overwhelmed by the demands of his senses, fought a weakening battle against the images that beckoned—all of them ending with the glorious pleasure of—

He stopped himself, shaking with need. This was his Taryn, barely recovered from a loathsome experience with her family, and he was taking advantage of her shaken emotions. During his week of confinement in the cave, he had thought over and over of her plea for independence, for the time to become confident of his love—and he had promised himself he would honor her wishes.

On the other hand, he thought as Taryn snuggled closer, a few more encounters like this and they would both go up in smoke. She had no idea how seductive her actions were—and someone was going to have to think ahead.

He groaned against her cheek, trying to think clearly. "I know we discussed a sensible engagement period, Taryn, but just in case, I believe we'd better let the banns run this Sunday." Taryn pulled away to look up at him, her swollen lips open in surprise as he explained. "The banns are effective for thirty days, and frankly, we may wish to marry sooner.

"Besides," he said shakily, in what he hoped sounded like a confession of chagrin, "Asada will cease his endless lectures if we let him think his plan is proceeding smoothly." He managed a smile for her benefit, trying to coax her into a playful mood. "Perhaps I should turn him loose on you and let *you* fend him off for a while."

As she hesitated, Woolfe threw in his best argument. "My father's been hinting strongly for grandchildren. I could defer him to you as well."

That did it. She grinned. "Don't you dare, you wretch. He's so charming, I'd give in without a fight."

"Fine, then." He stepped quickly out of the curricle and reached for her hand. "I'll go in and drag Asada out of Cook's kitchen, for my father wants to show off his cutter to Asada and me."

A scant half hour later, Woolfe and Asada strolled toward the waiting boat that would take them to the cutter. Thinking about Taryn, Woolfe sighed heavily, a signal that Asada quickly caught and questioned.

"You are unhappy with the heiress." There was panic in Asada's voice.

"Nonsense, Asada. She needs some time to go from being a slave to her family, to marriage with a rough, dominating boor like me."

"Tell her to behave herself, Woolfesan. She is only a woman."

"For heaven's sake, do not voice that aloud to Taryn," he warned. "She has agreed to have the banns finished this Sunday, but we have set no date for the wedding." To Woolfe's relief, Asada's thoughts turned inward, and he said not another word during the trip to Esteban's boat.

Esteban-Justin greeted them, beaming with pleasure. "Welcome aboard, gentlemen."

"Thank you for inviting us . . . Father."

Justin smiled at the familiarity and ushered them around the compact vessel, finally settling them aft and below decks in the captain's quarters. After showing them his innovations for comfort, he waved them to chairs. "I've been trying to put myself in your boots, trying to understand what you went through after I disappeared for so long, Woolfe, and I believe that you'd better hear my story."

"That's not necessary, sir. I trust you had good reasons."

"I don't believe that goodness had much to do with it, son, but once it's told, you can decide yourself." Woolfe nodded, and Asada's eyes lit with anticipation.

Justin's voice was low as he began. "As you know, I'd lost your mother the year before and was still grieving. The nights were the worst, so I walked a lot. I was surprised to find myself captured by the local smugglers and on my way to sea."

"Where to?" Asada asked.

"I ended up in the Mediterranean." He smiled at Asada. "I

was rescued just as you were, but not by friendly American merchantmen. We were attacked and boarded by a local corsair. Since I was just so much cargo, I was transferred to their ship and told I was new meat for the slave trade in Algeria."

Woolfe shuddered. Matching expressions of disgust settled upon the faces of Asada and Justin.

"I thought things were bad on the smuggling ship, but the seamen who manned this corsair were the dregs of the sea—they were even hunted by their own. Worse yet—or maybe good fortune for me—was that they had grog aplenty and, being drunk most of the time, forgot I was there. Since their food rations were poor and the ensuing disease had made ailing sailors of most of them, I decided to become a doctor."

Asada chuckled, and Justin's eyes twinkled at the remembrance. "How they had ever conquered our ship was a wonder, for most of the time any exertion caused them to pass out or even die. They had swollen legs, putrid gums, and bullock's liver—terrible ulcers. The telling symptom, of course, was that their old wounds would open and bleed. Lord, what a mess.

"They were riddled with scurvy, of course," Justin said, shaking his head in wonder, "something our sailors had known about for years. And here they were, surrounded by countries that grew fruits and vegetables by the basketful all year round."

"So you cured them?" asked Asada, partly horrified and mostly disbelieving.

Justin shrugged and chuckled. "By the time we all got friendly, I knew who were the villains and who were the sheep. I saved the sheep and did not stand in the way of the villains as they sped to their just rewards."

"Ah, so," Asada said with bloodthirsty satisfaction.

"So you came home?" Woolfe asked.

Justin went quiet. Woolfe could see him sorting through painful memories before continuing. "It was many years before I could manage to slip home, for there was a price on my head. By that time, I owned several ships and had made a healthy fortune."

Justin clasped his hands on his knee and mused, "Life's hell sometimes. By the time I made it back to England, you were gone." He looked at Woolfe, a rough tenderness in his voice. "So I came here to wait for you." He cleared his throat and smiled at Asada. "That's the bare bones of it, gentlemen."

"We'll hear the rest another day," Woolfe baited, surprised

and chagrined when Justin agreed with a thoughtful nod of his head.

"But after Geoffrey died, why did you not step forward to claim the title?" Woolfe asked. "And when I came home, why didn't you make yourself known?"

"I was tempted that night you showed up here, Woolfe, but I didn't know what kind of man you'd become—if you might be ashamed of me. I just thought I'd see which way the wind blew before I decided."

Irritated, Woolfe retorted. "I've been here for weeks. Hadn't you figured it out yet?"

Justin chuckled. "Truth to tell, I was having such a fine time doing business with you, I hated to upset things."

"But if you decided to remain Esteban, you couldn't claim the title."

"Hell, Woolfe, the last thing I want is the fuss of being Lord Kingsford. After all, there's no one's nose to rub it in but yours, and I liked seeing how well you were handling it without having to die to do so." He grinned. "You just keep all that nonsense, and I'll sit back and enjoy it."

He added sheepishly. "Not only that, but as a dead man, I have been able to continue operating my ships under an agreement with the Crown that allows me to attack their enemies on the ocean. If I were to suddenly pop back into the limelight as a privateer, it might prove embarrassing to several prominent officials, not to mention my becoming persona non grata in your social circles. No, after establishing my identity as Señor Esteban, I would rather leave things as they are.

"Now," he said brusquely, rising from his chair, "the reason I asked you and Asada out here is to offer a small gift that might please you. I thought you might like to bid a fond adieu to Oliver and Quinn."

Asada brightened. "They are to be slain?"

"I considered it, Asada," Justin said, "but their sins are too numerous to be blessed with a quick slide into Hell."

"Ah so." Asada nodded in agreement, waiting eagerly for Justin's explanation.

"I've brought them here, down in the hold, and they'll leave on the morning breeze. The cutter will take them to a country ship, which in turn will take them to a ship bound for the Barbary Coast." He led the way down the ladder into the hold.

Quinn and Oliver, chained against the wall, stirred as the hatch opened. Oliver, his eyes blinking against the light, pulled against the chains that held him to the wall. "What the hell do you think you are doing, Esteban, treating us like this? If it's a ransom you want, why just—"

He blinked and stared at the other two. "What the hell is Woolfe doing down here with you?"

Justin bowed to Woolfe and waved him forward to speak for them both. Woolfe smiled, savoring the moment, then dipped an insulting bow to Oliver. He turned to his companions, smiling at the look of anticipation on Asada's face.

"Oliver, allow me to introduce my father, Justin Burnham."

"Justin?" Oliver's eyes widened in disbelief, frantically examining Justin's scarred features. He stared as if Justin had turned into a monster before his eyes. Then he began shaking, wild with terror. "Justin Burnham?"

Solemnly, deep satisfaction in his emotion-filled voice, Justin said, "Oliver Chastain, in payment for your sins against my son, I sentence you to the same fate you allotted me so many years ago. I have friends on the Barbary Coast—"

Oliver's face broke out in a sweat, and he rattled his chains violently. "For God's sake, Justin, you can't do this to me!" He threw himself forward, but his chains jerked him back against Quinn.

Quinn growled, pushing Oliver aside. The hold echoed with the sounds of Oliver's piteous cries.

The three men turned to make their way back up to the deck, silent as they contemplated the fate of the two vile creatures they had left below. They drifted to the railing and looked out to sea. The wind picked up for a few moments, blowing their coats out behind them. Without speaking, they automatically turned their backs to the wind and looked up at the Heritage.

Grinning, Woolfe opened the conversation. "I believe we have a little negotiation to handle, Father."

"Oh?" Justin's eyes lit up.

"Yes, you see, Oliver falsified the sale of the property your inn stands on."

"What!" Justin roared. "You mean that you now own my inn?"

"You only have to claim the title to have it back."

"Damned if I will, you Arab peddler!"

"On the other hand, I still need money to invest in the East India trade. You pay a fair price, and we'll split the profits three ways between you and me and Asada. Plus," he added, watching his father's eyes beginning to twinkle, "have one of your ships bring back a cozy little Japanese wife for Asada."

"Woolfesan!" Asada protested.

"The idea came to me this morning, Asada. It's taken over my brain, you might say; reminds me of your grand scheme for me and Taryn. A comely little wife," Woolfe told his father, "one with enough spirit to keep Asada minding his own business."

Woolfe laughed as Asada remained speechless, and Justin joined in, saluting his son in admiration. Justin leaned back against the railing, watching his son with a grin. "However, I believe we do have another bit of negotiation to conduct, and that's the disposition of our guests below decks. I think it's only fair that we split the money we receive from the sale of these two."

Woolfe choked and had to cough before he could speak. He studied his father's expectant expression, then willingly joined the argument. "But, Father, you only suffered at Oliver's hands, while both of them gave me grief. I shall take the price of Quinn, and you shall profit from Oliver's sale." Woolfe dropped into a slatted chair and closed his eyes, enjoying the sun on his face while his father deliberated.

"Oh, but Quinn is an able-bodied man, able to do more work. On the other hand"—Justin wavered, considering the alternatives—"Oliver is still a handsome man, and I know a pasha who likes . . ."

Asada found his own chair, a lounging affair with room for his outstretched legs, took out his large handkerchief, and leaned back with his eyes closed. He flipped the white cloth over his face and settled down for a long, restful nap.

Asada strode into Cook's kitchen and bestowed upon her his most respectful bow. "Your mistress has put herself in danger of losing Woolfesan. She is willful and disrespectful—and Woolfesan will not compel her to do her duty."

Cook threw her hand over her heart. "My heavens, whatever do you mean?"

"Woolfesan believes your mistress wishes to delay the wedding. Until she is sure of his love. She wishes to be an independent woman. Bah!"

"She never said such a foolish thing!"

"So I have told him, but he has vowed to honor her wishes."

Cook sat on the bench, fanning herself. "Well don't you worry, Mr. Asada, they'll work it out, you just wait and see."

Asada paced across the kitchen and back again. "We have no time to wait. Woolfesan is going to London to invest money, and when that happens, he loses all sense of time. He might not return for years."

"Lands' sakes, I don't believe such a thing."

"Already, he stays away from her for fear he will force her to his will. Already they look warily at each other, unable to speak with honesty. When minds drift apart, hearts will soon follow."

"Oh, my Lord, whatever shall we do?"

Asada bowed, *a pronouncement bow*. "I have a plan."

On Sunday morning Taryn went for a long walk through the woods, mulling over the expression on Woolfe's dear face when he escaped—yes, escaped—from her yesterday. Oh, his need to attend to things was real enough, but the relief on Woolfe's face was so telling that it frightened her. Every time they began to get close, he backed off like a skittish colt. He was regretting his offer to marry her, she knew, and longing for his freedom. A man like him, so full of ambition and energy, could never be content with a simple life in Kingsford.

She couldn't even work up a good argument with him anymore, for he'd given up telling her what to do. She would rather have him bossing her around than this *gentlemanly* disinterest. Even his heartstopping kisses were a thing of the past. And the more *properly* he treated her, the more uneasy she became.

Take, for instance, his plans to go to London to invest money in the East India trade. His eyes had been filled with pure excitement as he described his schemes. Determined to fight for his love, she'd invited herself along, insisting that Cook and Alyce had never seen London, and would lend them a modicum of countenance. Just think, she had said, several weeks together in London. His response had been a tug at his neckcloth and a stammered agreement, followed by the disheartening suggestion that it would be a good time to consult with the solicitor about seeing that her independence was secured.

She had almost crawled away in defeat at that moment, but Cook and Alyce and Asada joined in, feverishly naming places to see. If it wasn't for the fact that she would need to have her affairs in order, she would send the others on without her.

She leaned against a tree, remembering Asada's unusual visit several days ago. He had looked at her warily, then gone to the kitchen to talk with Cook and Alyce. Soon, even the vicar had joined their conclave. Every time Taryn came into the room, they stopped talking and looked at her strangely.

Then she knew.

Woolfe had confessed his disenchantment with her to Asada and was planning to leave. The crew in the kitchen knew all about it and were already feeling sorry for her. Their numbers soon grew from Cook, Alyce, the vicar, and Asada, to include Spaulding and Mrs. Maloney.

By this morning she was resigned to it all. She had packed her bags herself, pushing Alyce and her hovering kindness away. She knew if she heard one pitying word from anyone, she would lose her self-respect and cry all the way to London.

She sighed. It was time to go. She pushed away from the tree and walked briskly toward the Hall. If she must endure it, she might as well endure it bravely, for she certainly did not want to see Woolfe feeling sorry for her. No, she'd act as though she didn't care, and he would never know.

In fact, the only consolation she could find was that Woolfe seemed just as confused as she was by everyone's strange behavior, so at least he wasn't aware of how they pitied her.

She hurried to the Hall, and found them all waiting for her in the kitchen—except the vicar, for this was Sunday. Asada and Cook were hovering over Woolfe as if he were an invalid. They bullied her and Woolfe out of the kitchen and into the dining room, where the table was beautifully set. So, she thought with a little catch in her throat, this was to be her last meal with Woolfe.

Woolfe was everything that was proper, kissing her on the cheek like a maiden aunt and trying to bring up all the things he thought she wanted to hear. The more he talked, trying to find some subject she would enjoy, the more frantic she became. Was this truly the last time they would be together?

Her heart beating, she stretched out her hand and laid it over his. Startled, he looked up, and his hand turned to capture hers. "Taryn—"

Their hands separated guiltily when Cook bustled in, bringing more coffee for Woolfe, and placing a tray of freshly baked buns on the table. Taryn waited until she left, then she began, "Woolfe—"

Asada wandered in and separated their fragile link once more. They invited him to sit with them out of politeness. Although he seemed jumpy and anxious, he accepted their invitation and promptly began a string of fulsome compliments for Taryn.

Then Asada turned his gentle, *concerned* smile on her, saying gravely, as if his words held momentous import, "Woolfe-san is a worthy mate, able to defend his land and his people, and to raise his own sons to be great warriors." He bowed and said to Taryn, "A prudent woman espouses such a man quickly before he chooses another. *Zen wa Isoge*—do quickly what is good."

Clearly agitated at Asada's obvious matchmaking, Woolfe responded quietly, *"Yamai wa kuchi kara."* Then, watching Asada with a warning look, he translated the proverb for Taryn, "Some men dig their graves with their teeth."

Asada gave Woolfe's scowling face a hesitant glance, then quickly announced it was time to go. Taryn panicked—how could she talk to Woolfe when the coach would be filled with their friends all the way to London?

She grabbed his hand as they walked behind the others. He squeezed back and looked at her strangely. Her hand burned at his touch. Oh, why had she wasted these past days? Why had she not just asked him what was wrong?

Woolfe led her to Hawksley's repaired coach, which Asada had confiscated from the Heritage, and Spaulding and Mrs. Maloney came behind in the curricle. Then Alyce remembered something. "You and Woolfe need to be present for the banns this morning."

"No, let's just keep going," Taryn protested. She couldn't bear it if Woolfe said it first. Woolfe looked sharply at her, then turned to stare at the landscape.

"Taryn!" Cook scolded, "how would it look if you left the vicar with such an embarrassing moment?" They looked to Asada for approbation, and he nodded approvingly. This maddening argument went on all the way to the church until Taryn wanted to scream. Woolfe looked out of the window, ignoring everything that went on around him.

"I shall not go to London if you behave so badly," Cook said as the coach stopped. She stubbornly refused to budge until Woolfe sighed and said, "I cry quits; what about you,

Taryn?" and he pulled Taryn out with him. She was so grateful to hold his hand that she didn't care that Cook mumbled all the way up the front steps.

When they entered, Taryn stopped in dismay, for they had barged noisily in, argument and all. She pulled back, but Asada was behind her, nudging them all forward.

The congregation that awaited them was a more subdued one than the week before, although the numbers had swelled. The gamblers sat doubled upon their rented chairs so that bunch of socials she had seen arrive this past week from Brighton could park themselves on the rest.

Justin sat in the Burnham pew and looked up cheerfully at their entrance. Taryn was so humiliated, for there her party stood, filling up the center aisle of the church with everybody looking at them. She was sure Reverend Sefton must be appalled as well—but, no, the vicar looked down from his pulpit with a strange gleam in his eye, and with a confident tone in his voice, began to speak.

"Just in time to call the third banns for Taryn Burnham and Woolfe Burnham, Earl of Kingsford. Are there any objections?"

Taryn turned into Woolfe's chest, whispering, "Do something."

The vicar said clearly, "Miss Taryn, do you love him?"

Taryn raised her head and sent the vicar a scolding look. "Of course I love him, but—"

"And do you want to marry him, cherish him and—?"

"Eventually, yes," Taryn sputtered, her temper rising as she pulled away from Woolfe, for Woolfe was no help at all, standing beside her with his mouth open in surprise.

"And, Woolfe Burnham, do you want to marry her and—?"

Woolfe looked down at his fuming bride-to-be, concern in his dark eyes. Impatiently, he waved at the vicar to shut him up. "Yes to all of it. Now be quiet for a moment."

Unfazed by his lord's grouchy mood, the vicar intoned. "Why then, the only thing left is to declare you man and wife, which I now do."

Cheers broke out from the back and the side aisles, while the ladies in the front of the congregation sniffed into their hankies. "Sign the book," someone said, handing Taryn a pen. She took the pen and looked at Cook, suspicion spreading over her face.

"Cook, are you trying to—"

"I am sorry," Cook said, blushing. Alyce slipped behind her mother, blushing even brighter.

"Just sign and we'll leave now," Asada said in her ear. "Everyone is staring at us. I'll fix it all later." He led her hand to the book, and she signed, willing to go through any farce to leave this humiliating scene. Oh heavens, what if Woolfe thought she'd had part in this?

She turned to look at him. He was grousing at Asada and looking anxiously at Taryn. Oh, if only they could have a few moments alone! Asada convinced the reluctant Woolfe to end the confusing, noisy moment by scrawling his signature as well, for by now the congregation were pressing around them, asking questions about their wedding trip and offering good wishes for a happy life together.

Asada somehow got them moving back down the aisle, this time with the addition of Woolfe's father, who in his ignorance believed they were really married and kissed Taryn on the cheek. Asada pounded Woolfe on the back and spooned him into the coach, and Cook and Alyce did the same for her. The coachman whipped up the horses just as the door closed, and Cook and Alyce squealed their good-byes.

"But, Cook and Alyce . . ." Taryn said in a weak voice.

Woolfe stared out of the window, his eyes narrowing at the sight of their friends waving cheerfully good-bye and hugging each other like triumphant conspirators. He looked back at Taryn—and grinned.

"So you *do* love me? I thought you were having second thoughts about it all." His grin widened and, looking at the ceiling of the coach, he roared with laughter. He pulled her onto his lap and kissed her forehead.

She struggled for a moment, then her eyes drifted closed. "Imagine them trying to pull a trick like that on us."

"Did we stop it in time?" he asked innocently, pressing his lips against her closed eyes and weaving his hands into her hair.

Just as he angled her face for a real kiss, she protested in a languid voice, "The vicar thinks we are married."

"I'm wondering about it myself." He lowered his mouth to hers and she shivered at his touch. Encouraged, he gave up breathing for another minute just to melt her down a bit. When he stopped to look at her, she sighed and, to his great surprise, lifted her face eagerly, searching for another kiss. They didn't talk for quite a while.

"I like that," she said dreamily. "Shall we do it a lot when we marry?"

"You know," he exclaimed, "we both signed the registry. What does that mean?" He untied her bonnet and threw it on the opposite bench. "Something official?"

She looked alarmed, a frown upon her brow. "Oh, no—"

He kissed her pursed lips. She clung to his shoulders when he pulled away.

"It's bad, then?"

"The worst," she sighed.

He unbuttoned the top button of her dress, kissing her as he did so. All the way down he went, kissing and unbuttoning. "Are you cold?" he asked, slipping the dress off her shoulders. "Shall I give you my coat?"

"Umm." She nodded, so he wriggled out of his coat and threw it over beside her hat.

She eyed his wide, shirt-covered shoulders and reached for his neckcloth. Tugging it loose, she tisked, "It's a terrible knot, Woolfe. You're a hopeless barbarian." It fell to the floor. She slipped her fingers between his shirt buttons and stroked dreamily. "Just as I thought."

He groaned, but equal to the struggle, slipped the white, lacy delicacies off her shoulders in return. "I never dreamed . . ." he said in wonder. Shaking, he touched her.

She arched into his hand, and her mouth sought his. In her frantic bid for closeness, she severed the buttons from his shirt. Finally, she gasped, "We're in a coach, Woolfe."

"A very large coach."

"You know where this goes, don't you?" she scolded.

"I know. Babies."

They named their firstborn Hawk in honor of Hawksley's coach.

Author's Note

Many interesting events were unfolding during the Regency Era, one of which was that the Dutch, who were the sole Europeans to have trade with Japan, used American vessels for a short time. The traders were restricted to docking at Nagasaki Bay—on an island off the mainland. Japan's meaningful trade with the outside world did not begin until the late 1850s.

Asada's story could have happened in every detail. As for his friend with whom he escaped, he would not really have been sent to the island—if a fisherman was blown off course and rescued by non-Japanese, he was executed when returning to Japan for having interfaced with foreigners.

The Japanese proverbs used in this story are authentic, collected by the author while living in Japan, but Asada's general philosophy of life may be considered suspiciously convenient for the story.

The East India trade did indeed open up in July of 1813, and provided many enterprising businesses and individuals the opportunity to make a great deal of money.

As an epilogue to this story, Taryn's father's prophetic notion did, indeed, come true. The prehistoric lead mining area—through which the Terenig River flowed—once again flourished. In 1866, the Plynlimon lead mine was opened and had its most successful year in 1874, when 404 tons of ore were extracted.

My husband, the historian, advised against my use of the word "poufy" for Mrs. Maloney's cap, but I loved the word and decided that Woolfe's sassy housekeeper made up the expression, and the fashionable world did not catch on until 1817.